Barbara Francesca Murphy was born in Austria in the 70s. She started writing at an early age, some of her short stories were published in local magazines. As a child and teenager she travelled extensively, getting a taste and knowledge for foreign cultures, fuelling her imagination.

She graduated from high school in America and went on to study tourism and management shortly after completing her college course. She settled in Ireland, where she has been living ever since.

Lucina's letters is her second published book.
Her first one, *Second Chances*, was published in 2019.

For my mum, love you always
For Daniel, Chris and Ryan.
For Lena, one of my own.
For Kathrin, in loving memory.

Barbara Francesca Murphy

LUCINA'S LETTERS

AUSTIN MACAULEY PUBLISHERS

LONDON * CAMBRIDGE * NEW YORK * SHARJAH

A CIP catalogue record for this title is available from the British Library.

ISBN 9781398406452 (Paperback)
ISBN 9781398406469 (ePub e-book)

www.austinmacauley.com

First Published 2022
Austin Macauley Publishers Ltd®
1 Canada Square
Canary Wharf
London
E14 5AA

As always, I want to thank my family and friends for their support in writing this book. Thanks to my computer wiz, who patiently explained the simplest steps over and over again whenever I needed him to. A big thank you to my first readers, your critique was much appreciated.

Thank you, Austin Macauley publishers, for publishing my second book.

A big thank you to Mindbuck media and their campaign to promote my book. It was a great pleasure working with you guys. Special thanks to Emily for all your hard work.

The editorial department and the marketing department for your collaboration in bringing this book into the world. Thank you to all the fellow authors I got to know after completing my first novel, for sharing your wisdom, expertise and friendships.

But most of all I want to thank the small community I live in. I am so grateful for your excitement and all the support you showed me.

The woods are lovely, dark and deep.
But I have promises to keep, and miles to go before I sleep.

(Robert Frost)

Family Tree

Alfons, born in 1916, marries Hettie, born in 1926; they have one daughter
Lucina, born in 1945.

Hettie marries Martin O' Cuinn, born in 1924; they have five children.

Rachel, born in 1950, has two daughters: Samantha, born in 1970, and Kelly,
born in 1974. Kelly's children are Paige and Alexander.

Marie-Anne, born in 1951, has a daughter Lora, born in 1970.

Rosie, born in 1952, has two children: Grace, born in 1969, and Ewan, born
in 1973.

Theresa born in 1955

Trevor, born in 1961.

Prologue

I cross my heart and hope to die, stick a needle in my eye.

Wait a minute I spoke a lie, I never really wanted to die.

But if I may and if I might, my heart is open for tonight.

Though my lips are sealed, and promise is true, I won't break my word to you.

But if by chance I should somehow slip, accidental words tumbling from my lips, if this solemn vow I should break, then no more breaths shall I take.

Thus, you know this promise is not a lie for I am not prepared to die.

They did not mean to hurt the boy, much less kill him.

They only wanted to teach him a lesson. They thought he had no manners.

Interrupting their play, pestering them, following them to their secret location.

The snot-nosed, freckle-faced imp, hiding in their base, deep in the woods.

He demolished their stash of cookies; he ripped up the soft blanket and threw it out into the bushes. He ransacked the place. All their lovely dolls were naked, scattered around the damp ground of the forest, covered in pine needles: dolls' dresses and aprons floating in the nearby river.

The boy behaved worse than normal. They forbid him to set foot in their makeshift home; he was not allowed to take part in their games. They told him to go home and leave them be.

He said nothing, just stood there with his sulking face and mean eyes.

When they returned from mushroom picking, he had vandalised their house, their little slice of paradise.

They grabbed him by his skinny arms and legs and marched him over to the bank of the river.

They swung him high in the air, letting go by the count of three, dropping him into the black water beneath them.

He screamed, landing with a big splash.

"That will teach him!" one of them said.

They assumed the boy would resurface in a minute, calling for help. They would reach out their arms and help him back on shore.

He would stand in front of them, water dripping from his T-shirt and shorts, telling them he was sorry. Later, they would all laugh about it.

But the boy did not come up for air, as the merciless current of the river dragged him down, never giving him another chance to breathe.

The three girls stood and waited, for what seemed like an eternity.

When they finally realised the boy would never call out for them, would never crawl out of the waters, soaking wet, never torment them again, wanting to be part of their fantasy, they silently went back to the base. They did not speak a word; at first, it was not necessary.

In complete mute agreement, they tidied up their camp, collected all the dolls' clothes that had washed up on the edge of the river, and picked the ones tangling from brambles. They folded what was left of the soft blanket and cleaned away the biscuit crumbs.

Only then they sat down; heads bent together.

"I cross my heart and hope to die, stick a needle in my eye," Samantha spoke in a soft voice, cutting a small line into her index finger. She passed on the white pocketknife. When the fingers of the three girls were bleeding, they pressed them together, vowing to never utter a word, so help them God.

Part One

Chapter 1

August 1978, County Waterford

Towards the end of the day, when meadows glistened in the golden evening sunshine, Rosie went looking for her boy.

Although the day was still warm, she felt a chill, pulling a light cardigan around her shoulders.

She had asked the girls whether they had seen Evan in the woods.

They confirmed he had followed them but said he had left, after a while, to play on his own.

Not being able to locate her son, Rosie grew anxious, alerting a few neighbours, and soon a search was on the way.

Tommy, Rosie's husband, who was working a late shift, was notified at the factory.

He hurried home as soon as he got the word.

The police sent out as many men as they could, but they came up empty-handed and had to abandon the hunt for the boy a little past nightfall when shadows around them made it impossible to see.

The only item found, by one of the younger garda, was a red polka dot doll's dress near the water.

Rosie stayed up all night; Rachel, Marie Anne and a couple of neighbours kept her company. The women kept the kettle boiling, dishing out endless cups of sweet tea. They prayed for the boy. May he be safe, may he have only lost his way and will be found as soon as daylight crosses the sky.

Rosie refused to give up hope. Not for a single second did she allow bleak thoughts to enter her head. Her precious boy would be well.

Sunday, at mid-day, the sun high above the trees, a fisherman called the police.

He was out early, far down the river—where the water became quiet—setting up his rod, bucket of bait and a small camping chair. It wasn't till later when in need of stretching his legs, he wandered down the river path, smoking a cigarette.

Scanning the river, he spotted something colourful caught in the shrubs that grew close to the water. He went back to fetch his binoculars. Looking through the lens, his heart stopped. Leaving his fishing gear behind, he ran to his truck, racing over to his mother's place to make a call.

The boy's skin was bluish-white, his eyes sunken back in his face, and a band of freckles across his nose.

He could have only been four or five the most. He was slight, with skinny legs and knobby knees.

Harry McBride's, the officer in charge, son was of similar age.

His son was out playing football while he held this dead boy in his arms.

Surely his mother had forbidden him to go near the river. But boys were rascals, ignoring boundaries, oblivious to danger.

It probably never occurred to the youngster that playing at the river's edge put him at risk; he must have stumbled and fallen into the water, the sheer force carrying him to his death.

He must have drowned in minutes.

McBride swallowed hard. Not often did he come across a casualty as juvenile as this. He gently closed the boy's eyelids. Tonight, he would pray to St. Nicholas in the Cathedral of the Most Holy Trinity. May rest this boy's soul in peace.

First, though, he had to deliver the sad news to the boy's mother.

Rosie listened without hearing. The word 'dead' filled her entire being, leaving no space for any other information to filter through. Someone handed her a glass of water.

She sat still, rigid even, unblinking. The tears and screams would come later.

Endless dark days of depression, unbearable sadness and guilt would follow.

Her life would change forever; her beautiful, fun-loving, naughty, yet gentle son was no longer.

Samantha, Grace and Lora would each face their own struggles, trying to live their lives with this heavy burden on their shoulders. The memories of that day haunting them in their sleep, making it impossible to forget, impossible to master normality, bound together by their pledge, the promise to stay silent.

Chapter 2

Dying is a funny thing, really.

You are confronted with death pretty much from the very beginning: parents' constant warning of looming dangers, an accidental fall, crossing a busy road, an illness…

The persistent reminder of death's presence in our lives. Such a fine line between the here on earth and the beyond.

Death never scared me. I had been contemplating it all through my childhood and adult years like a shadow that never left my side.

I knew in my heart that one day I would lie down and fall asleep.

I assumed I would be an elderly lady, and I was right.

I envisioned floating out of my human body and gliding into eternity. There, I would be amongst angels and the spiritual Creator.

I never liked to call Him God. For me, He always was the Saviour of all lives, the Redeemer we could count on. He would examine your life and the person you were. He would be loving and understanding. This wasn't about religion; it was only about a higher power, a force out there so strong you could not ignore it if you tried. Most of all, He would be delightful. I was right again.

There simply was nothing to fear. My relationship with the spiritual Creator was always a good one. We understood each other. I talked with Him almost every day, confiding in Him, sharing my secrets, and asking for guidance in times of trouble. The answers always came.

I never doubted my relationship with Him, and I believed that once your last breath was taken, we would join the many gentle spirits that are watching over us.

And this is exactly where I am now.

Chapter 3

I was born with a silver spoon in my mouth.

My beloved father, Alfons Wilson—born out of wedlock to a Swedish mother and an Irish father—made his fortune during the great depression.

After a brief stint at Cork University, he threw caution to the wind and partnered up with his mother, Klara. She provided the finances, and he the brains. The world was preparing for war. Workers in need of jobs were out there by the bucket load. Cheap labour was slaving away for minimal wages. Klara and Alfons were able to buy up bankrupt businesses and abandoned houses for bargain prices.

Alfons was a young man with a vision.

Determined from an early age, with capable hands and ruthless nature, he transformed derelict buildings into modern units and apartment blocks..

He employed electricians, plumbers and plasterers; paid them a pittance, and fired them without warning if they displeased him in any way.

Soon he earned a reputation as the man who could turn any old site into something beautiful. He was called upon by the rich and famous for remodelling their homes into heavenly mansions, aesthetically pleasing to the eye; experimenting with pioneering architecture, he always exceeded the clients' expectations.

My father made his first million by the age of 26; he continued to work till he reached his mid-thirties and then retired to enjoy a life of glory.

Alfons was generous with his money and his love. I never harboured an ounce of doubt that he wasn't the best father anyone could wish for. I was his princess, and he was my hero. His wicked sense of humour rubbed off on me at an early age; his solid advice accompanied me through my life.

After courting my mother, Hettie—a beautiful but naïve woman—for a short period, he refused to marry her when she fell pregnant with me at the age of 19. Hettie's looks were strikingly similar to his own mother, Klara. Tall and fair with porcelain skin and wide blue eyes. Hettie's smile was so sweet that bees mistook her for blooming flowers, frequently landing on her.

Her physical good looks were not enough to hold Alfons. He vowed, however, to always care for me, financially and emotionally.

He abandoned her to make amends with her family, strict catholic people, who were burning with shame. Their eldest daughter had committed a mortal sin. The only support he offered was a large sum of money for Hettie and he requested that his baby was to be named Lucina Viola, should it be a girl. This is how I became me, the love for Italy instilled at birth, my grandmother's obsession with the southern country passed on through generations, sealed with an authentic Mediterranean name. When my father returned, a year later, on the day of my first birthday, Hettie had reconciled with her mother and grandparents but was never to speak a single word with her father again. My maternal grandfather shunned my mother and me till the day he died, suffering a stroke behind the wheel of his automobile, crashing headlong into a tree.

From my first birthday onwards, my father became a huge presence in my life, filling my head with wonderful ideas, glamour and endless possibilities. We spent a lot of time together. Even though he possessed the magic of any rich man, making things and servants appear at the click of his fingers, he also showered me with love and kindness, listening to every word I spoke, revealing the most extravagant tales in return.

Chapter 4

Alfons, my father, was a child out of wedlock himself.

Knut Karlsson, my great grandfather, a six ft five-inch-tall, blond Swede with eyes so hard you would never dare look into them for longer than a split second. Knut got rich in exporting iron; he was part of the association owning the iron mines in Gallivare. Like his father, he was not a supporter of the Lantmanna party, which consisted mostly of smaller peasant proprietors, opposed to the nobility. Knut's primary focus was to accumulate wealth, indifferent to the suffering of his fellow countrymen, he employed ruthless methods to reach his goals. Knut was in charge of overseeing the iron export to numerous foreign destinations. He ruled with an iron fist as tough as the metal itself.

His only child Klara was his pride and joy. Since his wife had died at childbirth and he showed no interest in remarrying, his only companion was his daughter. He spoilt her so outrageously that everyone around him knew with certainty that nothing much would become of her. No one dared to say a word or point out his errors in fear of Knut's violent temper.

Klara grew up doing as she pleased, and when she finished her schooling, she simply did not know what else to do with her time.

She had a fascination with Italy, a land filled with lemon trees and olive groves. She spent her days daydreaming of sunshine and the cobalt-blue waters.

Realising his daughter had no talents at all, Knut suggested sending her to America to learn English. Another language surely would come in handy for whatever she decided to do.

Since the Swedish emigration to the United States came to a halt in 1914 as World War I broke out, the alternative was Ireland, a country still ruled by the United Kingdom at that time.

Klara Karlsson did not mind where she was going. As far as she was concerned, she was on an adventure to an unknown land, one step closer to her fantasy of Italy. She convinced herself a boy would be waiting for her on the Irish shores, red-haired and pale-skinned. They would fall in love instantly, living happily ever after.

Klara stayed in a beautiful stone-built guest house in a small town on the Irish east coast. The tall, blond, and foreign-looking beauty stuck out like a sore thumb in the village. Everyone was curious, and everyone was helpful in assisting her with learning the English language.

Toby Wilson could not have cared less about the language barrier, and he did not give a toss whether Klara fulfilled her dream of mastering English.

All he wanted was to get the gorgeous blond into bed.

Toby had come from the west, a bricklayer by trade with fast hands and an appetite for women. He was tall and fair, muscular from manual labour with broad shoulders and a wide smile that convinced most women to give themselves to him freely.

He had left a long trail of broken-hearted girls scattered along the west coast. He had promised eternal love to all of them, with absolutely no intention of keeping his word. They were fleeting pleasures in his young life, meaningless encounters. He made sure though that he never revisited any of the towns he had been in.

Klara was only another conquest to him, but one he had to have.

He took his time, sussing out the situation, striking at the perfect moment.

Klara, enthralled with her new and somewhat mysterious pursuer, was of the opinion that at the age of 20, she had held on to her virginity for long enough.

His words were magic in her ears as he talked of marriage and family, vowing she was the only one for him.

And it was time to have some fun; fun, they had. There was not a place that stayed untouched by their sexual desire.

Klara's favourite was the shed behind the guest house where Mr Miller kept hay and straw for the animals. There they would roll around for hours, delighted with their nakedness, pushing boundaries as far as they dared.

It never occurred to Klara that she could fall pregnant, but she soon realised that something was wrong. Eventually, she confided in Mrs Miller, the guest house lady, who had taken her under her wing.

The village doctor confirmed she was two months on.

Mrs Miller thanked the Lord above it wasn't one of her own daughters who had committed such a sin. Since Klara wasn't her flesh and blood and had come from a faraway country where morals and Catholic faith obviously did not matter, Mrs Miller promised to look after her. Klara wrote a letter to her father explaining her situation, stressing that she had believed Toby would be with her till death do them part. At this point, Toby was long gone. As soon as he got wind of the pregnancy, he packed his duffle bag with his few belongings and was on the way up north in search of more good times.

Knut, initially disappointed, quickly came around to the idea of a grandchild.

He increased her monthly allowance so that Klara could live a comfortable lifestyle. Once a year, Knut would board a ship and make his way to the island to meet up with Klara and his grandson Alfons.

Mrs Miller delivered Klara's baby on the first of June during the year of the Easter Rising. She wrapped him in a towel and proudly showed him off to anyone who came to visit.

Klara stayed with the Millers for a couple of years before she bought her own place. A cottage at the edge of town, covered in ivy with a small garden to the back where she planted fuchsias, rhododendron, pots full of bay laurel, and a border of foxtail lilies. Alfons became her world.

When Alfons repeated history, getting Hettie pregnant and initially leaving her to deal with her dilemma, something inside him changed. It took him a year to figure things out. He fled to Italy, where he travelled in a lavish fashion till he stumbled upon a magical place far down on the boot's heel. His ostentatious nature got him noticed within days in the picturesque town of whitewashed buildings.

Money made it all possible. But Alfons was not only pretentious; he had a funny and sincere side to him that quickly won over most of the Italian villagers' hearts. He purchased a beautiful old building of trullies made of Lecce stone. The grounds of the medieval Masseria, were decorated with ornate fountains and marble sculptures of voluptuous women.

When the year abroad drew to an end, he realised he could either hide forever or become part of something bigger.

He chose the latter.

I thanked all my lucky stars that he decided to come back to meet me.

I felt blessed with the most wonderful father anyone could imagine.

Alfons apologised to Hettie, but he did not take her back.

He had no interest in marriage or a big family.

He told Hettie to move on, to find someone to love, and so she did.

She met my stepfather, Martin O' Cuinn, a local builder at Saturday's set dancing in the pub. Martin was a good decent man with a heart of gold. Hatred, greed and jealousy were unknown to him. He loved to smile and crack jokes with his friends. He was also a secure confident man. These attributes allowed him to take me in as one of his own, treating me fairly, loving me as if I was his blood.

He was a great stepdad, giving me enough space to be with Alfons and never questioning our relationship.

Martin knew that whenever I spent time with my father, I was well looked after, and Alfons, in return, allowed Martin to raise me and teach me everyday values along with my siblings. They never spoke more than a hello to one another. Their agreement was a silent one, as was the acceptance of Alfon's generosity, which greatly benefited Hettie and us girls.

My mother Hettie gave birth to Rachel in 1950, a year later to Marie-Anne, another year later to Rosie, and a couple of years after that to her last daughter Theresa.

Trevor, the only son, was born after a considerable gap in 1961. We never found out if he was an accident or the result of the last try for a boy.

We girls sure had fun in a house full of laughter, pranks and sisterly love.

My sisters always meant the world to me. It did not matter one bit that our biological father was not the same.

We all shared a wonderful childhood, and a bond only sisters know.

We were fused together by something magical, a spell that I could not allow to break. We were one.

I understood early on, being the eldest, that it was my responsibility to keep the family intact, to guard secrets, and to bring people together again when life had torn them apart.

My sisters and their daughters all got caught up in the web of a complex family situation, fighting or surrendering to their own demons.

I needed to support them; I needed to be there for them when tragedy hit.

I would turn to my beloved father Alfons for strength, praying to the Creator to allow my dad to guide me in the right direction.

When everything seemed lost, when the family was ripped apart, when secrets were aired and a devastating occurrence revisited, I needed to take charge. I needed to bring them together again even if it meant to orchestrate from beyond the grave.

Chapter 5

You would never think the bunch of people gathered near gate 23 at Dublin airport's terminal one were heading to a funeral.

The flight to Bari, Italy, was on time. The Ryanair plane was cleaned and ready to embark again, a line of passengers queuing to board, passports in hand.

Only the party of thirteen was making no attempt to take part in the commotion. They seemed oblivious to what was happening around them, still talking, shrieking with laughter. The brief was to be jolly.

They were dressed in bright colours of orange, yellow and vibrant pinks. The men were clothed in Hawaiian shirts and chinos; the women were in printed dresses, sandals and broad-brimmed straw hats.

To the on-looker, a family was on the way to a sun-drenched relaxing holiday of pool and beach time.

Amongst the loud and happy individuals, one member of the group sat quietly in an assistance airport wheelchair. Her face was bent downwards, her lips moving, releasing a constant stream of unidentifiable mutter.

She was a corpulent woman dressed in a pale blue sleeveless dress, revealing her meaty arms. Her wispy brown hair combed to the side and held in place by a tortoise clasp.

When the line cleared, and they were the only ones left to step on the plane, the group finally made its way to the last identity check.

Grace bent down to whisper into her mother's ear. "Mum, time to walk now. We cannot take the wheelchair on board."

A furious shaking of the head followed, and Grace signalled her Aunt Rachel.

"Rosie, honey." Rachel's voice was soothing, like summer rain.

"You are well able to walk, come, lean on me. We have another chair waiting for you in Italy. Come on now, that's a good girl."

With a firm grip around her waist, Rachel guided Rosie down the aisle and to her allocated seat. In her head, Rachel knew her sister understood what they were saying to her. She was taking it all in.

Rosie chose not to participate in life anymore, and Rachel did not blame her. Her loss was just too grave all these years ago; her heart broke into a million pieces. It pained Rachel to see her sister like this. Rosie was a shell of her former self, but nobody was able to draw her out, and God help them, they had tried. It took all their efforts and strengths combined to get Rosie to the airport. When they got word, Rosie let them know she was determined to join them because it was Lucina's funeral. She would not make an effort for anybody else; they believed her.

Marie-Anne, of course, did nothing to help. She only made things worse, being her stubborn self. It made Rachel's blood boil. The silly cow even travelled on a different day, arriving a day earlier than the rest of them. Rachel rolled her eyes; when would it ever end? She will have to pull herself together for the sake of Lora; after all, it wasn't Lora's fault that her mother was unable to put herself in someone else's shoes for once! Marie-Anne had not allowed Lora and her family to travel with the others; they had to join Marie-Anne. To be completely honest though, Lora was a piece of work herself. The apple certainly did not fall far from the tree.

Lord have mercy on Lora's kids; they surely did not have it easy.

The crew was ready for take-off. "When I am afraid, I put my trust in You." Rachel quickly crossed herself and fastened her seatbelt. She kissed the golden cross she always wore around her neck, stealing a glance at Rosie, who was sitting in her usual position, an untouched magazine in her lap. Grace was busy strapping Noah into his seat.

That child is the colour of a jellyfish, Rachel thought. Grace never let him out into the sun, too afraid the child will get a burn. Her niece was afraid of her own shadow. In Rachel's modest opinion, Grace needed to get a grip. Was Grace always like that, even as a child? Rachel tried to think back. The cousins were best friends during their childhood: Sam, Grace, and Lora joined by the hip, always in cahoots, roaming the neighbourhood, free and wild. Nothing like over-protected Noah. Noah was small in size for an eight-year-old; by looking at him, you would think he was three years younger, drinking out of a beaker cup, like a little baby.

Grace's husband could not join them, always tied up at work. Always too busy for family events. What a silly man, missing out on so much.

Next to Rachel was her own husband, Paul, who was already snoring. He despised flying and had to take a tablet to calm his nerves. The side effect was extreme drowsiness. Rachel patted him on the knee, *sleep well, darling*. Paul was a good man; he never got involved in any drama, a man of few words, content in his own right. Then there was Theresa at the window seat. In contrast to Paul, Theresa loved flying, always claiming the seat near the window. Her youngest sister behaved like a child in some ways; never having married, Theresa certainly maintained her youth. Her baby was her pooch, a little Yorkie, Mr. Bruno, named after Bruno Mars.

Rachel thought of the name as quite juvenile but had not said a word, as Theresa was only besotted with her four-legged friend.

Such a little yapper, that dog!

Unable to get seats near the others, Rachel's much younger brother Trevor and his partner Garry sat near the back.

"As gay as Christmas." People would comment about the pair. It never bothered them as they were both of a happy go lucky nature, not letting unpleasantries into their lives.

Rachel's parents, Hettie and Martin, had always stood by Trevor, urging him to be his true self. They insisted God had made him stand out from the crowd, perfect and unique. Their support made Trevor resilient, confident and fearless.

In the row in front of Rachel were her grandchildren: Kelly's son and daughter. Sixteen-year-old Alexander, a quiet musical boy far too soft for this ruthless world. He had pudgy cheeks, his body not yet having shed the puppy fat. Rachel worried about him, while her daughter Kelly only doted on her son. There was nothing quiet about her granddaughter, Paige. A rowdy girl, who at a little over twenty—Rachel was sure of—had lived more than most sixty-year-olds. Kelly did not seem to notice any disturbing signs with Paige. Rachel, on the other hand, had seen many red flags; her granddaughter's aura was all wrong. And then there was Paige's boyfriend Reuben, who thankfully didn't join them on the trip. Rachel felt he had a strong and malign influence over the girl. It was quite unsettling. Kelly was blindsided, her head permanently stuck in the clouds. Rachel should have had been tougher with her.

Her daughters, Samantha and Kelly, plus Kelly's husband Ben, were seated another row up. Poor Ben, overweight and bald, always looking awkward next to her gorgeous Kelly. Kelly, with her remarkable resemblance to Grace, the most splendid woman to have ever graced the silver screen. Yes, and there was the name. Had Rachel known her second-born would look like the star when she searched through name books of the 1950s? Perhaps, she wasn't sure anymore. She, for one, loved it when people commented on the striking similarities and the coincidental naming. Kelly was an exquisite gentle creature, always calm and collected, yet flaky.

Kelly was nothing like her older daughter Sam, who had equally lovely looks, and a glamorous foxy lady style. Sam was diligent in her advertising job, obsessed with her appearance, too vain and self-absorbed to ever consider a family of her own. Sam's meek voice tricked people into letting their guard down too soon, believing she was a pushover. Sam always waited for just the right moment to reveal her true hard self, just like a scorpion rearing its venomous stinger. Rachel though chose to believe her daughter's heart had a soft centre.

Both of her daughters reminded Rachel of her sister Lucina; in Sam's case, the looks only.

Lucina, a magnificent creature in every way with a heart of gold and a highly addictive lust for life, drew you in whether you liked it or not.

Their rock, the foundation of the family, was her beloved sister, who lived her life like a movie star.

Oh, Lucina, why did you have to die? And who would sort out their lives now?

Chapter 6

It is unbearably hot when Samantha stepped off the plane. A sudden wave of heat hit her, making it impossible to catch her breath.

Along with the others, she made her way across the boiling tarmac to the main building of the small airport.

Greeted by a modern interior, clean white floor-tiles, and best of all refreshing air-condition, Sam started to relax.

She was worried that her face was puce with the swelter. Discreetly, she tried to smell her armpits and discovered an unpleasant odour of light sweat.

Damn deodorant, promising 48 hours protection! She should have opted for her tunic with light sleeves and not the halter neck.

Sam quickly checked herself in her pocket mirror. *Good, God!* Her face and neck were flushed in various shades of red. She left her family at the luggage carousel and dashed into the ladies room to powder her face. *Stupid weather!* Sam preferred to stay nice and cool, maintaining a perfect ivory complexion.

Standing in front of the large mirror, silver eyes were staring back at her. Kelly, of course, got the spectacular colour, an unusual shade of blue running into lilac. Sam had tried coloured contacts, but it never looked natural. Sam was very pleased with her hair though. Cutting it this short was the right thing to do; the pixie style suited her.

Now she practised her breathing exercise: two long breaths in and out, count to ten, and again. There was no point in panicking; panic would only make her look worse. All was under control; all would be fine. She would settle in nicely in her lovely climatised hotel room; having all her garments and beauty products at hand. She would look great again. The funeral would be over in a flash, sad as it was. She would be back home in no time, getting on with her organised predictable life.

Poor Lucina, her fun auntie, was so positive and full of banter with no worries or inhibitions, it seemed. Life was plain sailing for her aunt; no wonder she managed to live it to the fullest. *Where was she now?* Sam wondered. She didn't want to think about death too much; it made her uneasy. If she kept in control she would be safe. She tried to banish all disturbing thoughts from her brain; nevertheless, she was overwhelmed with the urge to knock on wood. She must oblige for all to work out and for good luck. She pulled a small perfect square of elmwood from her shoulder bag and knocked on it three times. Relief washed over her.

The piece of wood was her constant companion ever since that embarrassing taxi ride in Philadelphia. She had been over there for work. Her team had delivered the advertising pitch to 'Grossman Foods,' one of the biggest food processing companies. She was in a cab on her way back to the hotel when a persistent, bad and worrying thought would not leave her head. She tried everything: breathing, counting, etc.; silently obviously. Even a quick prayer, although she was an atheist. Nothing got rid of the horrendous images in her mind.

She simply had to knock on wood. Mortified and disgusted with herself, she asked the taxi driver to stop near some trees that lined the street. She jumped out of the car and knocked on the nearest one. Reassurance made the hugely awkward moment nearly bearable. Sam pretended to study her blackberry for the rest of the ride, avoiding all eye contact with the bemused cab driver.

Ever since then she carried the little treasure in her bag for those exact moments. It sure made her life easier.

Chapter 7

The window on the third floor of the small charming boutique hotel was wide open. The air tasted sweet with the scent of ripe citrus fruit.

Across from the cobblestone pathway was a piece of land, reddish dry earth covering the ground. Ancient olive trees stood there, thick trunks with hard-worn bark and majestic crowns in an unidentifiable green.

The sky vast, white clouds weaved through the pale blue, the light so bright that Kelly has to squint. She was nearly finished unpacking her dresses. Obviously, she has put away Ben's clothes first. He has already parked himself downstairs in the open-air bar, enjoying a drink. She did not mind. It was nice to take care of her family while she still could.

She would check on the kids. Paige would be furious when Kelly asked if she needed any help. Her daughter's usual state of mind was angry.

She used to be a lovely placid child with a constant smile on her lips. The change came in her late teenage years. Suddenly, Paige was boy crazy, constantly arguing with her and Ben, staying out late, and sleeping all day. Kelly was concerned but did not want to step on her daughter's toes in fear of rejection and verbal abuse. Paige managed to sit her leaving cert with minimal efforts, accumulating just enough points to get into a second-rate art course. Kelly was not sure what Paige was studying or what the degree would be. She was trying to have as few confrontations with the hostile young woman as possible.

Alexander, on the other hand, would appreciate his mother's efforts to straighten his shirts and shorts. Such a gentle and handsome boy. Kelly loved his rounded cheeks, his solid arms and legs. He did not socialise much, but Kelly knew his time would come. What was the rush? His heart was in his music, a gifted piano player with a voice so sweet it made angels cry.

Alexander sang in the choir and Kelly made sure she attended every one of his performances. At least, she used to.

Kelly gazed out into the countryside. *How beautiful!* She marvelled at the divine scenery, mesmerised by the chirping of the crickets below her. No wonder Lucina chose this to be her home. Kelly was filled with a warm pleasant feeling. Happiness was oozing from every pore. She just knew things would fall into place.

This part of the world was divine. They all made the flight over without hiccups. There was some commotion on the bus from the airport to the hotel, but it must have been minor. Kelly did not really pay attention. Her mind had wandered, and she felt at peace in the knowledge that her aunt had lived a spectacular life and had died a happy woman.

This was not a goodbye but a celebration of a unique lady. They would all attend in loud colours, as requested by Lucina. Her aunt had written a letter with specific instructions of how everything was to unfold.

Typical of Lucina, Ben had said when the letter was read out to them.

Always having the last word, orders from beyond the grave.

Kelly thought it was endearing and thoughtful of her late aunt. *Why not have a send-off Lucina style?*

Sure, her aunt had been a strong woman, and people usually did what she asked them to do.

Lucina had been on Kelly's case before she passed away. She wanted to talk to Kelly, but Kelly had managed to avoid her. This very action filled her with regret now.

She was determined to honour Lucina at her farewell. She would try to send positive vibes through the family.

Anyway, they were all here. Everyone on the flight this morning stayed in the 'Porte del Paradiso' boutique-hotel.

Marie-Anne, Lora, Oscar and their brood were staying in a guesthouse at the edge of the small town closest to the cemetery.

Kelly was hoping they would all get along. It surely was what Lucina would have wanted.

Kelly was looking forward to catching up with her aunts, cousins and kids. It was not often that they all met.

Thinking of it, they mightn't have been together since the horrid argument between her two aunts all these years ago. Poor Rosie, she had been in such a state. Kelly was a kid back then, but she remembered it well. The fight had caused a rift that split the family in two. They had all sold their Waterford homes and moved towards the city, one by one. No one could bear to live in close proximity to the place that had changed their lives forever.

Now Kelly's heart was overflowing with sadness. She was a right mess lately. She felt too intensely. Ben had said as much before in this accusing tone. He did have a point. Kelly did get swept away by her emotions. It's a Pisces thing, her friend Antonia had pointed out. People born under the fish sign were dreamers; they feel deeply, and they carry the world on their shoulders. The last bit, Kelly was not so sure about. She certainly was a dreamer but the weight of the world? Not so much. It was more accurate to describe her thoughts as flitting around in her brain, like confused butterflies.

Kelly smoothed down the last dress and hung it into the wardrobe.

It was her favourite piece, green—the colour of a peacock—dainty ruffles flowing down the middle like a delicate waterfall.

The same dress she had worn when she had said goodbye to Jannick. He had held her close, running his hands down to the small of her back. She closed her eyes, smelling the scent of his musky aftershave, feeling his soft stubbles on her cheek. She must not cry; she must not long for him. Not today. She simply must not think at all.

Chapter 8

They passed one grimy bar on that horrible drive from the airport to the hotel. Of course, there was a bar in this shitty hotel, but she can hardly drink herself senseless in front of her parents.

The minibus was too hot, no air con and it stank. The driver had been confused because of their ridiculous, happy outfits. "Are you not here for a funeral?" His eyes wide with surprise, his voice dripping with a greasy Italian accent.

Rachel, who else, had seen it as her duty to inform the guy about crazy Lucina's wishes. Paige felt like punching someone.

She took a seat next to her aunt, Samantha, and stared out the window, not interested in making conversation. Only when she saw a guy in a Fiat nearly ramming into a big SUV, peeping his horn loudly, screaming some obscenities, Paige opened her mouth. Her innocent observation on the crappy Italian driving had sent her aunt over the edge. She might have mentioned the irony of getting killed attending a funeral.

Samantha had practically freaked out. She literally shouted at Paige not to talk such rubbish and to take it all back.

Paige had lost the last bit of respect for her aunt, there and then.

Paige threw her clothes into the drawers. She was dying for a smoke. At least they got her a single room. Her mother had used her noggin for once. Paige pulled a Marlboro from her purse and opened the window. She leant out far, blowing smoke through her pierced nostrils.

Fucking countryside. This hotel was literally in the arse end of nowhere—complete boring isolation. Of course, everyone else found the location idyllic. It was total shite, and anyone in their right mind could see that. What was Lucina doing here all day long? There was nothing but quietness and annoying sunshine. But then again, Lucina was a bit soft in the head, wasn't she?

Paige had been forced to buy a colourful dress; her mother had insisted on it. As if Lucina could see them. Seriously! Paige only wore black and leather; she despised colour. Now, the funny-looking orange dress lay in the bottom of the wardrobe like rotting fruit. Her mother had chosen it at the end when Paige had lost her nerve completely; shopping with her mother was excruciating. Kelly had rushed her from store to store, begging her to try on one disgusting garment after the other. All Paige had wanted was a cool drink and a smoke.

Paige shuddered.

She scanned her Facebook.

And there he was—the first story on her news feed.

Smiling with those dimples. Blond hair cut short, sticking up in all directions. The familiar eyes. His arms around that bitch. The bitch looked like she had won the lottery, grinning like a dumb ass.

She had long red hair, and if Paige hadn't hated her so much, she would have admitted that the bitch was pretty.

"After a few ups and downs, we have finally tied the knot!" was written under the photo, and a gazillion people liked, loved and commented on it.

A few downs… was that what he called it? A down. That was what he called her. Just a down, a little unimportant smidge of a thing. A nuisance. Like a mosquito, squash it and be done with it. Forget it. Already forgotten and moved on.

Fuck that, Paige hurdled the phone across the room, and it landed with a thump near her bed. She felt like chucking it out the window into the wilderness.

But then she would not hear it when Reuben called. And he would call, sooner rather than later, checking up on her, and whatever she would say, she'll be in trouble.

Everything was folded nicely in the cupboard. He was stretched out on the comfortable bed, relaxing and listening to the insects of the south playing their concert outside in the warm evening air.

There was a piano arranged for the funeral; Alexander would play and sing, "Con Te Partiro," Lucina's favourite song.

Music was the only thing he was good at. His great auntie, as he had called her, had often asked him to sing and play for her on the grand piano, the centrepiece of her living room.

Alexander was very fond of the elderly lady, as she, like his mother, never judged him. She only appreciated his gifts.

Unlike his father, who wanted him to be a ballplayer, a soccer star, and a tough guy who bragged about girls and fights. A real lad. He was none of that too sensitive for this world full of bullies and roughnecks. Like his sister, a mean creature, whose pastime consisted of making fun of him. That and staying out all night, getting in trouble. Paige was a small girl with a hard body and a strong resemblance to their dad. There was nothing pretty or feminine about his sister. Her countless piercings, tattoos, and God knows what else. She was not like their mother, who ws a gentle Goddess like creature, even if she was a bit flaky and distracted

Alexander was the male version of his mother, a fact Paige teased him mercilessly about. Sissy, she called him. He was too soft looking, not masculine or handsome at all, she told him.

Alexander did not care, nor did he get back at her. He simply stayed out of it. He knew, for example, that Paige already had an abortion over in the UK. He heard her creeping back into the house in the wee hours of the morning, drunk and stoned. But he kept quiet. He would find no pleasure in telling on his sister or upsetting their mum any further.

Alexander enjoyed his own company, his music, and quietness. He liked to sit still, surrounded by nature, daydreaming of a life without hardship. A life in which he was not the target of horrible pranks by his peers, a calm place where music made up time, a destination far enough away from the present all-consuming days of school torture. A different era where he would meet a lovely tender girl who would adore him for what he was.

Chapter 9

The day of the funeral was a scorching hot day.

The sun splitting the stones shortly after 9 am, the temperature climbing up the thermometer quicker than you could imagine.

By midday, the asphalt will be boiling, hot bubbles rising to the surface, and only the bravest cicadas will attempt their song.

The funeral party will have a hard time picking out the lightest outfits, as none of the clothes they brought will be cool enough. They will stand at the grave in shimmering colours of pastel blues, emerald greens, crimson, and gold like the sun itself. Sweat dripping down their cheeks, mixing in with tears, running from their eyes hidden behind dark glasses.

Marie-Anne was up early before everyone else. She made use of her time alone to go for a brisk walk through the village. She was dressed in white linen trousers, a blouse and a big straw hat. It was just bearable outside, but she did not plan to go too far as she knew the sun would soon burn down relentlessly.

She admired the old stone buildings—small low dwellings in faded colours that lined the bumpy road. There was a white church, a couple of shops and restaurants. The piazza will be filled with people in the evening once the day had cooled down a bit. People will mingle, children chasing each other begging for ice creams.

Marie-Anne could see how Lucina felt at home here. Wherever she looked, she saw beauty. A strange calmness surrounded her, making it hard to swallow. And if she would not know any better, she would think she was about to cry.

The solid shell around her heart slowly started to melt away, and she felt nothing but deep remorse to have distanced herself from her family for so long.

There was absolutely no point in showering before the funeral. The light breeze that filtered through the open window was as hot as the air itself and brought no comfort at all.

Breakfast in the guesthouse did not start till 9:30 am, but luckily, Lora had packed some digestive biscuits and fig rolls into her bag.

She sat in the deep armchair at the window in the small but sufficient bedroom.

Oscar was still asleep, quietly snoring.

Nina and Cillian, her kids, were asleep, no doubt, in the room next door.

Her mother and herself were the only early risers. Lora saw her mum, Marie-Anne, leaving the inn at the crack of dawn.

Lora could have joined her on the walk, but she wasn't interested in exercising in the slightest. She preferred to sit here, nibbling away on her stash.

She thought of the fuchsia dress she bought for the occasion. The salesgirl promised that the wrap-style was flattering to her figure. She had, of course, bought the dress only to cry at home in front of the mirror.

The only thing that had calmed her nerves were two bags of Taytos and a Ben & Jerry cookie dough ice-cream. Afterwards, she felt sick and vowed to go on a diet, starting right after the trip to Italy.

Lora did not remember the last time she was truly happy. If she ever was.

Her kids had been extremely tiring with their endless activities. She had put a stop to all the demands some months ago, informing them that they either got themselves to their training sessions or not go at all. She was done driving.

Her job in the credit union bored her beyond belief, and her love for Oscar had dried up . She wasn't sure if she ever was in love with him in the first place. He was there, he proposed, and she accepted. It was as simple as that. She got pregnant quickly, and her fate was sealed.

One day flowed into the next one , hours melting into years. Years of nothing.

She was irritated with herself for having gained so much weight, but food seemed to be her only pleasure.

Her childhood had been fun, at times; running around with her cousins, playing endless games of 'house' down by the river. Of course, all that came to an end too after Ewan. After the big fall out between her mother and the aunts.

She missed the bond she had with Samantha and Grace; they were not close anymore. Lora wasn't close to anyone, really.

She was in a constant state of annoyance, she was moody, and she was very afraid.

She knew for a fact that Ewan came back for revenge.

She felt his presence for a long while, and the medium asked for advice had confirmed her suspicions. Obviously, she had not shared this piece of information with anybody. They would all think she had lost her marbles, especially Samantha and Grace.

But Lora knew it was the truth. What they had done all these years ago cannot go unpunished. A secret this big cannot be kept; it simply was not possible. Ewan was trying to get her. He appeared in different shapes and forms. He could take on the body of a man across the street, an animal cowering in a corner, or a shadow looming above the cherry tree. One day he would succeed, and there was nothing she could do to stop him.

Her phone beeped loudly wakening Theresa from a sweet dream. She turned beneath the feather down blanket reaching blindly for her mobile. It was 11 am, and surely she had missed breakfast. It did not matter; she got a good night's sleep, feeling refreshed after the day travelling. She probably wasn't missed either this morning. As the youngest of the sisters, Theresa felt like the odd one out. The rest of the women were closer, more alike. Well, Rosie was struggling now, but before, she was just like them. Theresa had always sensed that she was different. She even looked different for heaven's sake. The sisters shared voluptuous figures and childbearing hips, beautiful light skin, grey eyes and fair hair. They were all like their mother, Hettie; natural beauties whose cheeks turned rosy from the Irish air.

Theresa was like Martin, their dad. Olive skin with large, hazel eyes and unruly dark hair.

It wasn't only her appearance that was different. Theresa never felt included in the sisters' games; she could never follow their jokes. She was never asked to take part.

Theresa was also unable to have children.

All her sisters were extremely fertile, having their babies young , popping them out as if it were no trouble at all, bringing them into this world effortlessly.

Except for Lucina, who although a sought-after godmother, had none herself. And she never regretted it, as she had reminded them more than once.

But this had been Lucina's choice when Theresa would have given her right arm to have a child.

Theresa smiled. Lucina was never afraid to do what she wanted regardless what other people thought.

Her aunt was ruthless in a kind sort of way.

Theresa checked her WhatsApp messages. She ignored one from her colleague and went straight to Tina, her dog sitter.

"All happy and chilling out," Tina wrote, sending multiple photos to prove her point.

Bruno Mars, relaxing on the brown leather sofa. Bruno Mars, sniffing around the garden. Bruno Mars, fetching a ball. Her beloved dog on Tina's lap and sprawled out on the big swing seat.

Oh, how she missed her baby.

She was so glad she found Tina, a gem of a dog minder. Without her, Theresa would not travel. It was hard enough to say goodbye to her darling, as it was.

At least he was in great company.

She knew the rest of the family thought that she was a bit nuts, treating her dog like a child.

But what could she do? Bruno Mars was the only thing that kept her going.

Chapter 10

The funeral was a big affair.

Lucina could not have picked a hotter time if she tried. It was all so perfectly fitting. Lucina loved the heat, a real sun worshiper, always sitting out till the last rays of the day had vanished behind the tall cypress trees, leaving an orange stripe across the sky.

It was like Lucina was directing her last goodbye from heaven.

There they were in their brilliant vivid colours. Standing in small groups waiting for Lorenzo, the priest, to call them in.

The villagers were gathered near the entrance of the small mediaeval church. The stone building had turned yellow in places, underlining its maturity.

In the middle of the cobbled stone square before the church stood a single lemon tree, fruitless but green, providing the only shade around.

Sam was perspiring. She could feel pearls of sweat running down her temples. Thankfully, she was wearing waterproof mascara. She hoped no one would bother to take pictures. She would look horrendous, all pink-cheeked and puffy. Kelly probably would; she always photographed every occasion. *Silly girl.* Well, if she did, Sam would get her hands on the pics and airbrush the hell out of them. She blinked behind her Prada glasses and saw Lora standing close to Marie-Anne on the far side of the group. She waved quickly. Sam had not spoken to Lora since their last lunch together; maybe they would be able to catch up later. Grace, next to Sam, was topping Noah up with more sunscreen, rubbing the white lotion into his pale skin. Grace had made Noah wear long cotton trousers. Sam was sure the boy would have preferred shorts. Grace was fussing over the child, swatting away flies with an endless stream of instructions coming out of her mouth. Sam was getting annoyed. Would Grace not leave the boy alone for two minutes? And what was taking so long, she was literally melting away. She hated nothing more than being kept waiting. She might as well do something useful. Maybe, her pelvic floor exercises. She needed to be beautiful inside and out. And with inside, she did not mean her personality; she referred to her organs. Sam must be the whole package. She was proud of her liver detox weeks and of practising breathing techniques to strengthen her lungs (everyone should maintain a good pair of lungs) and her picture-perfect pelvic floor. She could squeeze the muscles and count to one hundred without breaking a sweat. She smiled over to Lora who was discreetly nibbling on a piece of dried fruit; she threw a 'this is taking forever' look over to her mum whose hand was resting on Rosie's wheelchair, without letting on that she was working her pelvic floor.

Rosie's eyes skimmed over the cobbled stones. There was a thin film covering her left eye, making it hard to see. Maybe she was going blind. She could not detect a single weed sprouting on the church piazza. It was immaculate. She wondered how they keep it this way. She had always been so careful to pull all the unwanted plants from her garden, but they just kept coming. This was a long time ago, of course. She hadn't worked in the yard for years. The sisters and sometimes her nieces came over to help. Nowadays, Rosie liked to sit in her chair, looking at the world. There was not much she needed to say anymore. In her sleep, she talked plenty to her boy. He visited her all the time. During the day she felt him too, but he liked to keep his distance. One day she will hold him in her arms again. It was the only thing she was looking forward to. She will ask for forgiveness. She will cry that she had not been a better mother, that she had not watched over him, and that she had not minded him enough. He will hug her like he had done a thousand times, and all will be good.

A hint of a smile appeared on her lips, so quickly and so faint you would have never noticed if you weren't expecting it.

Above, the sky was so blue, an incredible shade of azure, that Rosie felt pained by it.

She knew her sisters were worried about her. Lucina had visited often when she was in Ireland. Lucina used to sit with Rosie, holding her hand, never forcing her to speak, understanding her silence. Understanding her guilt and her longing to be reunited with her boy.

When Rachel told her about Lucina's death, Rosie wept without making a sound, without tears. She surprised everyone when she indicated that she wanted to travel to Italy to attend the funeral. She had not set foot outside her home in more than ten years, except for the one and only time when Lucina had invited all the sisters to Puglia. Like the time before, it was a big undertaking for her

43

sisters, but they made it happen for her and for Lucina. Rosie was forever grateful. Lucina was not only her sister but her friend; a truly merciful compassionate person. Besides, Lucina was now with Ewan, delivering all her messages, and letting him know that she would be there soon.

Just as the 'Padre' ushers the men and women into the house of God, Paige's phone begins to ring. 'Highway to hell' is blaring into the stillness. Paige frantically fumbles in her shabby tote to locate her phone, ignoring the disgusted looks around her. Her hand grabs the iPhone, skinny fingers with bitten off nails. It's Reuben. Paige hesitates for a moment, then switches the phone off. The service is about to start. Reuben will be hopping, but what can she do? He would have been even angrier if she answered, explaining that she cannot talk. Either way, she is in deep shit.

The Balotelli family ran the quaint trattoria close to the church, located on a tiny side street of the village. Inside the stone-walled house were a cosy restaurant and a traditional kitchen where papa Giulio was the boss.

In the summertime, everything was happening outside in the courtyard under the vine-covered pergola. Guests enjoying their antipasto and Giulio's secret recipe of orecchiette washed down with local wines. Delicious smells of herb-infused bread drifted over from the outdoor pizza oven. The Chianca stone patio of the alfresco dining area was covered with terracotta pots full of colourful azaleas, geraniums and lavender.

Right next to the property stood an imposing maritime pine, a guardian looking over the Balotelli family.

It is too early for the Italians to have dinner, so the noisy clientele with their laughing bambini in tow has not arrived yet, giving the funeral party some peace and quiet. Lucina's village friends had politely declined the invitation to dinner except for Ilaria, Lucina's best friend, who sat at the head of the table. Ilaria was halfway through an enormous plate of black olives, speaking without bothering to swallow first, gesticulating wildly.

Rosie was watching Rachel nod in agreement to everything Ilaria was chatting about. Rosie might not say much herself, but she was a great observer. She was comfortably seated in an armchair the patron of the house had brought out for her especially. People in the south were so nice. She can easily see why Lucina spent most of her time here. She also understood why Lucina and Ilaria became such good friends. Both possessed the quality of living life to the fullest. Ilaria was loud and funny with an appetite for adventure. Rosie had no doubt, however, that the two women had many heart to heart conversations too, sharing their deepest secrets. Lucina's final farewell was beautiful. The church was packed with village friends and the family. Ilaria made a moving tribute to her friend, Alexander sang a wonderfully touching song, and a local girl played the organ. The priest spoke in Italian. Whatever he said was music to Rosie's ears. It must have been meaningful too, as the villagers were moved to tears. One of them, an elderly impeccably dressed man with a white moustache, read a poem. Rosie did not understand a word, but it was like the angels had spoken from heaven.

The service was the single most beautiful thing Rosie had ever attended.

This place had something magical about it. Rosie was not sure if it was the sweet smell of oranges, the waft of tomato sugo escaping from the kitchen or the parasol like pine trees against the sapphire sky. She only knew she felt calm for the first time in years, enchanted by the Italian surroundings.

When the waiter brought another drink order, Rachel took the opportunity to leave the table. She was tired; she had been taking care of Rosie since they arrived, tending to her every wish.. The church service had been classy, just the way Lucina would have liked it. Tasteful flowers, a simple but surely expensive coffin. She had cried quite a bit. After the ceremony, the coffin was brought to the cemetery where it was lowered into the ground. The priest spoke a few words, and a letter from Lucina was read out by a friend. Rachel did not think anyone was surprised by this. It was Lucina after all, having the last word. She looked around and saw people smiling. She caught Ben rolling his eyes and Paige playing with her skull-earrings. Her daughter Sam looked worryingly red, the colour of her face a stark contrast to her peroxide blond hair, cut way too short, in Rachel's opinion. What was her daughter thinking, going around like a little pixie?

The letter started out in Italian; Lucina had mastered the language in her own time. It must have been funny as the villagers laughed. Then Lucina had addressed the family, saying how grateful and happy she was to have them all here in one place reunited. She went on to say how she had loved her life, but her time had come. They should now go and celebrate, and they would hear from her soon. The last sentence of the letter went over most peoples' heads since they knew how dramatic Lucina inclined to be. Rachel though paid attention. She could not shift the feeling that this was not the end of it all. After the letter, it was Rachel's turn. She had prepared a short but moving speech in the name of all the Irish family. Just when she took the handful of warm earth to throw down the grave, she saw the angel—not at the burial pit—but far beyond the cork trees on the horizon, rising up into the soft air.

"The Lord gives, and the Lord takes," Rachel whispered. She walked out of the restaurant into the field, bordering the property. The tranquillity soothed her. She stood for a few moments, breathing in deeply. She did not doubt what she saw, not for a split second. Rachel knew angels were all around them. The sun was warm on her skin, and she closed her eyes. When she first learnt about her sister's passing, her right index finger started to bleed. Rachel did not even look for a cut or graze as she knew in her heart and soul that it was Lucina's absence that made the blood run from her finger. She simply wrapped some tissue around it and let it be. Only when Ilaria rang with the funeral arrangements and Lucina's request for sparkling outfits, the finger dried up.

It all fit together.

Lucina was still here.

Rachel would go back to the table and talk to the others. Maybe Marie Anne would take the first step and approach Rosie. Maybe there would be peace at last.

Anything was possible as a spell had been cast over them, bewitched by the Italian charm, Lucina smiling down from heavenly realms.

Chapter 11

My celebration of life was wonderful. I don't like to call it a funeral, much too old fashioned and dull.

My life was exhilarating in every way, and I loved every moment of it. My goodbye needed to be just as spectacular. I was careful to have every detail organised before I passed. I picked out the coffin and the types of flowers I liked long before I took my last breath. Everything was in place. I had left a list of instructions.

Although I had a fair idea of when I'd die, I could not know the exact date, so why leave things up to chance?

Ilaria followed the order meticulously, as I knew she would.

I especially enjoyed the splash of colour in the garments my loved ones wore. It was such a joy to see how much effort everyone made. They all looked happy and sad at the same time. I felt for Rosie; it could not have been easy for her, bringing back memories of her own son's burial. I was so thankful she came, as she seemed to enjoy the gem that I called my home.

How they all came together like one big cheerful family, making it work on my behalf. The way it was a long time ago and the way it should be again.

We would have to see how they would cope when I summon them again to learn about the secrets they had kept so close to their hearts.. It worried me that it had to be this way, but there would have to be pain before healing.

Like my beloved father, I died at seventy, and like him, it was my heart that failed me in the end. The circumstances were quite different, however.

My daddy loved to indulge in fine wines and cigars. He was also quite fond of gambling. He lived his adult years in luxury, never denying himself any pleasures.

He was an outstanding father who showed me the world, but most of all, he taught me how to live.

With plenty of money in his pockets, he spent his final years cruising on his yacht, entertaining his friends and trying his luck in Monaco.

It was there, at the roulette table in one of Monte Carlo's posh casinos, that he departed. He had placed his stack of chips on the 13 black, his favourite number, raised his glass of Dom Perignon to the crowd and with a cry of elation fell back into his seat. No one realised that he had died, as—in the very same moment—the ivory ball landed on the 13 black, and the onlookers assumed my father's call was one of triumph.

My own story is less dramatic.

Not known to anyone but myself and only confirmed in my mature years, I was born with a small hole in my heart.

When, after a routine check-up, the consultant investigated further and told me the news, I simply smiled as I had an inkling already. There was nothing to be done, so I continued to live as I had before, happy and fulfilled.

My heart would stop beating, doubtlessly earlier than if it were a healthy organ. But this knowledge did not make me sad or concerned. We all must go at some point. The only thing I sped up was the move to Italy. My house in Ireland was still there for me to stay in and visit, but Italy was where I belonged.

My life there was easy, filled with sunshine and delicious food. My days were spent walking in the olive plantations, reading and sipping cappuccinos in one of the cafes.

I learnt Italian. My teacher was Ilaria, who became my best friend. Through her, I was introduced to the villagers. Their hospitality was immediate, and their warmth contagious. I made many friends and participated in numerous village events.

I became acquainted with Pietro, my gentleman friend and lover. A retired barrister who claimed that he was waiting for me all his life. Our relationship was uncomplicated and full of banter. We spent many days on his little skiff fishing and many evenings with a glass of limoncello watching the amber fireball slowly disappear, leaving an inky sky behind.

Although proud of my Irish heritage, I felt I truly belonged here in this quaint part of southern Italy.

I feel nostalgic now thinking of my friends and the place I called home.

I always believed that eternity is rather a pleasant feeling than a place. My relationship with the Creator was solid and fun as we understood what was required of one another. I am taken care of, I am floating in a warm cotton-soft place, and still, I can get a glimpse of what is happening on earth. I was present at my farewell, although I could not physically take part.

I feel at ease, untroubled and content, there is no other way to describe it.

My last goodbye is over, but I have not completed my task yet.

There are too many loose ends to be tied, too much hurt in my family.

The ferocious act was so appalling, the deception so great; it ruined so many lives and, consequently, fear wormed its way into every imaginable crevice.

I always was and still am the head of the family, the confidant, the string that holds us together.

The truth will bring change for the good; it will fix the broken pieces.

I have asked the family to come together for my burial, and I will call on them once more.

Chapter 12

She sat in the same plane seat as on the way over. Looking out the window, Theresa could see brown vegetation and tall trees. Soon the aeroplane would climb high into the sky submerging itself into thick clouds.

The days in Italy had turned out better than Theresa had anticipated. Initially, she had been anxious about Lucina's strict instructions; she had been afraid that people might not oblige. She had also worried about her sisters.

There had been nothing to fret about. The ceremony itself was elegant and touching. Lucina's village friends were charming. Especially Pietro, who was clothed in a fashionable suit with a scarlet red handkerchief in the breast pocket. She did not understand his poem, but the vibe was that Pietro was more than just a friend.

The get together afterwards was, if she dared to say so, fun. Ilaria was a right hoot. No wonder she and Lucina were best friends.

Nina and Cillian were an absolute credit to Lora, so well-mannered and polite. Alexander had outdone himself singing this marvellous song and Noah, what a little cutie. She wasn't sure about Paige though; there was something off with this girl. She was distant and cross.

Even her sisters seemed somewhat united with Marie-Anne, exchanging a few pleasantries with Rosie.

The few days in Italy had been effortless. Now it was time to get back to real life and her job. Out of the siblings, Theresa and Trevor were the only ones still working. Theresa could have retired a couple of years ago but chose to stay on part-time. She liked her position as an accountant in the manufacturing company, close to where she lived. She enjoyed her co-workers, and the sense of purpose work gave her. The rest of her time was spent with the women's golf team, the hiking club and the love of her life, Bruno Mars. She simply could not wait to cuddle him again.

She had bought him Italian dog-biscuits, a checked raincoat and a diamanté collar in the airport.

Bruno Mars had rescued her; he had instantly filled the void not being able to have children.

The moment she laid eyes on him, she knew he had to be called Bruno Mars. Her absolute favourite artist. Yes, she was of the older generation, but that never stopped her from relishing his music. His songs resonated with her, and when she was alone, she danced to the beat, shaking her booty, like a young one.

"Do you not think it's strange that there is no will?" Trevor said to Marie-Anne when they left the restaurant.

He linked arms with Garry, walking down the narrow street. The air was still balmy, and the moon hung low.

Marie-Anne answered that she did not think it was peculiar. They were dealing with Lucina, who made her own rules.

Marie-Anne was mulling this over now. She boarded the same plane back as the rest of the family. Their separate trip over with Lora and her family seemed pathetic now. Being in that captivating white village had transformed her.

Why was there no will indeed? Maybe Lucina left everything to the villagers or the church perhaps? No, not the church surely. Although Lucina was spiritual, she had not been a great supporter of the catholic faith. Maybe Ilaria was the main beneficiary or a boyfriend? Either way, knowing Lucina, she had made some sort of arrangement. Had there not been something about further instructions in Lucina's letter? They would hear from her. Obviously not literally but in the form of a testament. Yes, that must be it. Marie-Anne is wondering who in her family has their eyes on the estate. She has a hard time coming up with a name. Rachel is far too devastated, Theresa and Trevor have their own things going on, and it has never even crossed her own mind to be left with money or property. No, the siblings are not interested. Ilaria seems to be well off herself. Marie-Anne couldn't help but notice the rather large pink diamond on her finger. There is still the nieces and her daughter Lora. Although Lora has such a hard strange edge to herself, Marie-Anne is sure it is not money that her daughter is after. Grace is completely consumed with her son; most likely, she is not even aware that there could be a will. And Sam? Sam, the affluent career girl, with her fat bank account and designer clothes. She also does not need the cash.

Best, all is left to Rosie.

Grace's hand squeezes Noah's knee. "All will be fine!" she promised. "Don't worry my little pet; we will be home soon."

"I know that, Mummy." Noah's high voice is irritable. He is concentrating hard on 'Super Mario' on his DS. Mario is running through the hardest level yet, jumping on mushrooms trying to rescue Princess Peach. His mother is talking too much. He is not the least bit concerned about the plane ride; he only wants to win this game.

Grace plants a kiss on his forehead. She smiles when Noah wipes it away. *Little rascal.* Of course, he loves her; he is only growing up. Too quickly, to Grace's horror. If she had it her way, Noah would have stayed a baby forever, sitting in his little bouncy chair gurgling. Safe, not getting hurt outside or dealing with children of his own age. Children can be so cruel.

Noah never complains about the kids in his class; in fact, he seems to be getting along very well with them. At the beginning of junior infants, Grace was surprised that all went so smoothly. She had spent restless nights worrying about bullying and the likes. But nothing happened. The transition from playschool to school had been a calm one. On day four, Noah had invited a friend back to the house. Grace had, of course, quizzed the little chap about his interests and parents, just to make sure he was a good influence on her boy. The school years gave Grace nothing to fret about. Noah was still enjoying it to this day. But a voice in Grace's brain keeps reminding her that life is never that easy, just wait and see. Life can be unbearably harsh.

She marvels at Noah, sitting there, absorbed in his game. He is so handsome and smart, such a lovable child. She could not take it if a single hair on his head was harmed. She only knows too well what can happen to little children. It only takes a moment of distraction, a split second of not paying attention and they could vanish forever.

At take-off, Rachel reaches for Paul's hand. The golden cross necklace is securely fastened around her neck.

"You are holding me by your right hand, never letting go." She quickly prays.

They have managed the funeral well. There were no arguments. There was also no reconciliation, but they have time. "All in its good time", the Lord says. The part of the world, Lucina had called her home, was stunningly beautiful and serene.

It is over and done. Only that it isn't really. There is a nagging feeling in the pit of Rachel's stomach, a sense of foreboding. Something is brewing. It is the silence before the storm. There is more to come, in what shape or form Rachel does not know. She is only certain of one thing. Whatever it was, they will not be prepared for the calamity.

Chapter 13

Sam shared the minibus home with Kelly, Ben, Paige and Alexander.

She was glad to be home; glad that the funeral was over. It was nice; everybody behaved amicably. They would always miss her aunt, but life must go on. She would be so busy at home, straight into work. A deadline was looming. Sam loved deadlines; she worked best under pressure. Tomorrow she would get up at 5 am, drive to work and check in with Hala, her very capable personal assistant. Perhaps Hala could bring some of her delicious Fattoush salad, the only dish Sam could savour without worrying about her figure. Obviously, Sam had been in contact with Hala every day, via emails and the odd call. It was imperative that the "Thorn House" project would take off without a hitch. Sam could not wait to be back at her workplace, making decisions, being in charge. She absolutely must be the very best at her job. She was respected and admired in the firm. People looked up to her. And she always got a big thrill before a project went. Adrenaline rushing through her veins, it was better than sex for sure. It was like playing God, life and death in her hands. Only the strongest survive.

When Sam was hired at "Shamrock-Advertising" three years ago, she made radical changes. She cultivated collaboration amongst her employees by facilitating proper communication. There had been no feedback system in place before Sam set foot in the company.

She secured new clients for the firm. She made them money. She terminated casual Fridays. From now on it was work-wear all week. Under no circumstances would Sam arrive at Shamrock in anything less but the most refined designer outfits. By week two, everyone knew who the boss was. She tried to be fair, never letting down her guard, never surrendering an ounce of authority.

She looked out the window. It was a dull day, the sky grey. She still felt a bit anxious. She counted red cars; if she saw five of them in the next 10 minutes, all would be good.

The minute Kelly arrived home, it was like she had never been away.

Crickets, olive oil and the dusty Italian air, became a distant memory—the white village with its cone-shaped houses something out of a dream. Kelly sighed, putting the first load of washing into the machine. Ben was barking at Paige, who had dumped her suitcase at the front door, unwilling to unpack. Her daughter was keen to meet up with Reuben. Kelly did not understand why Ben needed to be so regimental. Paige had not seen her boyfriend for a few days. And, at that age, a couple of days was a long time to be apart, it's when you still feel butterflies in your belly and every minute without your love is an eternity. Kelly only knows this too well.

Paige had been with Rueben for a few months, before that there was someone else. Kelly wasn't sure about the details, her daughter did not share much, but Paige seemed keen to be back in Reuben's arms. He obviously treated her right.

Kelly felt like that when she first met Ben, a million years ago. He made her laugh all the time. He was so funny. And handsome. Ben still liked to joke around, but Kelly's laughs were forced now. She tried hard to find him humorous. Sometimes, when he did succeed, she thought, *yes, he is back, he is funny*. The excitement was always short-lived. It was like they were going around in circles. They were polite to one another like strangers. Ben was a good man. He could be a bit domineering, needing to be right all the time; he liked to call the shots. But Kelly was not concerned with this. What puzzled her most was how her love for him just stopped. It simply did not exist anymore. She had no idea when it all changed. She liked him, for sure, but the love was well and truly gone. He was the father of her children; he was her husband. She once adored him. She knew it was true, but she could hardly recall the time when they were crazy about each other. No matter what she did or thought, Ben was just someone living in her house.

She had resigned to a life of a dull existence. If someone would had suggested she'd fall madly in love once more, she would have said they were bonkers. Not in her lifetime, she would have thought that her heart could pine so strongly for another man. She wouldn't have dared to dream that she would experience the best sex ever, carrying her to unknown heights, burning her loins with desire. The sex part was especially unexpected. Kelly never liked sex before. She felt that she was not good at it, but she understood it was part of a healthy relationship. She and Ben had plenty of it; she let him lead the way participating lethargically, never with any gusto.

She was unadventurous in the bedroom, sticking to a few positions and refusing anything too extreme. There was a time when Ben wanted to introduce some sex toys to spice things up. Kelly just laughed at him, telling him where to go. And yet, her sex life had done a 180-degree turn, changing her into a woman she did not recognise. It was like a drug. She became a minx, craving another man's touch. She now knew she would go further than she ever thought possible. A man had captured her heart, making her weak with yearning. The only problem was, the man was not Ben. She was an adulterer, a bad human being. Surely, there was a place reserved for people like her. The worst was that Kelly did not care. She did not even feel remorseful in the slightest. She would gladly take up permanent residency in the blazing hellfire for just one more night with Jannick.

Alexander's school uniform was laid out for tomorrow, beautifully draped over the back of his chair, so there would be no creases in his white shirt. He had no plans for the rest of the afternoon. He could call Donal. Sometimes they met up; mostly they talked about music and the odd time about girls. They never used any foul language or joined the male chauvinist bravado, so common amongst their peers. There were some nice girls in their year. Alexander and Donal would not mind courting one of them, not that they would have the first clue of how to behave on a date.

Because of the funeral, he had some extra days off school. Tomorrow he would have to bite the bullet and go in. One more year and he would be done. He would never have to face these horrid people again. He would be off, doing what he always wanted to do. Music. There were a lot of great music schools around, his top choice being the Juilliard School of Music in New York and secondly, the Royal Academy in Brittan. With their low acceptance rate, Alexander would be thrilled with either one of them. If he could ever pay for it. It would all work out; he was sure of that. He had inherited his mother's positive outlook on life.

But all the optimism in this world could not ease his mind or take away the knots in his stomach.

PE was scheduled in the morning, the worst subject of all. There would be no escape from the inevitable torture.

"Moobs, Alexander!" the other boys had chanted at the last PE session. "What size bra do you take? Your tits are bigger than the chicks." They had shouted when he changed.

It hurt, but Alexander tried to rise above it. He would keep his head down. Soon it would all be over, and he would be on to bigger and better things. One day he would think back and laugh about it. Well, maybe not laugh. Snigger perhaps, because he would be lucky enough to live out his passion while all the other tossers would be working in meaningless low paying jobs.

A smile flickered across his lips. It was time to get a thick slice of his mum's gorgeous Baileys brownies and forget his troubles for a while.

It was close to 2 am when Paige sneaked back into her house. Technically, she did not have a curfew anymore, but her parents didn't like it when she came home that late; especially, her dad. He was so set in his ways, the old prick. Paige did not particularly care if she upset him, but she was tired of the endless arguments. "What do you want to do with your life? What are your plans?" Why the fuck did she have to have any plans? She was young. She did not know. She would finish the college course, although she no longer was interested in it. And then she would see. What was the rush? These old people always needed to know exactly what was happening. She could be dead tomorrow. Like Lucina, woke up one morning and dropped dead in the evening. Paige had no ambitions; neither did she believe in the master plan. The one thing she really wanted was something she couldn't have. That ship had sailed. He was married now and happy. He would start a family and have a bunch of adorable blond kids running around. They would get a dog too, of course. A golden Lab that would catch every single ball he threw for it. He would take the dog for daily walks along the river in his grey Aran sweater, his 5 O'clock shadow, his rugged good looks. At home, the bitch would be waiting for him in their cosy, little cottage. She would greet him at the door in a rust-red satin morning gown that matched her luxurious hair.

Oh, how Paige hated them. Well, not Brodie. She still loved Brodie.

There was a sharp pain in her chest. It was heartache and it had been there for a long time, ever since Brodie dumped her.

She was with Rueben now. She should consider herself lucky. She had a boyfriend. So many of her friends were single, always on the prowl. Some were on Tinder, swiping left, swiping right. Paige did not have to waste her energy on any of that. She was spoken for. Rueben was such a babe-magnet with his dark messy mane, his chiselled cheekbones and his bad-ass leather jacket. Girls were always giving him the eye. But what really got the chicks going was his black

Kawasaki Ninja. Paige often called into his workplace at the mechanics, and they went for a spin on the motorcycle. Ruben completely disregarded speed limits and other rules of the road. Together they sped along the national routes, overtaking pretty much everything in their way, leaning dangerously close into the bends. For Paige this was nirvana. Her mind was blank when she was on that machine, her arms tightly wrapped around Reuben. She did not have to think or worry; she felt exhilarated and intoxicated by the nearness of death.

Of course, her parents knew nothing about the motorbike. They would have a canary blabbing on about the many dangers. But it was precisely the danger that electrified her the most.

The bike alone was worth putting up with Reuben's bad temper. He could fly off the handle as quick as a flash. The smallest thing would send him into a rage. And it was no picnic when he was in that state. Paige had learned to keep her head down, not to argue back. He smacked hard and had left many bruises. Once, after a bad episode, he had put his large hands around her neck and squeezed. She thought she would die. She saw black and must have passed out for a split second. His handprints were visible for days, and she had to wear a light scarf although it was summer. Reuben had apologised with flowers. He said he would not hurt her again. For a while things were better. Then the hitting started anew, but he never strangled her again. Paige knew she could be hard work, stubborn and irritating. She probably deserved a bit of discipline. After all, Reuben loved her. He could be so sweet, especially after sex, when he got her to do things she really didn't want to do. Yes, overall, he was a good catch. Most importantly, she was not alone. She had a boyfriend who wanted to be with her.

Not like Brodie, who tossed her away like a hot potato.

From time to time, Paige allowed herself to go back to the time when life was just bliss; when she and Brodie were an item.

The bitch had broken up with him because she moved to the States. Brodie was so over her and her drama. He said that much. He was so gentle, so smart and quick-witted. Paige just adored spending time with him. They went for walks; they kayaked, they went out, and he even brought her to art exhibitions and museums. Her parents would have thought he was the bee's knees, but funnily enough, she never introduced them.

And then the bitch decided to come back. Just like that. The bubble burst. All the sudden Brodie had feelings for her again. They wanted to give it another go. Paige was in the way. Their relationship had to end. So, he ended it and left her devastated. He called it a mistake. He said it wasn't serious anyway. Well, it kind of was, as Paige discovered a short while after.

It is all in the past now, she thought. She should be happy with Reuben. She was happy. She sat on the edge of the bathtub. She was still in her clothes, and she had not taken off her makeup yet. She took the razor blade from her beauty bag and cut three neat lines into her forearm. Blood trickled down onto the tiled floor. The release was awesome.

Part Two
1978–2018

Chapter 14

It was not Kelly's fault that everything came so easily to her.

It was like she was blessed, as if someone up there was looking out for her. Kelly was born with natural beauty, hypnotising eyes in shades of lapis lazuli and amethyst, creamy skin and an hourglass figure. But Kelly never used her looks to get her way; she did not need to, it all fell into her lap anyway.

She was popular in school without trying too hard. Her teachers thought she was a pet. She was never part of the cousins clique though. Sam, Grace and Lora were in a league of their own which did not include Kelly.

Kelly did not mind all that much as a child. She played her own games and put up with being bossed around by Sam. Her sister could be quite mean too. It was not till they were adults that one of Kelly's friends pointed out that Sam had obviously been jealous of her. This would not have occurred to Kelly. They were sisters and were supposed to love each other. Sam changed at some point. It was after young Ewan's tragic accident, Kelly thought. Sam became a bit withdrawn and even more fierce.

Besides the travesty and the horrible fall out between her aunties , Kelly's childhood was a very happy one.

She sailed through the school years with minimal effort, and she was cast as Annie in the annual school play when she was 14.

She had not even tried out for the part. She was singing in the shower after sports class, thinking she was alone. Her classmates had gone up ahead to the canteen. Mrs. Flynn, the drama and music teacher, happened to come into the change room to check on a window that had unhinged when the girls were trying to open it. Mrs. Flynn, an enthusiastic teacher, stopped in her tracks when she heard the melodic voice coming from the showers. The teacher forgot what she had come in for, transfixed, weeping silently.

So, Kelly played Annie. The title role was simply taken away from Siobhan, the girl who had worked so hard for it. You would think this incident made Kelly a target. It did not. The change was accepted without ever being questioned.

When school ended, Kelly went to her Debs, the school formal with Daniel, the most handsome lad in the vicinity. They danced the night away, and Kelly thought life just could not get any better.

Most of Kelly's friends had enrolled in college courses, but Kelly was not interested. She completed a secretarial class and was immediately hired into a small solicitor's firm.

Robert Brown employed her on looks alone. He hardly glanced at her secretarial certificate, enthralled by her eyes and substantial bosom. His desk was positioned opposite of hers, and he spent the best part of the day gazing at the divine creature across from him. His own work slacked behind, but as he was the boss, no one dared to comment.

Robert Brown's goal was to ask Kelly out on a date. He just needed to work up the courage, as he was a proud man terrified of rejection.

But before Robert got the chance Kelly was snatched away from him.

Kelly did not care about the job. She neither loved nor hated it. It was an easy life, and this was what she was after. She enjoyed making a few bob, spending the money mostly on herself. She hardly thought of the future, a career or beyond.

It was a Friday afternoon in 1994, the March winds blew harshly across the seafront, turning umbrellas inside out. The sky a slate grey, the rain coming sideways. In her lunch break, Kelly ran from the firm to the supermarket, and although it was a short distance, she arrived soaking wet. And she was not the only one. The place was packed with agitated people searching for a bite to eat or simply waiting for the downpour to ease up. She was standing in the enormous line to pay, when a row broke out between two women, arguing over a washing powder brand. Kelly, despising arguments, turned her back when, to her alarm, one of the now distressed ladies poked her in the arm asking for her opinion.

Kelly tried to make an excuse, but the two women had none of it. They stood, arms on hips, eyes gleaming, waiting for her to settle the matter once and for all.

Kelly did.

She only did what she would have done with a child—calming down the situation. She talked the women through it, listening to both, making the odd remark but really letting them find their own way. In the end, the pair laughed about their foolishness.

Kelly's work was done. She paid and was about to leave when a hand grabbed her arm.

"Excuse me; I did not mean to startle you." Barron Mulcahy's voice was warm and deep. He asked if she had time for a coffee; he had a proposition for her.

Barron's company specialised in executive coaching. He helped firms to reach their potential in eliminating barriers between management and employees. He was one of the pioneers in his field, as coaching was, at that time, unheard of in Ireland and perceived as a novice, American money maker.

Barron, however, was a clever and convincing man. He had come over from London five years ago where he had worked in a large company. He had noticed that communication was key and that arguments could fester if they were not addressed and could subsequently ruin the morale of a business.

He had proven that this theory worked, and enterprises started to take note. It was time for him to hire another mediator, and he wanted Kelly.

Kelly immediately liked Barron, the lean man in his mid-forties with his unruly grey hair.

She did not need to think twice about the offer. The money was good, and the position sounded interesting.

Kelly quit her job at the Solicitor and started with Barron. He arranged training for her, and she took to the job like a duck to water.

Barron assigned challenging cases to her, and she felt blessed to be doing something she liked.

Around six months after her start date, Barron asked her to attend an important meeting. He hoped to secure a business deal with a large and profitable company. It would bring Barron and his crews' pay cheque to new heights.

He needed Kelly's support. She did not let him down, her serene approach, her impeccable looks and that canary yellow outfit!

Barron, a highly superstitious man, was not only thrilled with the positive outcome but requested that Kelly should be present at every crucial sales pitch. What's more, he demanded she wore yellow and only yellow to every one of them. Kelly, who had noticed Barron's love for good luck charms, was amused by the intensity of his supernatural belief. She mentioned, half-jokingly, that there was no way she could arrive in a different yellow outfit for all his VIP clients.

The very next day, there was a cheque sitting on her desk. "Dress yourself in yellow!" Barron had scribbled in his messy handwriting. The amount was big enough to purchase a small car. Initially, Kelly was mortified; she felt she had ambushed Barron into shelling out money. But after seeking advice from her girlfriends and sister, who quickly reminded her that Barron could easily afford it, she threw caution to the wind and indulged in a frenzy of yellow. Dresses in sunflower and shades of primrose, pants suits in egg-yolk, saffron shoes and lemon handbags.

Kelly's life was one series of good fortunes. She breezed through her days smoothly without a care in her head.

She was not looking for a man; she wasn't even thinking about relationships when Ben came into her life.

He was the CRO of a business that used the firm she worked for.

Ben fell in love the moment he laid eyes on her. She was a goddess, swinging hips and the face of an angel. And although he was a good-looking chap back then, she was in a class of her own. Ben always aimed high, and there was no time to waste. A dozen pink roses were sent to Kelly's office with an invitation to dinner at an upmarket restaurant.

Kelly charmed by the worldly man and his wicked sense of humour, found herself falling for her prince in shining armour.

Ben knew what he was talking about; he was in charge.

They started spending a lot of time with each other. It was all good for Kelly; even the sex was bearable. It was part of the parcel; she just had to accept that. She did not feel confident in the bedroom, second guessing her every move. It was not an activity she would ever enjoy, mostly because she did not know how to be satisfied herself, but Ben did not seem to notice. In his opinion, he had hit the jackpot.

Kelly fell pregnant in 1996. She had not needed to worry about Ben's reaction. He was overjoyed, whisking her away to Paris, proposing on the Eiffel Tower. It all happened so fast; Kelly had no time to think. She was blissfully happy; her husband was a romantic, and they were starting a family. She would become a mother.

Kelly did not even have to plan the wedding. Ben and his mother, Mary, were only too happy to arrange all the details. Kelly ignored Sam's remarks about the bossy-boots future in-laws. Mary delegated some of the smaller jobs to Rachel, who good-tempered as always, did not mind. Her mother came along to help Kelly select a wedding dress. They had fun browsing and, in the end, picked a flowy dress made of beautiful ivory silk charmeuse.

Mary booked Dromoland Castle for the ceremony and co-ordinated the colour scheme.

Her best friend and bridesmaid, Isabell, wore a sage green satin gown, a colour Kelly wasn't particularly fond of. But it did not matter; Kelly appreciated Mary's enthusiasm and organisation skills. Sam, as the maid of honour, refused point-blank the dress Mary had chosen. "Not on your nelly!" Sam had barked at the elderly lady, leaving no room for negotiation. Kelly stayed out of it; she only wanted happy vibes. Her sister got her garment designed in London, a simple but elegant robe in bronze made of Italian satin.

The wedding was a memorable affair, Kelly's tiny bump well-hidden beneath her frock.

She gave birth a few months later and some years after that to her son Alexander.

Her luck was complete. She continued to work part-time, she adored being a mother, Ben made a great husband and father to the little ones.

Things were fine. Ben was busy at work; Kelly was occupied with the children. They still went out together as a couple; they still were intimate. Ben wanted sex all the time, and Kelly obliged. It was nothing new.

Kelly's favourite time was playing with the kids. They spent hours building with Lego and making all sorts of funny creations out of play dough. They went for walks and to the playground in the park nearby.

Kelly considered herself a sunny and content person when Ben seemed to be grumpy and irritable.

"It is probably because he is jealous of the kids," Isabell said. "He is not your priority anymore." But Kelly dismissed such silly suggestions. Jealous of the kids, his own brood? No way. Nothing had changed; she still adored her husband. But his aura was different; it had turned from scarlet to rust.

Kelly avoided bringing up his moods. There was no point. She convinced herself that things would get back on track. She was sure that it was all normal, so why open a can of worms?

Only Ben became more irascible by the day.

He arrived home one Wednesday evening to find the kitchen covered in flour; butter was melting on the counter and egg running down the breakfast bar. His wife and two kids were in a heap on the floor in convulsions of laughter, jam smeared across their faces and a banana squished into Kelly's hair.

Ben stood and stared at them. He believed they had lost their minds. Then he started to roar. He shouted at the top of his lungs. He ordered them to go and wash up and clean the filthy mess. Had they lost their marbles? He screamed. What on earth was going on? Paige and Alexander now terrified, ran off to have showers while Kelly just looked at him blankly.

"We were baking," she finally said in a small voice. "It got messy, we had a floor fight; we only had some fun…" she trailed off.

Ben regarded her as if she had two heads. His face was bright red, a large vein pulsing at his neck, sweat beads forming on his forehead.

Later, when he had calmed down, he told Kelly that all he wanted was dinner on the table when he got home after a long day's work. A clean place and a normal wife. Was that too much to ask for?

No, it was not. Kelly made a mental note to be more of that. More normal. Less mess and supper on the table. She could handle it.

That night she held her kids close, mumbling sweet nothings into their ears, promising them that all would be fine.

She would rein herself in whenever her thoughts drifted to happy places and dreams of carefree laughter.

She would try to make it work.

Chapter 15

The breakfast bar was covered with used coffee mugs, plates and crumbs. A cereal box had tipped over, and its contents spilt across the table onto the linoleum floor. The orange juice carton sat in a deep yellow puddle. Crackling noises came from the radio on the sideboard; nobody had bothered to tune into a better station.

It was a Tuesday morning in early May 2013 when Lora's children and husband finally realised that there was something terribly wrong with her.

Lora should have gotten ready for her job. She should have cleaned up, gone upstairs and got dressed. Instead, she sat frozen on her chair, cradling an ice-cold coffee cup in her hands. The kids were no longer talking to her. In fact, they hated her. Even Oscar refused to speak to her after she came clean this morning.

It was the endless questions that had bothered her the most—the hope in the kid's eyes, their willingness to do anything to find Toby.

In the end, Lora could not take it anymore. She felt the anger built up; she became impatient with them. They would not stop, and would not shut up about that damn dog.

When the irritation overwhelmed her completely, her cheeks flushing in various shades of pink, her mouth turning into a bitter, thin line, she just blurted it out. She had killed the fucking dog.

The effect of her confession was catastrophic. After a moment of stunned silence, all hell broke loose. Nina roared and cried. Cillian went as white as a ghost. He barely made it to the toilet where he vomited all over the seat. Oscar stared at her. Why? But why on earth? He kept asking in disbelief.

What was there to say? Lora could have told them that the dog barked too much, that he was annoying, that she was tired of cleaning up the shit in the garden and taking him for walks. But did it matter? She could not tell them the truth. They would have put her in a loony bin. Or, at the very least, Oscar would have made an appointment for a psychiatric evaluation. She stayed quiet, letting them assume whatever they wanted. She did not care.

Oscar tended to the kids, while she remained in her spot. He got them out to school, leaving her in the kitchen without saying goodbye. No one asked how she had done it or where the dead dog was now.

Grace carefully steered her station wagon away from the Montessori's drop off area. The salesman at the car dealers had assured her that station wagons were one of the safest vehicles. Safety was so important when she was driving her child around. Noah was four and had recently started in the preschool. Not that Grace particularly wanted him to go to school, but everyone had urged her to sign him up. It would be so great for his development, they had said. His mind would expand. The mixing with other kids would do him good. As if she was not enough for him. Not enough as a mother. From the moment she had learnt that she was pregnant, Grace had done nothing but minded her body. She quit her job immediately, as stress was bad for the unborn child. She nourished herself with only organic produce and carefully selected lean meat cuts. She exercised gently; she listened to classical music and the sounds of the rainforest. After her boy was born, she spent every second of her life making sure that he was cared for and protected. Her baby was her world. Nothing else mattered any more. When he started to walk, she ran alongside him, catching him before he could fall. She read to him, sang him to sleep, fed him the best baby food on the market and tended to his every whim. "You are spoiling him; he will end up like a typical only child." Her husband warned her. But Grace did not listen. She understood that it was all up to her. She had only one shot at this, every single minute needed to be devoted to her child.

Noah did not turn out spoilt. He loved other kids and had no issues sharing his toys. He gravitated towards children of his own age. Grace tried to keep the contact to a minimum. She was worried about too much exposure to other children. She refused to let him go on playdates without her because she could not supervise. The more she held him back, the more he wanted to get away from her. Noah was excited when Montessori school started. He could not wait to go. Grace longingly watched other kids hanging onto their mothers' pants, refusing to let go. Kids screaming and crying for their mums. She would have gladly traded places with those exasperated mothers. She would have scooped Noah up into her arms and brought him home. She would have had an excuse to keep him with her. But oh no, her son was only too glad to stay and play.

She kept watching out for signs of misery, but there weren't any. Noah was always happy; he mixed well and adored his teacher. No matter what way she looked at this, Noah was growing up, he was slowly but surely cutting the apron strings and soon enough she would be all alone.

Chapter 16

It was an unusually warm day for February; the air was moist with humidity, daffodils and crocuses already blossoming on the edge of the sidewalks.

Grace drove along the wide street lined with beech trees when the death notifications came on the radio.

"Caroline Mc Nabb died peacefully in her own home, surrounded by her loving family."

"She will be missed by her children—Angela, Mark and Lorcan—her beloved grandchildren, sister Kathleen and brother Liam and all the extended family. The memorial mass will take place on Thursday at 11 am in the Edgehillstown Church of the Immaculate Conception. The family is kindly asking for donations towards Cancer Support Ireland."

Death! There it was again. The one thing she dreaded most. Death and taxes, an inevitable occurrence. She did not care about the latter; death, however, was always in the forefront of her mind.

What if she died and left poor Noah alone in this cruel world? Without the love of his mother, her guidance and protection. Her husband would only do half as good of a job, being far more interested in his career than his son. Who would look out for him? Nurse him when he burnt up with a fever? Who would comfort him when a girl broke his heart? Who would give him advice when he had kids of his own? The answer was nobody. She was the only one who could do the job properly, who loved him unconditionally. She simply had to stay alive for him. Not that she was sick, or anything like that. But things could change. Very fast, as she knew. Bad stuff happened all the time, even to innocent little children. Grace could not even entertain the thought of losing him. She would die, on the spot, or kill herself. She could not go on without him; there was just no way.

With every bad deed, there had to be a punishment somewhere along the way. Grace knew that fate would decide its course for her. If she was not struck before, she would pay the price on judgement day. She could only pray that God would not settle the score with an eye for an eye.

A crime, like the one she had committed, would have consequences, no doubt. The only question was when? When would she pay for it?

Grace had not only murdered her brother she had also inflicted enormous pain upon her mother. She had ended her mother's life along with Ewan's as Rosie had given up. Losing Ewan and the incredible guilt that engulfed her broke Rosie's heart and spirit. And all Grace had done was watch her mother deteriorate. She never set the record straight; she never came clean and admitted to what they had done. She never eased her mother's torment.

She had tried talking to Lora twice about it. The first time was a few months after the incident when all her mum did was cry. The second time was much later when she realised that there was no coming back for Rosie. Her mother took up residency in a very dark place, one that let no one in. She no longer spoke; she no longer washed herself, or ate proper food.

The light from her eyes was gone, her look vacant. Her aunts were buzzing around her mother, helping in every way they could. Grace herself did everything in her power to make her mum's days more bearable. It was her own way of easing her guilty feelings. Even when it only was a drop on a hot stone.

When she spoke to Lora as an adult, her cousin refused point-blank to cooperate. She reminded Grace that they had committed a crime, that their sentence would be lengthy. Grace had tried to argue that they were children, but Lora had convinced her that this evil act would still result in a prison term. Most importantly, they had not confessed straight away. Too much time had passed.

Too worried to ask anyone and terrified she might have to give up her son, Grace kept quiet and watched her mother slowly die, riddled with grief, blaming herself.

One thing Grace knew for sure. It was only a matter of time before she would stand trial.

Misdeeds as terrible as theirs could not stay hidden away in the past. The aftermath would have a catastrophic effect. Grace was petrified.

Theresa and Julian were still in bed when Senora Del Toro gently knocked on their door.

It was just after 6 am, and the incandescent sunlight was already smouldering the stones of Mojacar's narrow cobbled streets.

They had both taken a week's holiday and travelled to Spain to celebrate the one-year mark in their relationship.

He was Theresa's first significant boyfriend, her first meaningful partnership that would surely lead to marriage and a family. She was happy. They were happy. They had spent the last few days at Palmeral Beach and roamed the whitewashed Moorish old town, stopping for tapas and sangria. They had laughed when they touched the breasts of the Mojaquera statue, honouring the legend that they would fall in love with the town and return.

They held hands and kissed in the shade of fig trees beneath the scorching sun. Julian had booked them into 'Sol y Luna,' the guesthouse closest to the Plaza Nueva.

"What time is it?" Julian turned to Theresa; the bedsheet wrapped around his legs.

"Six," Theresa answered. She rubbed her eyes and got out of bed.

She opened the door slightly to find the senora standing there in her morning robe.

"There is a phone call for you, senorita," she said in a thick Spanish accent.

Theresa was still wearing her pyjama bottoms when the taxi pulled up at Almeria Airport. She hadn't bothered to get dressed. She had simply pulled a T-shirt over her nightwear and thrown all her belongings into a case.

Julian had urged her to make a proper plan. To think things through. But Theresa had not even listened. She needed to get home as quickly as possible. She would find a flight. She would beg the airport staff to let her on. Her sisters needed her. Rosie needed her! Ewan was dead. Her godson had died. Rosie's life was in turmoil. Rosie was the only one who had made her godmother, the only one who had thought Theresa was mature enough to handle the responsibility. Now Ewan was dead, and she was not even there. It had taken Rachel a while to find her in Mojacar, to locate the guesthouse and place the call.

Julian stayed very calm during her meltdown. He had tried talking to her had wanted to figure things out together. He had put a hand on her arm when she stuffed clothes into her bag. He had tried to stop her. He felt the need to discuss everything; he did not understand that there was no time.

How would he know about her obligation? Rosie had just lost her beloved boy. Rosie, the only sister who truly had tried to include her. Theresa could not risk jeopardising that. There was no time to explain the intricate details to Julian; she needed him to act fast and come with her. He did not. He did not understand her urgency and refused to accompany her. He said they would talk when things had settled.

Theresa swallowed her pride and boarded the plane without him.

The days that followed were like a blur. Rosie was beside herself. There was a funeral to arrange. People were in a daze.

When Julian returned home a few days later, he wanted to contact Theresa, but she was too busy comforting Rosie to see him.

Days turned into weeks, and she still had not seen Julian. He had tried to get in touch. It was never a good time; besides, Theresa was still hurting over his decision to stay.

Eventually, Theresa returned to work, although Rosie was broken.

She wondered if things would have been different had she not gone on holidays. Would her godson still be alive? She could have watched him, spent more time with him. She could have helped more. Rosie had relied on her, but Theresa had been too occupied with herself.

Julian and Theresa only met up one more time.

They spoke in a quiet corner of a pub. Julian failed to understand her and Theresa was too exhausted to make him see that if he really loved her, he would have moved the earth to be with her. He would have simply trusted her decision and would have come with her, no questions asked. He would have accepted how important this was to Theresa. But instead, he wanted to talk, wanted to sit together and contemplate. No, he did not get her. There was no point in prolonging their relationship.

Theresa was sad and at the same time glad she had figured out what he was made of before they had gone any further.

She now comprehended what she needed most in life. She wanted a baby.

Rosie's bereavement had highlighted her loneliness, the need for her own little family. She wanted to be a mother, to care for someone, raise a child and show him the world.

She wasn't old, and still, her biological clock was ticking away fast. All her sisters had their children early; Rosie gave birth to Grace when she was only 17. By her family's standards, she certainly was over the hill as she wasn't even in a relationship any longer,—a babyless spinster.

Over the next few years, Theresa concentrated on finding a man willing to have kids. When that man did not materialise, she had to think on her feet. She would not leave a stone unturned to fulfil her dream. She would explore other options, search for alternatives. She would go down avenues she could never discuss, and never admit to, not even to herself. She would do things that would make her sisters' stomachs turn.

Chapter 17

Samantha's date was late by five minutes already. There was nothing that Samantha despised more than tardiness. Why was it so hard for people to be on time? And why was everybody so flipping blaze about it? Sam could feel herself grow angry, a lump rising in her throat. You just had to be fucking organised, that's all. How difficult could it be? She managed to be methodical in every aspect of her life, down to her daily routine. Always making lists and ticking off accomplished tasks.

She turned the glass of Pinot Grigio in her hand. The newly opened wine bar was the hippest place to be, and at six o'clock, it was already buzzing with customers. She pulled impatiently on her pristine shirt collar, she smoothed down her carefully ironed, crease-free, tailored linen suit. She became more agitated by the minute. She was on time, so why couldn't Bob be? Bob worked with her. Under her, to be specific. She had finally agreed to a date after him pestering her for weeks. Now she regretted it.

A tad shy of thirty and the millennium looming, she was still single. She would have never admitted to it, but she was starting to feel the pressure. Kelly, her younger sister, was married with a child. Most of her friends had tied the knot. To be honest, she did not have many close friends, but the few she had were blissfully happy. They all wanted a family. Melting away at the mere sight of babies, dreaming of tiny pudgy hands and feet. No thanks! What a nightmare: getting up at night, losing out on her vital beauty sleep, grubby paws, and shitty nappies. Sam never considered making all that part of her life. In fact, she could not stand kids. Not even her niece Paige. Sam tried to avoid spending time with the toddler at all costs. She made up excuses, blatantly lying to get out of her duties as an aunt. She was relieved, rather than getting offended, when Kelly chose her best friend Isabell as godmother. She truly hated children. They were loud and obnoxious, demanding and irrational, and most of all, slobby. Traits Sam made a wide berth around.

She had never felt maternal. When they were kids, she was always the boss, the instigator. She tolerated playing house and dolls with her cousins but only when they obeyed her rules. She never babysat for anyone, and her own sister was a nuisance to her most of the time. Nurturing was easy for most women but not for her. People often commented on how hard she was, as cold as ice. She was driven, and she knew what she wanted. She dreamt of a career and money and sought out the finer things in life. She wasn't easily pleased either, uncompromising and unforgiving. It was her way or the highway. She was successful and moving up in the corporate world. She would have liked a boyfriend, but since it was the only thing she could not control or could not make happen, she had failed so far. "You are too choosy," her friends would comment. "He would have to be 100% perfect before you would even consider dating him." And why not? Why not aim high? Why not search for the ideal man when she herself was striving for perfection in every aspect of her life.

Her job was challenging and prosperous, her apartment immaculate, her car brand-new and shiny.

She ate healthily, looked after her organs, worked out at least three times a week and would, under no circumstances, leave the house without a full face on. She prided herself on her appearance. And she had to work hard on maintaining it. The things she could not take care of herself, she placed in the capable hands of the specialists. She did not have the good fortune to be born a natural beauty like Kelly. Sam had to buy the coloured contacts to make her eyes stand out. She invested in the latest products on the market for a flawless skin; she worked her body hard to keep a slim waist. She lifted weights, keeping the bingo wings at bay and she had bought herself a fine set of boobs. Again, Kelly was blessed with the big bosom, and Sam had missed out. She gladly paid a substantial sum to have the best plastic surgeon, an Indian man, transform her. She started botox early in life , and she was constantly on the lookout for the latest treatment that promised eternal youth.

Sam loved nothing more than shopping. She left a stack of cash for a new designer bag without batting an eyelid. She handed over her credit card without flinching, walking away clothed in celebrity inspired garments, always bang on trend.

She never gave to charities, the homeless or any other organisation as she considered it a waste of money. She saw no point in sharing her hard-earned cash with the less fortunate. Sam thought of the needy as lazy and unwilling. Where there is a will, there is a way, was her motto.

She could not, however, apply her philosophy to the opposite sex. Besides dates and meaningless sex, one-night stands, more for her own gratification than a commitment, she was alone.

She not only used her hard-ass attitude at work but also when weeding out the less desirable candidates from the massive pool of willing men. One wrong move, one annoying habit, a bodily flaw, and they were out.

The handsome ones, the ones with trained bodies and washboard bellies, she took to bed. This was the first test. If they passed her bedroom requirements, they were given a second chance. Another date at which she subjected them to further examination. Work and ambitions, hobbies, tidiness and political views were all on the list of inquiries. Should one mention his desire to start a family, Sam dismissed him immediately. Not another thought wasted on the man.

So far, only two had moved on to the third level—the level of spending more time with one another. This was the crucial part. The part when you'd find out that your guy doesn't close drawers or replace the empty toilet rolls. The time when you find out that your man felt the need to call his mother, to run by her whether he should wear a tie or dicky bow to an important meeting.

At this moment, Sam would tell him that things weren't working out. That it was her, not him. Nobody ever made it past phase three.

Sam often watched the yummy mummies—the soccer mums in their white jeeps, dark sunglasses and leopard print ankle boots—darting into the cosmetic clinic for their three monthly botox top up before picking up their rowdy kids from school. Sam sat in her Lexus and sniggered at them. The only thing they had in common was fitting their procedures into their lunch break. Unlike the stressed mothers, she would go back to a job she loved and a clean, clutter-free house. She did not want what these women had, even the rich ones who did not need to work. Sam thrived at work. She pitied these ladies, seeing the stress on their faces, trying to juggle their own needs with the ones of their family, hardly ever having any time to themselves. Sam could do what she liked whenever she liked it. She did not need to answer to anyone.

She was always in charge. Letting go of her control would be like giving up, not caring anymore and if she did not care, she would find herself on a downward spiral in no time at all. She would be sacked, lose her home and end up living on the streets. Cold, filthy and vulnerable. The maniacs who'd share the shelter of bridges with her would probably rape and burn her, kick her helpless body, kill her. She would die in the gutters. No! This could not happen. She would not let go of an inch.

Even thinking about these possibilities made Sam break out in hives. An ultimate nightmare. There was no time to relax. Perfection all the way so that she could secure her place on top.

Bad stuff happened to people all the time, people who make wrong choices. Sam would not be one of them.

How did she let herself think these dark thoughts? Now her hands were clammy, and her date still a no show. She knocked on the wooden table for good measures and positive inspiration. All would be fine. She reminded herself to stay calm.

This was all Bob's fault. Normally she would have been at the gym working her glutes instead of sitting here like a moron, wasting her time, bad images racing through her head.

If the next person who came through the door was a woman, Sam would leave, knowing Bob was not worth it.

Too bad there would be no sex; Bob had a fine ass. *But what the hell*, she thought, *there was always the vibrator.*

The door opened, and a tall brunette sailed in. Sam stood up, grabbed her bag and left.

As she stood, waiting to flag down a taxi wrapped in her long merino wool coat, she felt a little sorry for herself. She would be alone in her apartment, watching ex on the beach or some other silly mindless show.

Sam whipped herself into shape again. It was her choice to leave and be alone. She was fine, perfectly happy; she did not need a man, especially not a loser like Bob, who clearly did not know his ass from his head. No, there was no need to feel sorry for herself. She was a strong independent woman. She could always call a friend, although they would be hanging out with their better halves. She could see if Kelly was free and willing to share a G&T with her big sister. She would allow herself one tall glass and seriously detox the next few days.

Then again, Kelly could be so tiring. She'd be better off chilling on her own.

Sam had recently spent a whole week with her sister. They had flown to Lanzarote for a bit of sunshine. Obviously, Sam was not a sun worshiper. She did not want to end up with leather skin and wrinkles so deep that no fillers could fix them. Kelly, on the other hand, baked in the sun without giving it any thought. *Silly girl.* She told Sam she used a natural crème from the health food store that kept her skin well nourished. Kelly was offended when Sam laughed at her. Sam thought the health food shop lotion was a joke; she had never heard of anyone buying beauty products there. Sam had to admit though, Kelly's skin was flawless, and for some strange reason, it did not burn in the heat.

After all her moaning, Kelly did not lift a finger organising the trip but left everything to Sam.

It turned out that all Kelly wanted was to sit by the pool, talk, and read. Sam became antsy after the first day. She wanted to see what the island had to offer. There was camel riding, cactus garden and Martinez's Museum of Art to explore.

She suggested to rent a car and drive around, but Kelly informed her that she was happy lazing by the water, drinking a few cocktails and yapping with the lovely couple from Belfast. Sam lost the plot. What in God's name was the point of a holiday when you did fuck all. They had an argument. Kelly called Sam bossy, dragging up their childhood and accusing Sam of being domineering and excluding her. Kelly could be so juvenile, never letting go and always playing the victim. Her sister might be gorgeous, and things fell into her lap, but she sure was meek.

In the end, they went their separate ways. Sam busied herself with activities during the day, and Kelly spent her time conversing with random strangers and laughing with the kiddies that splashed in the pool. How pathetic. There she was, her sister, trying to get away from her family and then drooling over every dumb child that looked her way.

In the evening time, the sisters met for dinner, keeping the chats light, although there was a visible strain between them.

Sam was not sure who was more relieved when Saturday came, and they boarded the plane home.

Sam only knew she would never embark on another holiday adventure with her sister. She would rather stick pins in her eyes.

A taxi finally screeched to a halt. Sam hopped in, already dismissing the idea to contact Kelly.

She was quite content again. Her life was good. Maybe the perfect man was out there, but she wasn't all that concerned anymore. She had never truly been in love anyway.

She held her place in the world: her career, money, nice things, and some friends.

She would continue to call into auntie Rosie; she could spare an hour here and there to keep her company. Everyone in the family did their bit. It was an unspoken agreement between them.

Sam felt bad for Rosie and the part she had played in making her aunt's life a misery. But she refused to feel guilty. They were kids. They could not judge the consequences. They did not know what they were doing. Or did they? The few times Sam let herself dig deeper, she realised that a tiny part of her had known. And what was worse, she had wanted it to happen. She had hated that annoying little snotface and she had been curious to see him struggle.

"Let's throw him in!" she had said. And, of course, they did what she demanded.

This world could be so bad.

Sam often woke in the middle of the night, her heart pounding in her chest and sweat pouring from her face. She'd dream she was in a car crash, her face horribly disfigured, leaving her unrecognisable.

These dreams would carry into her days, bolts of lightning, flashes of scary thoughts.

She would have to remind herself to stay still, not to panic, and breathe in and out slowly. Knock on wood, believe that if she kept her desk in order, hung her clothes in a neat row, continued with an orderly, predictable life, everything would be alright.

She had to squash feelings of remorse and sadness as soon as they surfaced. She had to stay in control.

Chapter 18

Rachel had that dream again. She was running up a steep hill. She was panting, her breath shallow. There could have been someone following her, but she was not sure. She did not dare turn around as she knew turning her head would have cost her valuable seconds. She was in a hurry needing to reach the top of the hill as whatever was urging her on was waiting up there for her. But like always, she woke just before she got to the summit.

Rachel's body was covered in light perspiration, the night sweats had started a few months earlier. The less she wore in bed the more she sweated so she had taken to wearing warm flannel pyjamas even in the middle of the summer. She climbed out of bed, taking off her nightwear to air it out. It was early in the morning, the sun peeking through the gap in the curtains and Rachel knew it would be another hot day. She made her way into the kitchen for a cup of strong tea. She tried to shake off the strange feeling in the pit of her stomach that always lingered after that peculiar dream. She sat down at the kitchen table, cuppa in hand, opening her Bible. Reading the verses calmed her down. She prayed that the day would be good, that the Lord would protect them. Slowly the tight knots in her belly loosened and a peaceful sensation washed over her. She ripped off the date on the small paper calendar she kept next to the fridge. 12th of July 1978. "Your intuition will lead the way, look forward not back." The daily quote read, and Rachel smiled, she loved these inspiring sayings.

Soon she'd have to wake Paul who was gently snoring. She would have his breakfast and packed lunch ready. Wednesdays were busy for him. She'd let the girls sleep till nine, then they could help her with the ironing. After that Sam and Kelly were free to go and play outside. Rachel would stop at the church on the way to Rosie's. Her sister had asked her to help decorate the last four cakes for the "Queen of Tarts" bakery.

All the sisters were accomplished cooks, Hettie had taught them well, encouraging them from an early age to experiment and try out difficult recipes.

But no one came close to Rosie when it came to baking. She was one of a kind. Rosie started baking at the tender age of four, propped up on a stool next to Hettie, kneading balls of dough, rolling out perfect squares with the wooden rolling pin, cracking eggs into the metal bowl and expertly garnishing cookies and other baked goods, refining her talent even further as she grew older. Nobody ever believed that her desserts were home-made and not shop bought. When Rosie fell pregnant with Grace, she left school, married and stayed at home. She soon discovered that she could make a living baking cakes for birthday parties and other occasions. People from near and far came to discuss what theme they had in mind and Rosie would make it happen. She made cakes that resembled shoes and handbags for teenage girls and clown and animal shaped ones for little children. It did not take long before Tamara approached her. Tamara owned the "Queen of Tarts" bakery in town and was keen for Rosie to work for her. Tamara, a strikingly tall woman with fiery red hair had named the store after Camilla, the tart who had seduced her husband. Camila and Tamara's husband had fled to London, the name of the bakery however was a constant reminder of their sordid affair and Tamara felt she had the last laugh.

So, Rachel and Rosie would be busy working in the kitchen. Thank goodness it was another fine day, there were only so many games of Ludo and Scrabble the kids could play before getting antsy. The women would shoo them outside and be left to tackle their intricate work in peace.

The egg cartons sat in a neat row on the countertop, next to clean steel bowls, mixing spoons, piping bags ,nozzles and decorating moulds. Pre-made cake fondant in violet, cerise and cornflower blue were waiting, tightly wrapped in soft plastic. Pots of buttercream and caramel, little bowls filled with sugar flowers, silver balls and chocolate cigarillos were all arranged on the kitchen table.

Rosie needed order around her when she baked. The setting up part was always first on her agenda.

Once she was done, she would drink a mug of black coffee and turn on the record player so Maria Callas could stimulate her.

Tom had left at the crack of dawn, she had heard the muted honk of Lorenzo's Ford, indicating that Tom's ride was here. The two friends worked in the same factory a few miles outside of town. The shifts were long and started early, but beggars could not be choosers. Money was tight even with Rosie's cake contributions.

Her children were still fast asleep, but Rosie would wake them soon and encourage them to play in the garden so she could work in calm surroundings. Baking deadlines had to be obeyed.

Rosie often wished that she had more time with her kids, taking them for walks, letting them explore. But money was a constant issue and Rosie had to help make ends meet. Life was expensive. She felt blessed that her talent made it possible to earn extra cash and work from home as she had left school when she was expecting Grace, one year before she was due to graduate. She had been dating Tom for a couple of months before they got frisky one cold November night. One thing led to another and before she knew it Tom's hand was under her skirt pulling at her panties. The first time they had sex Rosie did not enjoy it, but it got better as she learnt to relax more. He had promised her he'd pull out so that she would not get pregnant.

But she did get pregnant and was terrified to tell her parents and even more of Tom's reaction. He had just started the job in the factory and pay was low. When she was six months along and no longer could hide her bump, she fessed up. Hettie, having been in the same situation was supportive, her father was not pleased but came around and so did Tom, picking up more shifts at work. They married with only immediate family present, a small but lovely ceremony.

After Grace was born, they all stayed with Rosie's parents till they had enough money saved up to rent their own little cottage.

The early years were hard. Rosie struggled as a new mother. There was not a lot of space in the house, the baby sleeping in her and Tom's bed, keeping them awake for hours. Rosie walked the hallway, night after night with her colic daughter draped over her shoulder.

And although Martin and Hettie helped wherever possible, they never had any spare cash. Finally, Tom made more money, Rosie started baking and they could afford their own house. They tried for another baby and when Rosie fell pregnant with Ewan, she was ecstatic.

Grace was four by the time Ewan was born, an independent girl, a great help to her mum and a big sister to her little brother. Rosie relished every minute with her new child. He was a dream of an infant, sleeping right through the night, feeding well and always in good form. He was no trouble at all. It wasn't that Rosie favoured her boy over Grace, she just enjoyed the whole experience more.

The memories of having Grace so early and unplanned, the hard times that followed, had left a bitter taste in her mouth.

Ewan was her sunshine, her pride and joy. He turned into a boisterous kid who always had a prank up his sleeve, a real boy with dirty knees and scratches on his legs. Rosie loved watching him play football in the yard and chasing the hens. She laughed at his mischief and boldness. She simply adored him.

Work picked up, Tamara employed her part-time and along with all the other cake orders that kept pouring in, she was flat out busy. Baking was her passion, but lately she found it to be a strain rather than joy. She never had enough time for her children, for her husband and herself. She wanted to cut back, but Tom quickly reminded her that she had to keep on taking orders if they ever wanted a nest egg. The pressure often got to Rosie, she felt stressed with the kids under her feet, and she dreamt of the day when she could relax.

Rachel arrived at Rosie's house just after midday. Rosie was pulling a blue velvet cake out of the oven when her sister came through the door. Rosie handed Rachel an apron, letting her know what she needed her to do. Rosie was the boss in the kitchen, Rachel respected that. The window was wide open, cooler air mixing with the kitchen's boiling temperature. The children had left the house, talking about going into the woods.

It wasn't till evening time when they sat down with a cup of tea. The cakes had been baked, decorated and delivered, the sweet aroma still lingering in the house.

"Round up the kids." Rosie said to Rachel, the stew they had prepared for dinner simmering on the stove.

Soon the girls filed in, hungry and exhausted from playing all day.

"Where is Ewan?" Rosie asked. " Where is your brother?" She looked at Grace as it was her duty to keep an eye on the younger sibling. But it was Samantha who spoke first.

"He was in the woods with us and then he said he'd go home. We thought he was here already."

A search through the house, yard and streets followed.

"Ewan!" they all shouted. "Ewan, where are you?" Soon neighbours joined in, spreading out in all directions. When all efforts were fruitless, Rosie called the factory and the police.

They soon arrived with sniffer dogs, taking statements from the girls and conducting their own search.

Rosie sat at her kitchen table, panic turning into numbness and all she could do was wait. Wait for good news. Her sisters and neighbours made tea, talked in hushed voices, stroked her arm and asked if she needed anything.

She needed her son. She needed Ewan to be found.

Kids did that sort of stuff all the time. They got lost in the woods, time not a concern, absorbed in their games. Ewan simply did not realize how late it was, unaware of the chaos he caused. He would be found, safe and well.

Only, Rosie did not believe any of it, a feeling deep inside her gut told her that he wasn't coming back.

They buried him on a humid day, a sky covered in grey clouds heavy with rain, but no rain would fall.

The coffin Rachel had selected seemed tiny, too small for even a five-year old. It was just not possible that it contained Ewan's body. Rosie's eyes were glued to the casket, thinking it all had to be a bad dream, a nightmare she would soon wake up from. There were music and prayers, a poem read by Theresa and Father O' Neill's humble voice drifting through the church, not making any sense to Rosie.

She was sucked into a hellish vortex. *When will I wake up?* She kept thinking. *When will this be over?*

The days that followed were a blur, people dropping in food, offering help, her sisters taking turns staying with her overnight. Theresa cried all the time, Marie-Anne busied herself with cleaning and cooking and Rachel prayed and pestered Rosie to speak with Father O' Neill for guidance.

Lucina sat at the edge of Rosie's bed where she had taken up residency, unable to leave the darkened room.

Trevor, only a teenager at this time, overwhelmed and confused by it all stayed away.

Hettie and Martin were at a loss. Their hearts broke for their daughter, the grief they experienced over losing their grandson unbearable. Hettie stayed strong for Rosie, comforting her whenever she could, at night though she cried herself to sleep, and all Martin could do was hold her tight.

Rosie refused to leave her room, she stayed wrapped up in a duvet, a blank look on her face.

She did not scream or weep, she was silent.

Eventually Tom went back to work. It was better to be amongst people who spoke than with his wife who did not utter a single word.

After weeks of persuasion Rosie left the bedroom. Rachel reminded her that she still had a daughter and Grace needed a mother. In her head Rosie knew that the little girl missed her, but she could not do a thing about it, she was frozen in time, her mind vacant, her heart slowly turning to stone. Life was meaningless without her boy.

The world should have come to a halt, stopped in its tracks, everyone should have given up, just like her. But no one did. Life went on as it had before. Her sisters buzzing around, Tom going to work, Grace playing with her friends. The planet kept on spinning, oblivious to her pain, a cruel reminder that people carried on when her days were over and her beloved son was dead, buried in the cold earth. It wasn't fair and Rosie wished them all dead, she wanted the world to crumble into a thousand pieces, floating into space. She had no intention of participating in life again.

Her thoughts were dominated by her son alone, she wanted to see him, be by his side.

She contemplated killing herself, but the fear of God made it impossible for her to follow through. Suicide was a mortal sin and if she did away with herself, she would never reach heaven, never be reunited with her son. She would burn in the eternal hellfire and her afterlife would be as torturous as her living days.

She would have to endure this empty life, the punishment for not having looked after Ewan.

He had been taken from her because she had been too busy, too concerned with making money. Too focused on unimportant things, she had allowed him to play in the forest, unsupervised. Grace had been no help either, dismissing her little brother as soon as she was with her cousins. Selfish girls. They probably excluded him, and he went off, alone, deep into the woods, too close to the river's edge. He would have lost his footage, and fallen into the icy water, the current dragging him to his death. What were his last thoughts? Had he cried out for his mum, had he wondered why she wasn't there to rescue him?

He was fighting for his life while she baked cakes for other people to make more money for a better existence. How ironic!

She had so desperately wanted a boy and her wish had been granted. She had it all, but she did not appreciate it enough, she got careless, swooped up in daily demands.

She let her boy down and now he was gone forever.

Chapter 19

It had been four weeks since his boy had drowned. Every morning when Tom awoke, he hoped, for a split second, that it had all been a bad dream. But then reality came rushing back, propelling him into a dark hole filled with crippling pain. He could no longer stand being in his house. Everything reminded him of Ewan. Even his daughter Grace was a reminder as she was still here, and his son was not. He knew he wasn't fair; it wasn't Grace's fault, but still, he couldn't stomach even looking at her. None of it made sense. And then there were Rosie's sisters, always in his home, butting in, making meals, and asking questions. Of course, they were only trying to help, but they were suffocating him. He did not have a minute on his own. His wife refused to talk properly, only speaking the bare minimum. She never wanted to hear Ewan's name. She didn't even cry! Tom fled to work as early as possible each morning and stayed for overtime whenever he could. . The guys at work treated him with velvet mittens; they walked on eggshells around him. Tom hated it. He wanted to shout: Just say it, just say how awful it all is!

It was not till Maggie, the canteen lady, looked him in the eye while slapping a healthy portion of mash onto his plate and asked if he wanted to chat that Tom realised how badly he needed to confide in someone.

She took a break and sat with him at the far end of the room. Tom's food stayed untouched as he poured his heart out to a woman he had hardly noticed before. It was like a waterfall of words was unleashed streaming out of him. Maggie did not say anything; she asked no questions. She simply listened, her head tilted to the side.

When the shrill bell reminded Tom that his lunch break was ending, he got up and thanked her. Maggie hugged him, and Tom hugged her back hard, wishing he could stay in her embrace indefinitely.

Rosie only spoke when absolutely necessary. She did not find the need to participate in conversations.

She stayed in her bed only to walk to the kitchen by afternoon and then back to her bedroom again. She had not washed or combed her hair and oily strands were hanging from her head. Rachel kept pestering her to take a bath. She even attacked her one morning, rubbing a wet washcloth over her face but Rosie had pushed Rachel away. Her sisters did not leave her alone. Marie-Anne kept taking her bathrobe and secretly washing it while Rosie slept. The first time she had done this, Rosie had been furious. The robe still smelled like her son from all the times she had cuddled him. But Marie-Anne just said it was filthy and stank. The sisters also made too much food. Tom and Grace managed to eat most of it, but Rosie never touched a morsel. It was only when Rachel reminded her that starving herself was the equivalent of suicide and, therefore, a sin that would land her at the devil's feet, Rosie took to eating bread dunked in milk.

Rosie did not care that she became constipated, that her skin lost all colour resembling parchment paper, and her teeth started to rot away slowly.

Rachel slipped vitamin supplements into her milk. Rosie acted as if she did not notice because what was the point. Her sister meant well; Rosie knew that.

She refused, however, to talk to Father O'Neill or to anyone else her sister suggested. She had nothing to say as there was only empty space inside her.

When Dr McCluskey called, recommending pills, she took them, but the tablets made no difference to her frame of mind.

Rosie knew Tom was looking elsewhere; he was hardly home using every excuse to stay away but Rosie wasn't interested. She would not have cared if he had packed his bags and left for good.

Grace tried her best to behave like the model child. She made herself invisible , never creating any noise, never bothering her mother and she often stayed in her aunt's house. She seemed nervous and pale. At night, when Grace thought her mum was fast asleep, she crept into her bedroom and sat on the floor next to her. Rosie always woke as her sleep was light, but she never said a word of comfort to her daughter, who softly wept, telling her how sorry she was. She wished she could tell Grace that she was not angry with her and that she did not find her responsible, but Rosie could not bring herself to say these words. The truth was, she did blame Grace for her part in Ewan's death, she blamed the other girls too, and most of all, she blamed herself.

She had no forgiveness in her, not for anyone.

She was angry, and she was sad. Loneliness had penetrated every fibre of her being, spreading out like cancer, making it impossible to feel.

Grace was still her child, a child pining for her mother.

And still, Rosie could do nothing about it. She had to believe that Grace was ok, her sisters would look after her, she would survive while Rosie was dying.

It was a weekend, and Lucina had arrived early at Rosie's house. Tom was nowhere to be seen. Lucina washed some dirty cups and swept the floor. She never cleaned too much as she felt it was an invasion of privacy. She had brought fresh vegetables from the market and a loaf of bread, still warm, wrapped in wax paper.

Grace came out of her room, sleep in her eyes, her little face crumpled.

Lucina made some tea, and they sat in silence.

Lucina often stayed with Grace. They did not have to speak to understand one another. Lucina's eyes were kind, and the girl relaxed in her presence.

"I did not mean it," Grace finally said in a whisper.

"Of course, you did not!" Lucina reached across to hold her niece's hand.

It was obvious that the girl struggled with feelings of guilt for not having watched her brother. But she was only a child herself.

Rosie should have made sure her daughter knew this, but Lucina also understood Rosie's grief made it impossible for her to act. Her emotions could no longer be rationalised. Her sister's spirit was quenched; her soul was destroyed.

Lucina could only be there for them, in whatever way they needed her to be.

She told Grace firmly to put the travesty behind her, to try to move forward and make a life for herself. One day she would become a mother , and it would be her turn to give back all the love that was lost.

Chapter 20

Later that day, the other sisters arrived with their kids in tow. Theresa brought a roast, and Marie-Anne a dessert. They helped Rosie out of bed, trying to get her into the bathtub, and when that failed, they resorted to sponging her down.

Food was ready at five, and they sat down to eat together.

Lora and Sam were being their usual obnoxious selves, chatting away about school and their friends.

"Why aren't you eating the roast, auntie Rosie?" Lora asked. Rosie ignored the girl, cramming the milk-soaked pieces of bread into her mouth so she would not have to answer any silly questions, milk dripping down her chin. Lora pulled a face in disgust.

"That's so yucky…" The words were out before Lora could stop herself.

Rosie's eyes fixed on Lora. For the first time in ages, she actually focused on someone. The girl was sitting there—all smug in her seat, alive and well enjoying a roast dinner—criticising her and finding her distasteful, brushing aside her suffering.

The same girl who had happily played in the woods, leaving Ewan behind, not caring what would become of him.

Lora was here, going to school, meeting her friends, riding her bike.

All of them were.

While Ewan's life was cut short, he would never again kick the football around the yard; he would never again look up at her with these startling blue eyes, that freckled face, and smile.

These girls had no idea.

All the sudden enormous rage engulfed Rosie; resentment so strong it could have broken metal.

She jumped up, sending glasses flying, shouting at the top of her lungs that they should all burn in hell. They all had blood on their hands; they all had played a part in Ewan's death.

Tears streamed down her face, so hot they left red marks on her cheeks.

Rosie kept screaming till Lucina grabbed her, holding her trembling sister close to her chest.

There was a stunned silence around the table. Grace cried, her lips muttering inaudible words.

Sam's eyes were wide with fright, the peas on her plate in a neat row.

Then, Marie-Anne got up, taking Lora by the arm.

"I will not listen to this, Rosie." Her voice was stern. "We all understand how terrible losing Ewan is for you. For you all. But I will not have you blame my child. She did no wrong. It was not up to her to mind Ewan. This was your job, but you were too busy…"

"Stop!" Rachel interrupted before Marie-Anne could say any more. "Please stop; we are all upset."

But it was too late. The irreversible damage was done. Hurtful words were spoken and could not be taken back.

"I hate you!" Rosie screeched. "The devil will get you in the end…"

Lucina and Theresa dragged her off to the bedroom. They held down her body while she thrashed around, crying all the tears she had stored up inside her.

Marie-Anne left with Lora, while Rachel comforted the bewildered girls. Grace and Kelly were both weeping, but Sam's expression was hard; her face had closed over.

Much later, when they had calmed down, and the kitchen was tidy once again, the sisters sat in the living room, cups of sweet tea in their hands. Rosie had fallen asleep, emotionally exhausted.

She would not shout again, and she would not shed a single tear till the day Lucina died.

There were no more words. She refused to feel anything; her insides had turned to concrete and her heart to a rock that sat motionless in her body.

She was a shell of herself, still on earth, only waiting for the day to come when she could finally die—waiting to be united with Ewan once again.

The sisters stayed in Rosie's house till midnight. They all agreed to do everything in their power to help and they would chat with the girls again. Accusations like these could have fatal consequences, especially since the girls were at a fragile age.

Of course, they all forgave Rosie for her outburst, and they sincerely prayed Marie-Anne would come around too. There was no way of telling as Marie-Anne was known for her fierce, stubborn streak.

Anyway, they would all do their best.

Rachel would once again speak to Father O'Neill; there ought to be something the parish priest could do. In any case, she would put her petitions before God.

They would rally around Rosie, as they had done before. They would care for Grace, would cook and clean and persuade Rosie to eat and wash. Or at least they would sit with her and keep her company.

Surely the girls would do their bit too.

They would all console Rosie when Tom would leave her, escaping into the arms of another woman. It was only a matter of time. But perhaps Rosie would not even notice; anything was possible.

Chapter 21

It was the day Lora took matters into her own hands. The day she stopped the demons for good, she hoped.

The kids were off to GAA practice; Oscar was out running errands. Lora had stayed behind, furiously mopping the kitchen floor. It was a never-ending job with no rewards whatsoever. She hated it. The kids said they were careful removing their dirty shoes, shoving filthy clothes into the laundry chute and keeping their rooms neat. But Lora never saw any real evidence; all she saw was work piling up. She certainly was sick of it all.

And then there was Toby, the dumb dog. He did not help matters either. The kids had to have him. She had been against it from the start, but Oscar gave in, rescuing the creature from a puppy farm. The kids were ecstatic, making all sorts of promises. "Yes! We will clean up after the dog; we will walk him, you don't have to do anything, Mum!" Ha! They named him Toby. A Jack Russel mix, a mongrel of some description.

Obviously, Lora ended up doing everything for the stupid animal. She fed him; she cleaned up his shit, and she brought him for walks.

The mutt wasn't even grateful for her work. It was like he despised her when he managed to adore the rest of the family. He wagged his tail on end as soon as Oscar came through the door. He jumped up and down, yelping in this ear-splitting way of his when the kids woke up in the morning. He accepted cuddles from all of them, except from her.

She knew right away that there was something seriously wrong with the dog. So, she kept her distance, never getting too close. She noticed how Toby watched her. He would sit in a corner glaring at her, following her every move. Lora was afraid to turn her back on him in case he bounced on top of her, sinking his sharp teeth into her neck.

Lora was petrified and things only got worse. The animal behaved all cute and friendly when other people were around, but as soon as she was on her own with him, he turned evil. He'd fix her with these horrible, yellow eyes; he growled when she slid a bowl of food across the floor, he snarled when she opened the patio door to shoo him out.

Then, on that Saturday, he spoke to her.

She had just finished washing up and as she turned around, she found the beast sitting there, leering at her, blocking her way, a low guttural sound coming from his throat.

"Go!" Lora shouted to make him move. The dog let out a long, strange bark that resembled the howl of a wolf, hissing the words 'get you' . Someone else, a dog-friendly person perhaps, someone with no bad experiences, could have easily missed the vicious warning. Not Laura, she understood precisely what he meant. The dog had spoken to her. He had threatened her. The dog was not really a dog; it was Ewan. He had come back.

Admittingly, it was not the first time Ewan had made an appearance.

Lora had seen him in the nasty boy who had waited for her every day after school, chasing her, ripping her schoolbag from her, pushing her around. Eventually, she had dealt with it. One day she was ready for him—a rock wrapped in a sock in her hands. When he attacked, she smashed the rock against his head with all her strength. She watched the boy tumble back, blood running down the side of his face.

She never saw him again. He simply disappeared. That was her first Ewan. There were many more after that. She knew he surfaced again and again, taking the shape of mean people in her life, their cruel comments, and hurtful suggestions. He turned events that were meant to be lovely and relaxing to dust right in front of her eyes. Yes, Ewan was out there, and he wanted revenge. He had, however, never managed to sneak into her home.

This was serious.

He was the devil and she had to save herself, once and for all.

Lora grabbed a piece of bread from the kitchen counter and held it up for the dog to see. He might have wanted to end her life, but he could not resist a quick snack.

She lured him outside, into the yard. She closed the door and ran upstairs to fetch Oscar's hunting rifle. It was sitting there, idle, in the glass cabinet. Oscar hadn't even bothered to lock it; he was that sure nobody would ever touch it. She checked for bullets. She had never handled a weapon before. She briefly contemplated hitting the cast iron skillet over the dog's head but she might miss, and the animal would escape. No, she could take no chances. She raced back downstairs, leaping over the last few steps. She had to hurry.

Toby was still sitting in the same spot. Unmoved. He was waiting for his treat. Grateful for no immediate neighbours Lora aimed. Pointing the gun at him she hesitated unsure if she could pull the trigger. But in that split second of doubt she saw a red flash in the dog's murky eyes. She shot. The bang was so loud she squeezed her eyes shut, the force of the blast making her stumble backwards. Had she missed? Was he dead?

When she finally dared to look, she saw parts of flesh, blood and skull. The wall behind them was stained crimson. She had blown his head off. She felt nothing but relief. It was over. It had to be.

She fetched a large black rubbish bag, put on some latex gloves and set about cleaning up the mess. The dog's torso and his legs were intact. She threw the body into the sack. The scattered bits gave her more trouble. She found soft parts of his brain as far away as the fence on the opposite side and oozing fractions of flesh in the flower beds. When she was sure she had gathered every bit, she hosed down the murder scene.

She removed all her clothes and put them into the washing machine, selecting the intensive cycle; then she had a long hot shower. Later, she placed the garbage bag in the trunk of her car and drove across town to the waste disposal site. She tossed the black bag onto the piles of rubbish and went home.

When the kids asked for Toby at dinner time, she explained that he had done a runner when the front door was left open yet again. She scolded the kids for not closing the door. But after the tears had started, she assured them that the dog would make his way home, that some decent person would find and return him.

Toby never came home. With each passing day, the kids grew more worried, hanging up posters of the missing animal, asking around. Oscar made phone calls to the local vet and beyond.

The intensity of the situation rose until Lora could not take it anymore.

She told them that the dog was bad. He had to go. She had killed Toby. And now Oscar believed that she had lost her mind, and the kids hated her but Lora did not care one single bit. They would forgive and forget. She felt calmer than she had in a long time. She truly thought that her torment was over; the past firmly put behind her. She could finally sleep at night. She had no way of knowing that this was only the beginning, that the secret the three cousins had sworn to never speak of could not stay buried. That it would rear its ugly head when least expected.

Chapter 22

The blue skies, the warmth on her face, Lanzarote was just bliss. Kelly was standing on the balcony of the room she shared with her sister. She had been looking forward to this trip so much, away from the daily demands, her little daughter and Ben. Sure, she missed and loved them, but she really needed a break, a change of scenery. And if they wanted to have another child, there would be no more escaping.

The hotel was lovely, the weather gorgeous, the beach clean, the pool water inviting. Everything was as she had imagined it to be except for her sister. Sam was her usual uptight self. No, in fact, she was even worse.

They had no sooner sat down in the plane, the nice, young stewardess asking Sam to hang her jacket on the coat hook when Sam started an argument. What was the reason for hanging up the jacket? Did they think the jacket would jump up and attack someone? She wanted an explanation!

Oh, it was all so embarrassing. The poor girl, probably on her first-ever flight as an attendant, was completely flustered. She kept repeating that these were the rules, and would Sam please hang up the garment. She literally begged her. Sam, naturally, was unmoved, demanding a decent answer, her waspish tongue ready to insult. Why! Was it this way? Why had the coat to be hung? Seriously, Sam was like a bold child, one that needed to be ornery at all cost. She even got the man with the acne scars across the aisle to agree with her. Yes, why?

It was bad. Kelly felt ashamed to be associated with Sam. She pretended to study the menu; she wished Sam would stop. In the end, the senior flight attendant came over and wrapped things up, in a matter of fact manner, leaving no room for further discussions.

A bit later, when Kelly went to the toilet, she thought she heard a sniffle coming from the plane's kitchen. Sam had made that girl cry. Kelly was disgusted with her sister.

The check-in at the hotel wasn't any easier. Sam insisted she had booked a sea view room; the partial view of the ocean was just not good enough.

Then she criticised the evening buffet. The meat was too dry, the vegetables not fresh enough, the juices watery, and so on.

All Kelly longed for was some peace and quiet and a nice relaxing time. But Sam made sure that this did not happen. The very next day, she was on Kelly's case to go sightseeing. It was boiling hot, and Kelly had been looking forward to lounging around by the pool.

Sam was resolute. She wanted to do things. She did not come here to sit on her arse; she wanted to explore. She even badmouthed that nice couple from Belfast whom Kelly had befriended.

She called her boring. She called her an old fart! She said Kelly had always been this way, spoilt, undecisive, a door matt. Sam could be so cruel and she loved to rake up the past.

Eventually, after hurdling the abuse at her, she stormed off.

Kelly did not give in her urge to cry. She stayed strong. She ordered a cocktail and read her novel; later, she joined the nice, polite couple for a game of tennis.

This was the last time the sisters holidayed together.

They managed to stay courteous towards each other for the rest of the days and kept their distance once back home.

Kelly soon got back into the swing of things, and after some time trying for another baby she fell pregnant again. Alexander was born on a bright Monday morning, her family was complete. She loved her life, her children and her part-time job. All was fine, except for her marriage.

Ben had always been close to his mother, but did he have to ask Mary's opinion about absolutely everything? Mary insisted orchid white was the new ivory, so the living room walls were painted in that shade. Mary said Greece was too hot for those poor children in the summer; they should rent a nice cottage in Kerry, and that way she could tag along. Mary demanded that they came over every bloody Sunday for a roast. When Ben did not visit his mother, he was on the phone with her. Sometimes multiple times a day.

Sure, Kelly knew from the start that Mary had a hold over him, but this was insanity. He had to cut his apron strings.

When she tried to talk with him, he became defensive.

It had always been just the two of them, Mary and her son. Mary was a single mother; his dad had died when Ben was a toddler. She had catered to his every wish and he was thankful for all the sacrifices she had made. He loved her. He owed her.

It was no use; no matter what way Kelly approached the subject, she ended up as the jealous bitch of a wife.

Ben acted irritated around Kelly, nit picking over tiny details. The house was never tidy enough; items were not put away correctly, the wrong pan was used for frying off meat, and his boxer shorts were not ironed perfectly. Certainly not the same way his mother had ironed them for him.

Kelly tried. She loved nothing more than peace in her home, good harmony.

She took care to erase all creases from his clothes; she rushed around before Ben was due home from work, making sure the place was up to his standard.

She smiled at Mary's advice, never speaking up.

Of course, she was still daydreaming. It was in her nature. Away with the fairies, as Ben called it. But she could not help it. She marvelled at a rainbow or two turtle doves sitting on the fence together, she reminisced about childhood memories and times when life was just simple.

She played with her kids, absorbed in a world of their own, forgetting to put dinner on in time.

She returned home with half the items on her shopping list, only because she helped an elderly lady find all the groceries she needed.

So, when Ben stood there, yelling at her, her mind was still far away. She wanted to tell Ben about her day, about the little things that happened in her life, but the words were frozen in her throat.

Kelly was well aware that she was a scatterbrain, she knew she annoyed Ben but she did not know how to make it all stop, how to focus, and become a proper wife.

She had adored Ben's organised resolute nature at the beginning of their relationship. She hadn't even minded Mary so much.

But as time went on, she felt more and more repressed.

"Ben is a control freak." Her friend Isabell kept saying. Ben liked to have the last word. He had also become far less romantic.

When they first dated, he surprised her with roses all the time. He lit candles all around the bedroom when they made love, be booked the nicest, Michelin star restaurants.

He would buy her jewellery on a whim. She only had to look at a piece; no sooner the sparkling chain was fastened around her neck. These days, even heavy hinting got her nowhere.

He used to compliment her; he always let her know that he was the luckiest guy in the world with such a beautiful woman by his side.

Now, even her good looks did not interest him much anymore. He barely glanced at her when she wore that tight-fitting little black dress that he used to find so sexy.

He still wanted sex all the time. But it was not the nice slow lovemaking from before. It felt rushed and emotionless.

Kelly longed for love and understanding. Her heart was lonely.

She had no idea how to improve her situation with Ben.

Her friends weren't of much help, and Sam had nothing but harsh critique for her. She did not want to burden Rachel. The odd time she let something slip in front of her mother, Rachel promised she'd pray for her. Her auntie Lucina was the better listener. She never commented as other people did, never gave advice unless being asked. She simply lent an ear when Kelly needed to vent and only occasionally reminded Kelly of the strong and beautiful vows of marriage.

Her prayers were never answered and her kids started to grow up. Alexander remained a lovely pleasant boy, dedicated to his music if not much else.

Paige was a challenge. But all her daughter needed was time and affection and not too much micromanaging. She needed to figure things out for herself. Kelly made sure she gave her that freedom without asking too many intrusive questions. She needed to trust Paige in making good choices and Kelly refused to believe anything other than that her daughter was a wonderful human being.

Everything in life had been handed to Kelly, her good fortune could not be over; it simply wasn't her time yet.

Chapter 23

Ben really lost the plot when the Range Rover was stolen and quite frankly Kelly did not know if there was any turning back from that moment on.

She had been over at Mary's helping out in the house, as her mother in law had taken ill with the flu.

Kelly washed the floor, stocked the fridge and prepared a pot of chicken soup.

On the way home, her boss phoned, informing her that the presentation for 'Frank's Beans' had to be on his table by 8 am the next day.

She quickly stopped at the butcher to pick up mince for her Chilli Con Carne. When she arrived home, she was frazzled.

Kelly set about cooking and finishing her work presentation.

A while later, Ben arrived home.

"Where is the car?" he asked without greeting her.

"What car?" Kelly was distracted. "Your flipping car." He barked, "the Range Rover."

"In the drive," Kelly replied. "Where it always is."

"Well, it fucking is not!"

They both went to look outside. The car was gone, leaving Kelly baffled. The guards were called to investigate.

Only when Kelly gave her statement, it occurred to her that she had left the keys in the unlocked car. An opportunist must have watched and taken advantage of the situation. It surely had been easier than taking candy off a baby.

The two officers felt nothing but pity for the pretty lady and her unfortunate mistake. The husband seemed to be an asshole.

Due to her own fault, the insurance refused to pay. The jeep was gone. Ben went ballistic.

He could not understand why she had been so dumb. Only his wife could manage to get her car stolen from right under her nose. She left the keys conveniently in the vehicle, so that the thief had no trouble at all stealing the car.

He called Kelly every name under the sun. Storming out, banging the door behind him with such force that a crack appeared in the wall, like a vein stretching all the way to the ceiling.

Kelly fled too. Alexander had been great and supportive as always, telling her not to worry too much; everybody made mistakes. Paige just stood in the kitchen, sniggering at the spectacle.

Without thinking, Kelly called a cab and went over to Lucina's.

She was lucky her aunt was in the country as Lucina spent more time at her Italian home than in Ireland these days. "My old bones need the sun," she kept saying.

They sat together while Kelly cried, cursing herself for being such an idiot.

Lucina calmed her niece down. She offered her a bed for the night, urging her to get some rest. Everything would look brighter in the morning, she promised.

At breakfast, early the next day, Lucina suggested that Kelly take a break from it all. Some time away, something different.

The kids were old enough; she could keep an eye on them too. Alexander could practise the piano over in her house. Ben would be fine. It would probably help their marriage to have a little distance between them.

Kelly mulled it over. It did sound enticing to go away. Find herself again.

She felt stronger after being in Lucina's company, and when she arrived at the firm, her mind was made up.

She organised time off work; she talked to the kids, informed Ben in a brisk manner, and confirmed with Lucina.

It was like she was on a mission. For the first time in her life, she got things done in a speedy and efficient way.

Would she still have dived in headfirst had she known what awaited her abroad?

If she had stopped for just a brief moment to examine her state of mind a little further, she might have reconsidered. She might have realised that she had reached a very fragile point. A crossroad. She might have understood that hasty actions had consequences that could ruin a life in the blink of an eye.

But before she paused for a single second, she found herself on a plane to Windhoek, Namibia.

Chapter 24

"You picked a boyfriend just like your father!" Paige's friend Emma had said to her. "Control issues." Emma drew the O out in that stupid, exaggerated way of hers. Controooool. They had a tiff about something silly. Paige could not even remember how it had started.

Of course, Emma had to hit where it really hurt. She knew Paige could not stand her dad. The comparison left her fuming.

Just to be 100% certain, she checked with Reuben if he liked his mum. Her own dad had a bizarre infatuation with his mother. Gross.

Reuben was cross with her for asking such a dumb question. "I fucking hate my mother." He spat. "I might kill her myself one of these days. Rip her throat out," he concluded.

She knew it! No-resemblance at all. Reuben was absolutely nothing like her pompous, overcorrect father. Reuben was a wild child, a free spirit. So what if he kept her in check? That wasn't necessarily a bad thing.

She probably needed to be on the straight and narrow.

Her dad clearly had lost control of her mother. Willy-nilly she had run off to Africa. She had hardly given them any notice or had asked for their opinion, behaving in her usual selfish way, not caring what they thought of it. Her dad had simply been confronted with the facts. Alexander, of course, had been his disgusting understanding self. Lucina promised to keep an eye on them, but what could Lucina do anyway? She was ancient, one foot in the grave. She only acted all hip and young. Pathetic. Her great aunt was on her way over now with promises of pizza, a movie, and some quality time. Yack.

Paige was very fortunate that she had Reuben in her life. He always made time for her; she could ride along on his motorcycle, and they had the most incredible sex. He wanted her all the time. He adored her. His temper and occasional slap were only minor things, things she could live with as Reuben truly loved her. Not like Brodie, who had just used her and then disregarded her as soon as his ex had come crawling back.

She had been so in love with Brodie; it still hurt thinking about him.

She thought she had found her soul mate. She knew he was on the rebound when they met and got together. Some mutual friends had said so. He even admitted it when she asked him about it. He talked about his ex for a while, and she could not help but notice how his eyes lit up when he mentioned her name.

They had sex first. He was great, and Paige was sure she wasn't too shabby herself. She never had any complaints from lovers. On the contrary, they all gave her the thumbs up and sometimes even came back for one last shag when they had already committed to another relationship. She was that good. And she liked it too. She let them do things other girls would never agree to. Sex was such a high, when the rest of her life was shit.

After many sessions with Brodie, Paige was convinced that his ex was firmly out of the picture.

He hardly talked about her anymore. All was good. They did not go out much, only sometimes they went to the movies or some gallery but mostly they stayed in his gaff, watching Netflix, drinking, and having sex.

She understood that he was completely into her when she fulfilled his dream. A threesome. Some girl, Paige had seen her on nights out herself and Brodie. It was an awesome adventure. Brodie was so grateful. He said so. He told her that his ex would never have done it, not in a gazillion years. Paige made him happy.

That was why her world collapsed when he told her, less than two weeks after the out of this world experience, that he was leaving her. For his fucking ex! She had changed her mind and wanted him back. What's more, he wanted her back too!

It was a travesty. Paige cried and cried. Her girlfriends were useless; her mum asked some questions in that helpless way of hers but Paige shut everybody out.

She wanted to be left alone with her grief. She slashed away at her wrists till she was so scarred she no longer could wear anything that did not fully cover her arms.

Then, as if things weren't bad enough already, she discovered that she was pregnant.

First, she was beside herself. But the more she thought about it, the clearer it became that this was the only way to get him back. This was her ticket.

She asked Brodie to come over to the house one evening when her parents and brother were out. She told him there was something important she had to tell him.

She made sure she looked amazing in her skin-tight leather pants and low top; he would not be able to keep his hands off her.

She cooked a meal from scratch when the most she had ever done was throw some pot noodles into the microwave.

She even tidied up the house.

At 8 pm, when Brodie rang the doorbell, she was ready.

Brodie wasn't thrilled to be there one bit. He never complimented Paige on her looks and wolfed down the food, eager to leave again. "What did you want to talk about?" he asked between hurried bites.

This was not the way Paige had planned it. She had anticipated a romantic evening, him praising her culinary efforts, holding her close, revealing that he simply could not live without her, that he had made a big mistake. When she envisioned telling him about the baby, Brodie was euphoric, exclaiming that now his luck was complete.

But the reality was nothing like her little daydreams.

Watching him grow more impatient with every passing minute, she blurted her secret out. She was pregnant. There, deal with it!

It certainly stopped him in his tracks, a noodle dangling from his mouth, suspended in time.

When he finally regained consciousness, he had the nerve to ask if it was his. Only after becoming hysterical and throwing a glass of water in his face, he came over, placing a hand on her back.

"Okay, okay..." he muttered. "We'll figure this out." We! he had said we. Paige started to relax. But not for long, as he went on to say that he'd give her money, enough to cover the trip to the UK to get an abortion.

Paige could not believe her ears.

She was too stunned and hurt to speak another word and when he left, she did not even clean up the mess; she just went to bed and wept.

She made the trip to the UK alone, refusing to think at all. It was quick, and when she got back, she banished the whole episode from her head, shutting away her feelings and disappointment, cutting her arms and legs to ease the pain.

From friends, she heard that Brodie was doing great, he was happy, and things were moving fast.

Paige ignored all the gossip.

She set about finding a new romance. She found Reuben. Even from the very start, she felt that Reuben was different. He was more intense. Their relationship was like an ecstasy trip.

Most importantly, Reuben did not have an ex he wanted to get back with; he loved no one but her.

Paige sat on the edge of her bed thinking of Brodie, listening to Shania Twain.

She had not allowed herself to even mention his name for a long time. But lately, thoughts of him had wriggled back into her brain but to her surprise, she did not mind; she let the memories drift.

If Reuben as much as suspected her indulging in the past, reminiscing about Brodie, he would have an absolute fit. He'd break a window or kick a door down. He'd punch her lights out, without a doubt.

Fuck, he'd even have a canary if he'd know what songs she was listening to. She deserved a bloody nose for her crap choice of music.

Paige smiled to herself. Sometimes she liked to be disobedient, sometimes she liked to dwell on the past, and sometimes she even liked Shania.

Chapter 25

When she stepped off the plane, all Kelly could see was a silky, clear sky stretching out above her. It was such a peculiar shade of powder blue; it made her eyes sting, and a lonely tear rolled down her cheek. On the plane, she had refused to think at all. There was no point in pondering the rash decision and thinking about what she had left behind. Ben had been stunned; Paige uncooperative. She hoped Lucina was able for the teenagers and the dissonance between the family members. Lucina wasn't exactly young anymore. Even though Lucina claimed to possess boundless energy, Kelly had her doubts. Kelly sensed her beloved aunt was ageing regardless of what she said. Lucina spent more and more time in her house in Puglia, relishing the quietness, letting the sun warm up her bones. She was due to go over again on Kelly's return.

Lucina had practically ordered her to take this trip, to get a fresh perspective on life, away from it all.

So, there she was, slightly tried from the long flight and the layovers.

Dutifully she filled in her emigration card at customs and was heading out to meet her driver and guide for the next couple of weeks.

The agency in Ireland had arranged a personalised tour, a small group of only herself and another couple from Amsterdam, staying in various lodges, exploring the vast, empty spaces of this African country. Jannick, the Namibian guide, would take them up to the Etosha Park down the Skeleton coast via Swakopmund to Sossusvlei. The travel agent had promised elephants, rhinos, kudus, hyenas, and wild dogs if they were lucky.

Kelly, who had never been to any exotic places, was looking forward to everything. But most of all, she was happy to be without her family. She desperately wanted to find herself again, not the mother or wife, but Kelly.

These emotions were new to her. She had always prided herself in spending time with her loved ones. She rarely needed that break from her husband and kids that so many of her friends craved.

But the last few months had weighed her down. She had found it increasingly hard to muster up good cheer and a smiling face. Ben's moods, his tedious particularities, his striving for a perfect domestic life, and Paige's hostility were exhausting her. Even Alexander's quietness got on her nerves.

She needed out for a while anyway.

Jannick shook her hand, a warm, strong grip. Kelly could not help but notice his toned, very masculine body. There was a flat, hard washboard where Ben's soft belly was, muscular arms with defined biceps, instead of mushy flesh, skin, browned by the continent's unforgiving sun, rather than the pasty, Irish one.

Athletic legs, broad shoulders and a ruggedly handsome face with clever eyes, tousled dirty blond hair and no bald head.

Kelly had to compose herself, realising she stared. It wasn't often she met a man that made her feel flustered. He was not the typical gorgeous hero of a novel. He was rougher around the edges; more Marlboro man meets Tarzan, more real.

Besides his appearance, there was a sense of strength to this man, someone who knew his exact position in the world.

And for the first time in years, Kelly felt alive.

Jannick brought her over to his jeep that would bring them on unpaved roads, covered in red sand, to places so remote you would question if they had ever been touched by human hand.

Once her luggage was stowed in the boot of the car, Jannick informed her that their adventures could begin. The Dutch couple, it turned out, had cancelled their trip last minute.

They had no business spending a minute longer in Windhoek, a town Jannick did not seem to be fond of. As Kelly took the seat next to him, she already knew she would leave out the missing Dutch couple when speaking to Ben later. She stole a glance at Jannick as he drove, one hand on the wheel, the other leisurely hanging out of the car window. She took in his delicious accent, the pronunciation of each word, describing his childhood in Swakopmund, talk of his grandparents who had emigrated from East Prussia in the 1930s. "I'm more German than the Germans," he said with a wink that told Kelly he wasn't in the slightest.

A true African with mere German roots.

They left civilisation behind, the countryside opening up, revealing a gigantic empty space dotted with a few trees providing the only shade around—

the blinding white sunlight mixing into the dry orange-brown earth, turning everything to dust.

As Kelly listened to the murmur of his voice, she closed her eyes, breathing in the sweet scent of aftershave and sweat, drifting off into a warm comforting place. In her heart, she knew what was going to happen. She had already decided on her own fate. Even if she tried to hold back, she would never win this battle. She would simply let herself fall.

Chapter 26

When Kelly awoke the next morning, she was momentarily confused. She stretched out her arms, feeling the cotton sheet beneath her skin. No Ben, and no familiar sounds of her house. She sat up with a jolt. She blinked, rubbing sleep from her eyes. She was here; she was in Africa. She was on her journey. Everything kept rushing back to her. The long flight, leaving her kids, husband, and Lucina behind. The four-hour drive to the Etosha national park. Jannick. Jannick!

An entire unfamiliar feeling spread out through her stomach, engulfing her heart, making her anxious and relaxed at the same time. And there was more. A sensation of utter longing. Something she had never experienced before. Not on her first dates in high school, not when she met Ben. Especially not when she met Ben. Ben had felt right and she had been intrigued by him, his self-assured personality winning her over. She had been more excited about the prospect of getting married and starting a family than him. Ben had been a perfect choice. Yes, she had loved him, and she had felt passion towards him in the early days, but nothing to the extent of what she felt now, an electric current zipping through her body making her lightheaded and dangerous. Ben and her had been doing okay for a long while. More than okay. They raised their family. Ben was stricter with the children while she had fun with them. She didn't like disciplining them too harshly. In her opinion, all they needed was love and nourishment. She provided that. Ben grew tenser with the years, more particular. There were constant arguments about the messy house, his mother his steady alliance, the ever-present thorn in Kelly's eyes.

They had drifted apart, living their lives—the routine of school and work, and sex without a connection.

Kelly pulled on her nightgown and stepped out onto the wooden veranda of the hut.

They had arrived at the lodge, outside the national park, in the evening. She had unpacked a few things and had joined Jannick for dinner, trying Springbok and pap.

They drank wine and chatted. It was an easy conversation; it was comfortable. Whenever their eyes met, Kelly's heart skipped a beat, her cheeks growing pink, and for the first time ever , she felt shy about her looks. Was her white top too tight, a bit see-through perhaps? She had seen him glance at her body, his eyes lingering a little too long. She had wanted to reach out and touch his tanned arms, and feel his hair between her fingers. Kelly thought she was going mad. She had never wanted anything as much as she wanted him. She could not understand what had come over her. All her life, she had felt asexual, the emotion of burning lust unknown to her. She had never particularly enjoyed being touched and caressed. And now it was the one thing she craved most. She imagined the sensation of his hand stroking her body, every last bit of it, allowing his hands to wander. She wondered what his touch would feel like, his skin against hers. She was dizzy with craziness, overcome with confusion and passion. She wanted to throw caution to the wind.

She drank too much last night, a dull pain lingering in her head as she stood on the deck, staring out into the Savannah, the brown grassland, the tall acacia tree, the bright golden African sun. The beauty of the landscape brought tears to her eyes. The longing for another man, deep inside her, overwhelming. But there was something else too. She felt at home.

She asked the African Gods for a sign, a tiny hint that she belonged.

She gazed far into the distance, and just as she was about to turn around to go back inside, she saw him. A majestic bull elephant, walking across the plain, without a care in the world.

They spent the day driving through part of the park, spotting wildebeest and zebras in abundance.

Jannick laughed at Kelly's excitement. Every time she saw another animal, her level of happiness rose to ecstatic. His eagle eyes saw far into the distance, making out giraffes and an eland long before she discovered them. He had grown up tracking animals, and finding wildlife was second nature to him. He enjoyed seeing Kelly's face brighten up as another creature crossed their path.

They found lions resting in the shade of a marula tree, too lazy to hunt in the midday sun, and a spotted female hyena walking alongside them, its posture comically slanted. Kelly was enthralled by the beauty of it all. Nothing could have prepared her for these nature's miracles. They stopped the jeep for snacks and cool drinks, and Kelly listened to Jannick talk about the Etosha's fauna.

She was mesmerised by his moving lips, his eyebrows that curled upwards whenever he went into great detail about the African species. Specks of her dream came flooding back to her. Images of naked bodies, making love…Kelly's insides lurched, and she had to restrain herself from wrapping her arms around his neck.

All of a sudden, Jannick stopped mid-sentence. He put one hand on her arm and a finger to her mouth to keep her quiet. "Look," he whispered close to her ear. She breathed in his scent, following his eyes and saw a small round animal scuttle across the earth. "It's an elephant shrew," Jannick said. "They are shy and very hard to spot."

They stood for a while, his arm resting on hers. And when he said, "It's good luck to see one of them." She knew for certain that he wanted her just as much.

After she had showered, Kelly selected a turquoise flowy dress for dinner.

They met in the only restaurant of the lodge, taking their seats overlooking the water hole. A rhino had appeared, a prehistoric looking animal , drinking its fill before nightfall.

Talking with Jannick was still easy, but there was an underlying tension between them now, a pull so strong it was hard to ignore.

When Jannick walked her back to her hut, his arm brushing against hers, she already knew she would ask him in. "Do you want another glass of wine?" She heard her trembling voice say.

"Are you sure?" he asked, and she understood what he meant. The question was not only directed at the here and now. He questioned her entire future.

"I am sure," she whispered, feeling worried.

Inside she poured them both some wine , and they clinked their glasses together, a toast to Africa and the amazing day they had. She held his gaze as he tenderly touched her face, leaning in, their lips touching. At first, the kiss was soft and gentle but soon replaced by urgency, sending their hearts into a frenzy. Ripping at their clothes, nails digging into soft flesh, a wine glass shattering on the ground, and their bodies falling to the floor. Jannick on top of her, inside her, a sensation so powerful she thought she would explode. Later, after their first passion-filled lovemaking, they laid down on the bed, this time slowly exploring each other. "You are so beautiful," Jannick said, stroking her warm belly.

"So are you," she replied. They made love again , with Jannick kissing every part of her body. She let him discover her, relishing the experience, taking sweet pleasure in her new-found romance.

Chapter 27

Her days in Africa were infused with euphoria born of hunger and yearning for a man that took her to new heights, stripped her bare, encouraging her to lose all her inhibitions. For the first time ever, Kelly enjoyed sex; she could hardly wait for their daily safari tips to end so that she could jump into bed with Jannick, letting him lead her to places beyond her wildest imagination. She felt like a new woman. She was finally awake. Every day brought a new discovery and she cherished every moment, viewing all aspects of her life in a different light. The sun was scintillating here, the sky a cobalt dome above them, the food scrumptious, and her mind relaxed far away from home. She hardly contacted Ben anymore; when she did, her texts were brief. She checked in with Lucina and her children, but she could not say that she missed them. A strange calmness had settled over her, a profound feeling of content and she knew that eventually, they would be okay without her.

When it was time to say goodbye, they both cried, holding each other till the very last moment; neither one of them wanting to let go. They declared their undying love for one another, and she promised to return.

Lucina did not particularly like going to Kelly's house. There was a sadness there that made it difficult to breathe. She was glad her niece was enjoying herself on the trip, not that Kelly kept in contact much. A cheerful short SMS occasionally that revealed nothing. Ben was working most of the time. When Lucina did see him, they exchanged meaningless pleasantries. Paige was a difficult one too. Always moody and downright secretive. She did not want to tell Lucina where she was going or what she was up to. Lucina tried but, in the end, she only made sure that the house was in order and that there was plenty of food in the fridge. She brought over casseroles and lasagne, and she invited Alexander to come to her place and practise the piano. The boy was well mannered and sweet, undeniably gifted, a musical talent that Lucina wanted to nurture. He played Chopin, Schubert, and Tchaikovsky while Lucina sipped her tea. It was wonderful. They chatted quite a bit too. At first, Alexander was shy obviously intimidated by his great aunt. But once he opened up, he told her about his constant struggles in school, the boys who teased him mercilessly, his dad who only saw flaws in him, and his mum who was too disconnected and dreamy to be bothered with his worries. Lucina did not reassure him; she did not pledge to help, nor did she say that all would be just fine. She simply listened but a plan formed in her head. Alexander could not wait for the day when school was done, and he could give himself to music completely and Lucina would make sure that his dream would become a reality.

They usually finished their musical afternoon around 7 pm, then Lucina drove Alexander home. She popped dinner into the oven to warm it up and set the table. None of them had eaten together ever since Kelly had gone on her trip. Ben ate in front of the TV, kicking off his shoes as soon as he came through the door, grunting a few words in their direction. Paige ate very little as it was. She picked on her food, tossing half-eaten portions into the bin even when it was her favourite tuna salad.

A few days before Kelly's return, Lucina stayed longer than normal. She loaded the dishwasher and tidied up. She could not wait to go back to Italy and her quiet life there. The glorious weather, her herb garden, the lovely village, and Pietro.

She now spent the majority of her time there, only visiting Ireland occasionally, mostly to catch up with her family. Of course, some of them came out to Italy too, but not as often as she would have liked. It was like she lived two separate lives—one here with her family and one, a more private one, in Puglia.

She decided to give the kids' shared bathroom a clean before she headed home. Paige was so messy, leaving her cosmetics scattered around the place; traces of kohl eyeliner and bronzer staining the porcelain sink. It made no difference to the girl how much her father shouted.

Lucina grabbed a sponge, cloth and bleach and went upstairs. It was quiet, the children in their bedrooms glued to their mobile phones, no doubt.

She pushed the door open.

Paige was sitting on the edge of the bathtub, a small razor blade in her hand. The cuts near her wrist were fresh, and blood was running down the side of her arm like a red piece of string.

They both stared at each other for a moment, then Paige screamed: "Can you not fucking knock?"

Her eyes wide and empty, her narrow face pale.

"What are you doing?" Lucina stammered. Fear lacing her voice.

"Well, I am not trying to kill myself if that's what you think," Paige answered. She looked at Lucina defiance in her eyes. "If I wanted that, I wouldn't do it here, rest assured." Lucina waited, and Paige continued, "I am just cutting myself, no biggie."

"No big deal?" Lucina could not believe her ears. How could her great-niece be so blasé, so casual about cutting into her own flesh, mutilating herself?

"What is going on with you?" Lucina tried. "Can we talk about it? Maybe I can help, I know I am…"

"No way!" Paige interrupted. "This is my own shit. I don't need to talk to no one. You didn't see anything, got it?" Paige stormed out of the bathroom, leaving a blood-smeared tub and the shimmering blade behind.

After Lucina thoroughly cleaned up, she went in to see Alexander. He did not know anything about the cutting but said Paige hung with the wrong people, her boyfriend was an idiot, and she was still in love with her ex.

Sunday morning, Lucina drove to the airport to pick up Kelly.

Her niece was virtually glowing as she stepped off the plane—no tired look around her eyes, the dark circles had vanished. And the radiant glow was not just from the African sun either, Lucina noticed. There was something else. Kelly looked different. Happy, fulfilled, but most of all, satisfied. Like a little child who had just devoured a delicious scoop of ice cream.

They hugged, and Lucina examined her critically. "Let's go for coffee," she said to Kelly.

Once they were seated in the cosy coffee shop, streaks of sunlight coming through the dirty windows, a cup of Latte in their hands, Lucina asked the only question on her mind. "You had an affair, right?" It was more a statement than a query.

Kelly could not disguise her joy. "I am in love!" she announced. Lucina took her time in replying; she chose her words carefully as she did not want to sound overbearing. She reminded her niece that an extramarital relationship had not been the purpose of the trip. There was her husband, even though he was a bit of a grump, to think about, and there were her children that clearly still needed her. But Kelly had an answer for everything. Ben and her marriage was long over, impossible to fix. Paige was practically grown up and would make her own way and Alexander would soon finish school and be on his way to bigger and better things.

Lucina agreed with her in regards to her son, although she insisted that Alexander was a sensitive young man. She could even understand Kelly's resistance in working on her partnership with Ben, but would she not at least give it one last try? Kelly fired back that she was finally happy, she had met her soulmate, she had rediscovered passion. She saw no need to tell her aunt that she did not rediscover it but had found real passion for the first time.

"Paige is not in a good way," Lucina finally said realising that her relationship advice fell on deaf ears. "I think she is truly unhappy and needs some guidance, some help…"

A phone call interrupted them. Kelly's face softened when she saw the caller ID. She swiped up to answer the call. "Sorry, I have to take this," she mouthed to Lucina, who was left with no doubt that this was the lover phoning. After she had hung up, Kelly said that she appreciated her aunt's concern but that she had to get home now. Paige would be fine; she would check in with her daughter and she would talk with Lucina another time. They drove home in silence, Lucina not finding the right words.. Kelly seemed too distant, too absorbed in her new-found love. Her niece would have to figure it out, but Lucina did want to speak to her about Paige again. If they did not see each other before Lucina left for Italy, she might write a letter. She just had to be careful how she worded it. She did not want Kelly to think she had failed as a mother.

Kelly thanked her aunt, and they hugged goodbye.

Lucina watched her walk towards the house. She could not have known that their paths would not cross again, that unforeseen events would prevent her from sorting out the mess. That voices from beyond would have to deliver the truth. That closure was all she could hope for. Her eyes lingered on Kelly's figure, disappearing through her front door, and she could not help but feel that all was lost already.

Chapter 28

It was 1985 when Theresa toasted to her 30th birthday. Theresa and her three best friends had booked into the Shelbourne for a night to celebrate in style. Marnie had driven them to the city; they had deposited their luggage in the room, reapplied their makeup, and soon were ready to hit the town.

"To our very best friend!" Connie held up her champagne flute. "To Theresa, may all your wishes come true!" They drank, they ate, and they sang drunkenly and out of tune when the birthday cake arrived. Later, they danced in one of Dublin's posh night clubs till their knees were weak, only returning to their hotel in the wee hours of the morning.

Theresa enjoyed the night of celebrations with her besties but what she really wanted was a baby. This was her one and only true wish. She had tried for quite some time but had not fallen pregnant. She had other boyfriends after Julian but had never conceived. Even fulfilling her duties as a godmother had been denied to her, and although years had passed, Ewan's death still haunted her.

At night, unable to sleep, she imagined the inability to welcome a child was her punishment for not having been there for Ewan, for not having looked out for him properly as she should have done as his appointed guardian.

She yearned to hold a baby in her arms, to nurture it, to love it unconditionally.

So, when she joined the jollification with her girlfriends, she vowed to make her wish come true this year. By her next birthday, she would be cheering with orange juice as she would be expecting. Theresa was certain of it. She would do it with a partner by her side or without; it did not matter as long as she got pregnant. This time she would give it her all, forgetting about her past failures, banishing all thoughts of limitations from her mind. She would succeed.

Jonathan loved having sex with Theresa. He could not believe his good fortune when the older, very attractive lady approached him after he had delivered the office equipment to the small firm. She had signed the slip on his clipboard, suggesting to meet her for a drink later. Her eyes cool on his; confident and poised,, as if she already knew his reply.

They had a beer in a pub close by, and as soon as they had taken their last sip she asked him if he was ready for sex. She certainly did not beat around the bush, she did not wrap it up in a "come over for a coffee or a nightcap." She went in for the kill, as straight as an arrow. Jonathan had never met anyone like her before. All the girls he hung out with had to be persuaded to go all the way. Maybe more mature r women were like that, no messing around, hungry for some action, knowing what they wanted and ready to be pleasured? His friends would not even believe him when he'd tell them. He'd brag about Theresa and the kinky sex they'd have. He would boast that she was willing to try anything, giving herself freely with no strings attached. And he would not be lying either, she had said as much. "I am only looking for a bit of fun, no commitment or relationship" were her exact words. It was like Christmas and all his birthdays had come together. She was a woman with morals of an alley cat. He had won the jackpot!

Theresa was no longer looking for love. She was searching for high sperm count, a suitable mate to father her child. And she had to be quick. There was no better way than target an unassuming young and healthy guy. All these juveniles wanted was sex, and she would give it to him. Plentiful. She would do whatever it takes; she would have to let him experiment, let him live out his fantasies. In the end, it would all be worth it. As soon as she got pregnant, she would dump him, nicely, of course. He would, blissfully unaware, go on to the next girl, and she would enjoy her pregnancy and child.

It was too good to be true when she saw the handsome delivery guy at work. She had no time to lose or muck around. So, she struck when the iron was hot. And, of course, he was game. She was looking her best these days as if her secret agenda made her shine from the inside out.

But some months into it, Theresa was getting frustrated. They had sex in abundance.. Having sex was the only thing they did as she refused to build a relationship with Jonathan. He had suggested to go out a few times, to show her off to his buddies no doubt but she had turned him down, only to reward him with more intimacy. It was an exhausting game, one Theresa was willing to play, reminding herself to persevere.

She had taken many pregnancy tests, all of which were negative. She so wanted to see that second blue line, but it never appeared.

Could it be that she had picked the only adolescent who shot blanks?

She decided to ask him a few questions about his previous relationships. He happily chatted away, telling her that he had slept with a few girls, obviously none of them as great or experienced as her. And certainly not as willing, no one he knew had such an appetite for adventure in the bedroom. Theresa waved away the compliments. She wasn't interested in sweet talk. No, he continued merrily, he hadn't always used a condom.

Shit! Theresa had picked an infertile one. She half considered asking him about childhood illnesses, mumps in particular but decided not to. What was the point. She already had wasted precious time. She was pissed. And it could hardly be her as her family was extremely fertile. Sure, she had never fallen pregnant before, but the issue must have been with the men she had dated as all her sisters had conceived straight away. Lucina had chosen not to become a mother. That was different. She had taken precautions. Theresa was gutted.

Firstly, she needed to get rid of Jonathan; then she had to hook up with another man as quickly as possible. Anyone would do at this point.

Theresa slept with whoever was available. She hung out in bars and took home anyone willing to have some fun. There were men who needed some variety, someone who went where their wives wouldn't go. There were the lonely ones, the rejects, and even a virgin or two. Theresa compartmentalised all feelings of shame, burying them deep within her. She simply refused to think. And she felt no remorse either. For her, it was like completing a task. She had one goal in mind, and she had to do anything in her power to reach it.

The sexual coaxing of a woman is a powerful thing, men left, right and centre fell under her spell, propelled into the land of endless pleasure.

One thing she made sure of was that she kept all relationships private. She did not confide in her best friends; she did not gossip with co-workers, and most of all, she did not come clean with her sisters. Her sisters would have been horrified to learn of her scandalous behaviour. They would have called her a slapper; they quite possibly would have forced her to stop, and abandon her dream of becoming a mother. Rachel would have hauled her off to the local priest, praying for her sin-stained sister. No one in their right mind would believe that Theresa acted in such a promiscuous way out of her own accord. Her sisters would not only be disgusted; they might even shun her, excluding her from the family.

No, Theresa kept things under wraps and she had no troubles with her male participants as they wanted to keep their affairs just as quiet.

In all the turbulence and mayhem, Theresa did not once consider herself to be the problem. She was so sure of her ability to host a foetus in her womb that the notion of sterility never crossed her mind.

Time passed, and after many lovers, Theresa was nowhere closer to fulfilling her desire.

All these men were useless. Maybe she needed to branch out further.

She started to read up on sperm banks. It was hard to find anything in Ireland, especially as a single woman as no facility here would accommodate her. It was far better to go abroad anyhow; this country had brought Theresa no luck at all. After many letters, faxes and hushed expensive phone conversations, Theresa knew for certain that she had found the right place for her. She would travel to Upstate New York in a last attempt to make her dream a reality.

The sperm bank was certified by the State; it catered for single women, and she did not need to have any previous treatments or IVF. The donors had to go through a screening process, so only promising candidates could be selected. The staff of the clinic had been very nice and helpful towards Theresa, answering all her questions patiently. She felt confident. America was miles ahead of Europe when it came to medical treatments. The clinic produced excellent results. This was it. She would pay an extra 500 dollars on top of the normal fee for a donor with a PhD. Theresa knew the father of her future child was smart, tall and blond. It all sounded perfect.

In a frisson of excitement, she booked her flight to NYC, telling her boss she was going to Rome for a break. She never breathed a word to her sisters. This was her adventure. She felt a thousand butterflies fluttering in her belly, anticipation, happiness and worry all rolled into one.

After a meeting with the consultant, a doctor would inseminate her with the sperm using a syringe. It all seemed so straightforward. Her timing was perfect; as she would ovulate in a few days..

Everything went according to plan. Theresa was booked into a guesthouse not far from the clinic. Her doctor was so professional and understanding, it made the procedure bearable.

Then Theresa waited. Work had not been too thrilled about the lack of notice she had given and the length of her vacation. She had to convince her superior that she was on the verge of a nervous breakdown, blaming a dispute between her and her sisters. She had cried in front of him, begging for some time to sort out her life. As she had always been a diligent hard worker, her boss had finally agreed on a once-off.

During the waiting period, she treated herself to good food, spa treatments, and a bit of shopping. She hadn't had a proper holiday in a while, and she figured after shelling out a lot of money for the procedure, she might as well continue to spend.

When it was time for her next appointment, she felt pregnant. She did not need a test to confirm it. Her breasts were tender, and her belly ever so slightly expanded.

She marvelled at the cherry blossoms on the short taxi ride to the clinic. The world was beautiful in a riot of colours and sunshine. She was excited and happy. Deep confidence had settled upon her.

A nurse ran the tests and left Theresa to wait in the consultation room. She returned a little while later.

"I am very sorry," the nurse began, "but unfortunately, you are not pregnant."

The sensation that accompanied these words was crushing. Theresa found it difficult to breathe, her hands flying up to her neck, a strange choking sound escaping her throat. The nurse rushed over with a glass of water. But it was not water Theresa needed. She needed a positive result. She started to shout, her voice laden with aggression. She demanded the test to be re-taken. She questioned the donor's credentials. How could these doctors even begin to understand her predicament?

She was ushered into another room, given more water, concerned looks on the nurses faces. A few minutes later the chief consultant appeared, a thick file clamped under his arm.

He spoke with feeling but certainty that left no room for arguments. He explained that the second test had come back with the same results, that the donor had indeed already fathered four children, that the sperm used was top of the range. The problem, therefore, had to lie with her.

The blow came fast and hard, and Theresa found herself grow dizzy and weak.

She was placed on a bed, the doctor by her side. From far away, she heard him mumble on about a series of examinations they could do to know for sure. They would be happy to arrange everything at no extra cost. Theresa only nodded, unable to utter another word.

Several days later, the final findings were presented to her on a piece of paper. Dr Gandolla sat in his leather chair, bracing himself for another outburst.

There it was black on white The AMH blood test unashamedly confirmed the ailing health of her ovaries. There was also the medical marker for her FSH level to consider. Not only were her ovaries hostile towards a baby, but her FSH level was as high as a menopausal woman's. Her body was decaying, her insides rotten. It hadn't been all these men's fault; it was her own. She was incapable of producing life. Unable to accomplish the one thing females were meant to do, the one and only thing that had mattered to her, that would have made her an equal to her sisters. She wasn't a proper woman, she was a failure; it was as simple as that.

Maybe she was being punished, taught a lesson. She had not done enough had not cared enough. Maybe she was denied her wish for a reason. Nothing mattered anymore. She had degraded herself; she had endured countless men and their sexual perversions. She was no more than a slut. And all without a positive outcome. Her sisters would never see her as one of their own. They probably never had, sensing that she was not made of the same stuff. A family with a long history of reproducing had no time for a fiasco of a woman like herself.

Theresa did not want to hear another suggestion of possible treatments, adoption, or anything else. She was done. She packed up her things and returned home.

She would put it all behind her, the sex, the sperm bank, the humiliation, the feeling of complete uselessness. She would have to carry on. She would distance herself from her sisters as much as she dared, walking proudly when she did see them, but knowing in her heart and soul that she could never hold a candle to them.

She would only cry in private, wailing for the child she would never cradle in her arms

Chapter 29

Lucina had invited her sister Theresa to Italy. It wasn't only that she wanted to celebrate her younger sister's 33rd birthday; she also wanted to spend some quality time with her. Lucina had noticed that Theresa had grown distant from the family. She often did not accept an invitation, making up excuses, and when she did meet with them she stayed for only the briefest moment. Theresa had become more quiet than usual, somewhat withdrawn.

It was time to get to the bottom of it.

Lucina had always seen herself as the head of the family, the leader of the sisters. She was, after all, the eldest. She was there to listen and to sort things out and she didn't view a bit of meddling as interfering. Sometimes it was enough to lend an ear, and sometimes, advice had to be given without being asked for it. Things had to be said or done. It was better when issues were out in the open. But it was hard to find the right time too. Lucina's conversations that took place in her head did not always translate to reality. She wanted to help but she did not want to offend anybody either. Nevertheless, she thought it was her duty to intervene in her sister's life. Her heart was always in the right place.

It was a tough job to convince Theresa to book the flight in the first place.

Then, when she was finally in her house in Puglia, Theresa behaved like a sulking teenager. Lucina had cautiously asked her sister how she was doing but had not received a satisfying answer. Even the long, beautiful walks through the vineyards did not draw Theresa out of her shell.

So, when Theresa's birthday came around, Lucina decided that this would be the evening of revelations.

She went to the morning market in the village, purchasing olives and a selection of cheeses. She got wine and flowers, seasonal fruit, and a loaf of bread, the delicious aroma wafting up her nostrils.

When the sun descended, disappearing on the horizon, she sent Theresa to freshen up while she set the table. Candles shimmered on the sideboard; soft music played in the background and Lucina made sure to fill her sister's wine glass to the brim.

Lucina took a sip from the Nero di Troia, smacking her lips. The intensely dark ruby wine with its woody flavour left a hint of liquorice on her taste buds..

Theresa looked beautiful when she entered the room. She was dressed in a simple, white silk dress showing off her great legs.

They clinked their glasses together, Lucina wishing her a happy birthday. In the beginning, their chatter was light, they talked about this and that, and Lucina could tell that Theresa made an effort.

Lucina refilled her sister's glass several times, and it wasn't long till the strong, austere wine loosened Theresa's tongue. When her eyes glazed over, Lucina made her move.

"What is happening with you, love?" she inquired gently. "I do think you need to talk."

Lucina got more than she had bargained for. Theresa did not only talk; she bawled, she sobbed, and she wept. The floodgates had opened, and Theresa's buried emotions came pouring out.

And so it was that Lucina learnt about the baby wish, the sordid affairs, the pressure to make her dream a reality, the trip to the sperm bank, and the failed conception.

Theresa talked about the love she had to give. She cried over Ewan and how she should have taken her godmother's duty more seriously. She said she was being punished. She told Lucina how helpless she felt when she could not get pregnant, that it tore her apart. She stated how inferior she was to her sisters, who popped out babies as if there was nothing to it. She voiced how she would never be fully accepted by her sisters, how they belittled her, feeling sorry for her as she could not produce an offspring. She felt she was not one of them; she was too different.

Theresa recited the many times she had a nice conversation with another woman, but as soon as she admitted to being childless, the discussion took a different turn. First, the other woman would struggle to find words of comfort as having no family could only be a tragedy, then she would make an excuse to leave. Children were the be-all and end-all.

Lucina listened; she only asked a few questions once in a while to clarify what Theresa meant as the combination of despair and wine turned some sentences to gibberish.

When Theresa had completely exhausted herself, Lucina guided her to the bedroom, helping her undress, tucking her in. She kissed her forehead good night.

The next morning was bright and beautiful, birds starting their songs early high up in the fig tree that grew in front of the house.

Lucina had prepared strong coffee. A tall glass of water and aspirin were waiting for Theresa.

She looked rough when she appeared in the kitchen, shielding the sunlight from her eyes.

She sat , gulped down the water , and took a long sip from her steaming mug.

"Now that you know what I'm really like, you must be repulsed by me," Theresa began. "You must think that I am a stupid girl, with no self-respect at all."

Lucina placed a hand over Theresa's. "I think none of that," she said. "Sometimes we want something so badly we forget ourselves."

"There can be no regrets in your life, no dwelling on the past. You did these things because you thought it was the only way. Your vision was blurred. You must forgive yourself and start to heal. I am here for you, but I also think talking to a professional would be a good idea. Someone who is impartial."

They spent the last couple of days relaxing in the golden sunlight.

When Theresa hugged Lucina goodbye, she pledged she'd seek help from a counsellor.

"Keep me posted!" Lucina said, kissing her face.

Theresa did honour her promise. Her initial fear of not being able to open up to a stranger subsided after a few sessions. Donna, her therapist, won her trust, and Theresa disclosed all her secrets, her fears, her hopes and her struggles with her sisters. She would continue to see Donna even when it wasn't necessary anymore, and years later, she would follow her therapist's advice and get herself a dog. A little creature she would shower with love.

Lucina had done good work with her sister. The depression had lifted. She had helped.

She vowed to talk to the other sisters, she wanted to let them know how Theresa felt about them.

But there were little opportunities, and attempts were often cut short. Life was busy. Sometimes Lucina even forgot about her mission, when life was running smoothly, endless days of sunshine stretching out before her. She did, however, monitor Theresa's progress.

Informing her sisters that Theresa considered herself flawed compared to them was often on Lucina's mind. She could not have known that when she finally did speak up, it would not be in person. That the divulgence, in the end, would turn everything upside down, leaving lasting effects on people that had unravelled long before.

Chapter 30

Sam is the first one to arrive at 'La Quinta' restaurant, managed by the avid foodie Francesca Murphy. Sam had been surprised when Lucina confirmed that she had secured a table. 'La Quinta,' the latest hype in trendy eateries, had a waiting list as long as Yonge street. But as usual, Lucina had her ways. Sam strongly suspected that her aunt had used one of her many connections to her advantage as she was well known in the city's culinary scene.

Sam jumped at the chance to dine in the Portuguese establishment. She would be the envy of her entire workforce and would, of course, indulge in lengthy illustrations of the avant-garde place.

She was sitting at the round table with its taupe linen tablecloth, lime-mint sparkling water in front of her, tapping her manicured nails nervously against the crystal.

Waiting made her anxious. She should have been accustomed to waiting as she always arrived before the appointed time. She inspected her shellac nails. She had gone for scarlet red this time, thinking it matched her mood but she wasn't so sure anymore, the red seemed overly bright and a tad vulgar now.

Lucina had invited her nieces for a luxurious lunch before she was off to Italy again. Her aunt spent a lot of time in her beloved trullo these days. She claimed she needed the tranquillity and the sunshine for her old body. She

Lucina had looked after Kelly's brood while her sister took a trip to Africa. Sam wasn't puzzled by her sister, choosing Lucina over her to check on the children. Sam's lack of maternal instincts must have been the deciding factor. Sam didn't mind, not really. To be completely honest, she had no interest in these kids, and she was far too busy anyway. She had sneaked over to Paris to see Dr Leg for a consultation. They had settled on a date in autumn. Even though she had played all her cards right, flashing her money, his dumb secretary could not fit her in before that, Sam would have no choice but wait for her new shapely legs. In the meantime, she made sure to freshen up, adding more collagen to her cheeks and lips, which looked rather plump indeed. She wore a Bitte Kai Rand ankle-length sleeveless dress and an arm-party of silver bangles. She looked good, and she knew it. She noticed the young male waiting staff checking her out. They weren't bad either, particularly the ripped dark-haired one. And who was to know what would happen after the luncheon. She decided it was time for a treat. She called over the David Gandy look-alike and ordered a Martini extra dry.

Taking the first sip on an empty stomach, made her mind relax and her tension ease.

She banished all the murky thoughts from her brain and allowed herself to loosen up.

"If the hot waiter looks over at me within the next three minutes, all will be fine," she told herself. He did, and Sam smiled.

Lucina breezed through the door. Her face slightly flushed; she looked gorgeous as always, dressed in an expensive tweed suit.

"Hello darling!" She kissed Sam on both cheeks. When the waiter appeared seconds later, she ordered a Bloody Mary for herself and another Martini for Sam.

"Lora and Grace are on their way," Lucina informed Sam.

"And Kelly?" Sam looked at her aunt. Lucina's complexion clouded over.

"She cancelled. She said she has a ferocious headache that she can't shift." Lucina let the sentence hang in the air as if she didn't quite believe Kelly.

Lucina knew full well why Kelly had opted out. She had been clever too, avoiding conversations with Lucina, texting rather than phoning and leaving it till the very last minute to let her aunt know that she would not come. So there was no time to ask any questions, to dig a little deeper. Kelly well and truly steered clear of Lucina. She must have known Lucina wanted to speak to her about the affair and about her daughter. But Kelly chose to close her ears and eyes to everything around her. She was trapped in a bubble of oblivious bliss. She no longer thought about real life, facts, or consequences, her niece had fallen for this other man, hook, line and sinker

Lucina exhaled; some way or another, the truth would have to be told. Things would have to be put right again. There was too much at stake, too much to save—a marriage with a long history attached to it, and a child who was crying out for help.

Sam looked at her aunt, who suddenly seemed frail. "Are you okay?" she asked. Lucina nodded, but Sam did not buy it.

Something was up with Kelly. Sam had only seen her sister a couple of times since her return. Kelly had changed somehow. There was a glow to her a strange gratification. She was hyper, not like the flaky Kelly she knew but her sister did not give away much about her vacation.

She only stated that she had a lovely time, that she saw an abundance of exotic animals, that the country was stunningly beautiful, captivating even. She had a dreamy look in her eyes when she spoke of Africa, a faraway stare as if she belonged to that place of sunshine and dried earth.

Sam could not make sense of her at all. Her sister had been on a fucking holiday; what was the big deal? Kelly could hardly have found herself on the trip, discovered something new?

In the end, Sam became irritated and bored with it all. She did not want to hear any more. Whatever her sister was going through, she would have to snap out of it sooner rather than later.

A little while later, Grace and Lora arrived. Sam nearly choked on an olive when she laid eyes on Lora. She hadn't seen her in some time, and she was both fascinated and appalled by her cousin's enormous frame. Her belly protruding outwards like a ginormous bulge in the magenta dress that did her no favours. Who on this planet had talked her into this outfit?

Thunder thighs were walking towards them; her bubble-gum-pink lipstick mouth curled upwards in a forced smile.

Behind her trailed Grace, mouse-like in a straight cadet grey frock and flat pumps.

They kissed, saying their hellos, extending greetings from their loved ones, and inquiring about Kelly's absence.

They ordered a round of drinks and finally looked at the menu.

Lora badly needed some alcohol. She had shared the taxi ride with a forever fretting Grace. Grace had not stopped talking for the entire drive, blabbing on about her darling Noah. How she hoped he would be ok at his playdate today, how she wished he would eat more greens, how her husband should make more of an effort with his boy, how she thought that Noah might occasionally lie to her. In the end, Lora had lost it.

"Oh, just shut the fuck up!" she had yelled at Grace, making her jump, the taxi driver giving her a curious look in the rare view mirror.

"What is wrong with you, anyway?" Lora had continued in a slightly softer tone as she saw Grace's face crumble.

"Your boy is fine; there is nothing to worry about. He is doing great. Why do you not just leave him be?"

"It's just because…" Grace had said, her voice quivering. "I don't' want anything bad happening to him. I mean, things can change," she had trailed off again. Lora had given her a stern look, and Grace had said, "You don't watch them properly, and they could vanish; it only takes a split second…"

"Why do I get the feeling that we are talking about something else here?" Lora had narrowed her eyes at her cousin and Grace had blushed.

"It is hard for me. I feel like I need to be on top of things all the time. I feel I might be punished for what we did to Ewan. That Noah will get hurt or worse." A tear rolled down her cheek, and as much as Lora wanted to smack her face, she composed herself.

"Listen!" Lora had said with authority. She knew where this was going. It was not the first time Grace had brought this up. She had wanted to come clean on numerous occasions. She had tried to convince Lora that it was the right thing to do, that they would sleep better at night, that they would be forgiven. What a bunch of nonsense. The damage was far too great. No one would understand, much less excuse what they had done to a young child, and that they had kept quiet about it all these years Rosie was beyond help. It would be a catastrophe.

It would tear the family apart. To hell with sleeping any better. Bad dreams, worry, and being haunted by Ewan's demons were the price they had to pay. She had endured decades of torment by his spirit. . Only after she had shot Toby, the dog, Ewan had taken a step back, bothering her much less.

Occasionally though she caught a glimpse of him somewhere—sitting at the street corner, giving her the evil eye, ramming a shopping trolley into her foot at the supermarket, calling her bad names. . But it wasn't anything to fret about, and as long as he did not invade her home again, she could handle it.

Lora had taken Grace's cold hand. She had to nip this in the bud once and for all. "We are fine," she had said as reassuringly as she could muster. "Coming clean would be a disaster for the family. You would break them apart. Do you really want to be responsible for more heartache? Besides, it would not resolve anything; it certainly would not bring young Ewan back." She could still see the concern on Grace's face, so she threw in her trump card. "We would still be prosecuted." She had insisted, her eyes as hard as diamonds. "Even if it was a long time ago. Think of Noah. There still is a lot of stigma attached to parents in jail."

"I don't think they would put us in prison." Grace had tried. "We were kids, after all."

"Yes, that's what I originally thought," Lora had lied. "But I looked into it, asked a friend of a friend who is in the force. It turns out we could still do time." Lora's demeanour had not changed when she spoke; she could be an accomplished liar when need be.

Finally, Grace had nodded. "Okay," she had said in a small voice. "My heart bleeds for mum and—"

"We are all the same," Lora had interrupted quickly before another emotional outcry was unleashed.

"Nothing will happen! We are all fine. As long as nobody knows the truth, your son will be safe."

And with that, the taxi came to a halt. The two ladies walked in; one with her head bent and shoulders hunched forward, the other straight, tall and secure in the knowledge that the past was buried forever, never to resurface again. That their lives would go on as they always had, not imagining for a second that all could come crashing down, the truth exposed leaving them vulnerable and distressed bringing no relief whatsoever.

Chapter 31

Lucina allowed her nieces to do most of the talking. She liked to observe. The food was outstanding, a palette of flavours exploding in her mouth, savouring the fresh produce the restaurant prided itself on. The drinks kept coming and the girls were getting louder.

Lucina noticed that Sam, in particular, seemed to have no limit, gulping down one drink after the other, her flirtatious behaviour spinning out of control. She became braver with each alcoholic beverage that slid down her throat. The young waiter kept his cool. He was probably used to older women hitting on him, giving him the eye. Cougars!

She only hoped that Sam would not deteriorate any further, leaving herself open for the embarrassment that would follow.

Sam seemed to loosen up as her alcohol level rose. Her niece was pretty uptight most of the time, paying far too much attention to her looks, worrying too much about other people's opinions even though she would never admit to it.

Sam's personal ticks escalated; Lucina noted with interest. Sam would always put her glass down twice. She placed the glass on the table, lifted it, and set it down again. She did this very quickly, and it might have gone unnoticed by the girls, but not by Lucina, her sharp eye taking in everything. Sam had her food arranged in neat little piles on her plate. Veg to the left, meat cut up in fine pieces in the middle and carbs on the right. She ate slowly and methodically in contrast to her other niece Lora, who wolfed down the balsamic-glazed steak rolls in record time, hardly bothering to chew.. She had gained even more weight since Lucina had seen her last, an angry aura surrounding her. Even when she spoke of an unimportant matter, like the weather or her hair colour, her tone had an aggressive edge to it, her voice reaching dangerous hights when discussing her kids, who seemed to be getting on her nerves a lot. And she was downright defensive when it came to her figure, although no one dared to make a comment.

"Of course, I will lose weight! Just wait and see," she randomly exclaimed, more than once.

Unfortunately, Sam had reached her peak; gentility cast aside, unfiltered words tumbling from her lips.

"Do you remember that dog of yours that you shot dead? Just because he was barking too much!" She hollered in a fit of laughter.

Lucina watched Grace swallow hard, looking uncomfortable. Lora's eyes turned to stone, a bitter hiss escaping her mouth. "The dog was very naughty. I could not put up with him anymore. I snapped. Leave it at that." But the warning was lost on Sam, who was barely listening, waving her hand frantically at the waiter shouting for another drink.

"Dessert, anyone?" Grace tried to save the moment. Lora snatched a menu from Grace burying her head deep into the leather-bound list of sweet afters.

Lucina's eyes locked on Grace, her niece was pale, her lips a thin line. That girl worried far too much, overthinking every aspect of her son's life. From what Lucina could tell, Noah was just fine. A young lad with a vivid imagination and plenty of friends. He was nothing like his mother. Grace agonised over every little detail. She seemed obsessed. She wanted to wrap that child in cotton wool, not letting him out of her sight, not letting him make any mistakes. Thank heavens for the father, who had more cop on.

Lucina wondered what made her niece fret so much. It certainly was unhealthy. There were no guarantees in life. Her brother's death must have had a big impact, possibly fuelling her anxiety. Maybe she would write her a nice, encouraging card. Sometimes it was better to put your thoughts in writing.

By the time they had finished their meals, Sam had to be helped along, swaying from side to side. As Lucina paid the bill, she saw Sam slip the waiter a piece of paper, licking her lips in a seductive manner, one that came across as utterly pathetic, bordering obscene. The waiter graciously accepted the scrap of a note without giving anything away.

Lucina felt embarrassed for Sam. She did a good job of making a show of herself.

Lucina hugged her nieces tight with the promise to see them when she was back from Italy, or perhaps in Puglia if they needed a few days of sunshine.

Grace and Lora both stepped into a taxi, and Lucina tucked Sam safely into another one with clear instructions of Sam's address.

She would have to look out for her nieces; they all had so much stuff going on. They were all struggling. Why, Lucina did not know but she would figure it out. And she could not forget about Kelly either. The sordid affair that would only bring bad luck. The daughter who needed a mother to understand, and the son who was too afraid to burden his own mum.

Lucina puffed out some air. She had a lot on her mind. A lot to do in the weeks ahead. But first she would travel to her home in Puglia. There, immersed in the calm, serene countryside with only the noise of crickets , it would all fall into place. She would know what to do next.

She felt relief wash over her when she climbed into the cab. As the distance between the girls grew bigger, Lucina felt comforted by the thought that everything would work out. She could not have known that it was the last time she had held her nieces close, that uncertain times were looming, that tragedy would strike.

Chapter 32

Sam had a sudden brainwave. She felt surprisingly fresh, not nauseous at all, just a little fuzzy in her head. As if it was stuffed with cotton, quite a pleasant sensation.

"Change of plan!" she yelled to the front, making the driver swerve. "Different address," she went on in a much too loud voice.

"Are you sure?" The taxi driver remembered the elderly lady's stern instructions. "The other miss thought that—"

"Ah, don't mind her." Sam interrupted, "I am a grown woman; I know what I am doing."

The driver's raised eyebrows indicated that he was not convinced.

Twenty minutes later, the taxi pulled up in front of a small dormer bungalow. Yellow paint peeling in places, the garden seemed well kept though, with royal blue geraniums, lily of the Nile and lavender planted to the front and flowering shrubs in pink and yellow to the back. You could see green thumbs were at work here, someone who preferred the outdoors to the slightly sad and shabby dwelling.

Sam jumped out of the car as if she was a nimble child. She would only stay for a bit as she might have a date later on. She was pretty sure that the waiter would call.

"Hello!" she screamed into the front door. "Rosie, it's me, Sam!"

While she sat in the taxi, snippets of the lunch conversation with her cousins flooded through her mind. It made her think of her aunt Rosie and the drama surrounding Ewan's death. It wasn't often they all hung out together anymore. There was something unsettling about them being in one room. Ominous, dark clouds had gathered over them. The secret they had all kept so close to their hearts. That day in the woods came rushing back, the years of denial, living her life despite the enormous grief she and the girls had caused. She hardly ever let her mind go back there, to the day and the dilemma that kept her awake in the weeks that followed the drowning. Her child's mind trying to understand her dislike for the naughty, snot-nosed boy, her actions, instigating the murder. One fact remained, she had wanted to punish him. In the end, she adopted the motto of living with no regrets. The past could not be changed after all and endless thinking would get her nowhere. She had no idea what had uprooted the past, maybe it was seeing her cousins, or maybe the drink was to blame . She wasn't sure anymore. Neither was she convinced any longer that going to Rosie's would help the matter now.

But it was too late. She was already inside the house, hearing the familiar, shuffling footsteps of her aunt coming towards her. She wanted to bolt and run, but she stood still, unable to move.

The dimly lit hallway felt eerie, a broken lamp on the floor, ancient brown wallpaper peeling in the corners where the walls met the popcorn ceiling. The whole place was dire, sad and as neglected as the woman who lived here.

Rosie stood before her. Her burgundy, threadbare bathrobe wrapped tightly around her bulging body. Hair plastered against her head, greasy, unwashed. A grey face with empty, sunken in eyes. Sam could not tell when her aunt had showered last, the pungent smell piercing her nostrils, making her retch. Sam wanted to hug her aunt but could not bring herself to do so. Instead, she quickly touched Rosie's arm and said hello.

Rosie did not reply to the greeting. "It's not your turn today." She snarled instead.

"I know," Sam answered. "I just thought it would be nice to call in and see if you needed anything." She spoke slowly, aware of the alcohol lacing her words.

Sam guided her aunt into the kitchen, drawing in a sharp breath. The heart of the home was in disarray but this was no surprise. Sam had lost count of how many times they had cleaned and tidied up only that all was undone again as soon as they turned their backs. A huge mess greeted her, unwashed dishes, encrusted plates, and rotting bits of food. She had seen it many times, but it shocked her nevertheless. In her peripheral vision, Sam saw something move. She turned and shrieked as a mouse ran across the cluttered worktop.

Rosie did not even flinch. The critter was either old news, or she simply did not care.

"Right!" Sam said once she composed herself. "I will scrub the place down. Maybe you could give me a hand?" Rosie just shook her head, sitting down on one of the tattered chairs with a thump.

"Fine," Sam said, rolling up her sleeves. "Go and have a shower, you stink!"

Rosie heaved herself up and slowly left the room. Sam could not hear the water running; but she did not care anymore. Cleaning the house was the only way to lessen her sins, to make amends in a small way. The alcohol in her blood certainly helped her cope with the filth. Normally her stomach would have turned at the sight of the squalor, bile rising, her face the colour of ashes. But now she grabbed at the decaying food, throwing it into the bin without the urge to vomit. The house was one thing, her aunt, a mountain of a woman reeking of sweat, another.

When the kitchen finally looked half decent, she went looking for her aunt, finding her sitting outside on the patio.

Sam had made them both a cup of tea. She would have preferred something stronger, but Rosie never kept booze in her house.

"The garden looks good," Sam stated. She knew how much Rosie liked to potter around; planting things and watching them grow were the only thing her aunt seemed to enjoy. And even that hobby slowly subsided as the years passed. Her other aunts and the cousins desperately tried to maintain that beautiful piece of paradise for her.

Rosie nodded. She loved her flowers and shrubs. Lucina usually drove to the garden centre , picking up greenery and topsoil. Sometimes Rachel went too. Rosie often marvelled at the colours; she muttered to the rose bushes and complimented the sprouting buddleia.

The garden was the only thing left in her life that encouraged good thoughts and a tiny bit of pleasure.

She knew people cared about her. Her nieces called in and cleaned.. Her sisters brought food and forced her to wash herself. Lucina held her hand in silence. And Grace, her daughter? Grace meant nothing to her and no matter how hard Rosie tried she could not bring herself to love her. In Grace, she only saw someone who had let her down, let Ewan down. A human so different to her boy she often wondered if she really had given birth to her. . There was a sadness that enveloped Grace, one that never left, and still Rosie could not forgive her. Their bond had been severed a long time ago and nothing would ever change that.

They all worried about her; they probably also viewed her as a burden to their lives, a nuisance they had to tend to. She was sure they felt sorry for her, having witnessed her downward spiral. Seeing the life seep from her eyes, knowing she was only waiting for one thing.

Rosie did not judge people. There were those who lost a loved one, grieved but continued on their path. For her, it was different. It was impossible to live after Ewan had died. She had died with him; only her body kept on going, kept breathing, kept pumping blood. There were no more words for her to speak. The world had become a meaningless, desolate place.

The minute she had heard the tragic news she had given up, there simply was no return.

Her son had been a planned baby, a child she wanted to have. She adored him even when he lived in her belly, kicking her sides, poking a little heel into her skin. He was the apple of her eyes; he could do no wrong. She loved everything about him, every fibre of his being. And still, she had neglected him, given too much time to her job, leaving him unsupervised. She should have been there every step of the way. She should have accompanied him into the woods, picked acorns with him, chased him around the trees.

She would never have the chance to make it right, not in this life on earth. She had forsaken the only person that truly mattered to her.

She could not wait to see him again. To take him into her arms and whisper in his ear: "I love you, please forgive me."

Rosie wanted to die. Everything else was of no importance to her. The world could go on spinning, but it would have to do it without her.

One day her body would give up, and she would be free.

Till then, she had to suffer, day in and day out.

Her penance would last an eternity .

After a long silence, Sam got up, clearing away the empty cups.

What was the use? Her aunt would not speak. Her eyes vacant, the lights were out.

"Whatever," Sam snapped , suddenly frustrated, the warm feeling of doing a good deed slowly draining from her insides.

She checked her phone. No message. What the hell? Why had that hunky waiter not texted yet? This day was turning to shit. She could not wait to get out of this ominous place. She wanted to run away from the silent creepy woman with a blank expression.

She cursed herself for coming here today; she cursed the drink that made her think visiting Rosie would somehow miraculously unburden her.

She grabbed her purse and dashed outside without a goodbye, running headlong into Rosie's neighbour.

"Oh, sorry! Pardon me!" the other woman exclaimed, dropping her shopping bag.

Sam heard glass shatter. "I am so sorry," she began. "I did not see you." She shielded her eyes from the sun. "I think something broke in your bag."

"Don't worry about it." The neighbour's face was round and kind.

"Did something happen with Rosie? Is she okay?"

Sam had seen the neighbour before, and had exchanged a few words with her. Lucina seemed to know the woman better. She had mentioned her name to Sam, but Sam could not recall it.

Lucina had said something about how fortunate they were for having a decent and caring person next door to Rosie. Right. What was her flipping name again?

"I am Sam." She stretched out her hand.

"Stella." The woman shook it, continuing to stare at her openly.

"Why don't you come inside for a moment. Have a coffee. You seem frazzled."

Sam exhaled. The day could not get any weirder. She might as well have a coffee with the neighbour, compose herself and then be on her way home. She threw one last glance at her phone. No message.

"Fine," she said. "Why not?"

She found Stella's house nicely decorated in natural colours with soft prints on the walls. There were no traces of anything personal, nothing disclosing the character of the owner. It was like a show home, soulless, pretty, pleasing to the majority.

"Take a seat," Stella said, gesturing to the large, grey sofa. Sam sat down. A simple glass coffee table stood on a shaggy rug. The curtains were pulled back, revealing a stone patio and a neatly mowed patch of grass.

Sam scanned the room but could not find a single interesting item. It was plain boring.

Stella appeared with a tray laden with a cafeteria, cups, sugar, and milk.

"Is Rosie ill?" she was asking now, peering into Sam's face, too close for her liking. "Should I give Lucina a call?"

"No, no, nothing like that," Sam said quickly. "I was actually out with Lucina today and some of the cousins. We had lunch, and I just thought it would be a nice idea to see Rosie afterwards, as she is, you know…" Sam trailed off.

"Lonely?" Stella offered. Sam nodded. Yes, Rosie was lonely, but Sam was convinced her aunt did not mind being alone. She had switched off, had left this world already. She was mouldering.

Stella cleared her throat, and Sam realised she had asked her a question.

"Sorry I was miles away."

Stella smiled her understanding smile. A little too sweet, too curious perhaps.

"Your auntie has been like this for a long while, yes? Lucina mentioned something about the loss of her son when he was only a small child. A terrible accident."

The day had been such a mess, a jumble of confusion, unpleasantries, and disappointments all rolled into one. Sam was done, exhausted with exasperation.

"It was no accident. We pushed him into the river. Grace, Lora, and me." The words were out before she could stop and think.

As soon as the truth spilt from her lips, her hand flew up to her mouth as if this would keep her from saying anything else destructive. But the damage was done; there was no taking it back.

Eyes wide, Sam sincerely hoped the woman had not paid attention, had not understood, but Stella's shocked expression told her otherwise.

Sam had gone insane. She could not even blame the drink at this stage. She had to escape before more harm was done. Then again, how could she make this any worse?

This was unforgivable; they had made a pact.

She needed to get away as quickly as she could, flee from this house and its nosy owner, run as fast as the wind, dismiss what she had done, never to think of it again, and pray that the secret would stay with Stella alone.

"I have to go," Sam blurted and raced from the house. She did not care that Stella was calling after her; she did not care that she had left her silk scarf on the couch. She did not look back. She kept on running till she was completely out of breath. She managed to hail a taxi, sinking into the car seat, the world turning black before her eyes.

Chapter 33

Stella Ludenberg was a quiet woman in her mid-thirties. She lived alone. She never was in a relationship long enough to reach the 'moving in together' stage.

She had grown up in West Brompton, an upper-class neighbourhood of London, in a gable-fronted terraced house with French doors leading to a secluded suntrap of a garden.

Her father, Gustav, a German business owner, spoiled his only child, lavishing her with material things to compensate for his lack of affection.

Stella's mother, Mary, a reserved woman, bitter and disappointed by her husband's aloof manners, never bothered to get to know her daughter. When Mary passed away, soon after Stella had finished her A-levels, Stella felt no obligation to stay on. Through her father's connection, she landed a job as an office administrator in a prestigious Dublin firm. Contact to her father went from the odd phone call to a single card at Christmas as they had nothing to say to one another. Gustav remarried only eight months after Mary's death destroying the last shred of their relationship as Stella refused to give him her blessing.

Stella stayed in her job, never even considering a change. She saved money as she spent little on herself. Her friends were her co-workers, a group of loud, chatty women who gossiped at work and went for drinks every Friday night. They had been kind enough to invite Stella along, although Stella knew they did not really care for her. As an introvert, cautious and boring, Stella did nothing to contribute to their wild stories of binge drinking teenagers and useless husbands. She did not even like going out with them but felt she had to join the weekly bravado at 'Moses' cabin.' She was well aware that these women were only polite, trying not to exclude her. But Stella and her mundane life did not interest them. Understandably so as Stella was not entertaining in any shape or form. So, Stella made small talk with these boisterous, confident co-workers, not because she enjoyed it but simply because it was her only connection to the outside world. The women and their anecdotes were her lifeline, her only glimpse of a place so different from her own, extravagant and fun. She listened and smiled, wishing she could be part of it all, wishing she belonged. Later on, at night, when she laid in her bed, restless and agitated, she replayed the stories over and over again in her head, like a film, only now she was the star of the show, the heroine.

Stella had befriended them all on Facebook, making sure she liked each and every one of their posts. It wasn't a hard task as her colleagues, a few acquaintances, and a hand full of people in the UK, made up her friends list of 27.

There, on this social media site, where everything seemed like endless fun , her friends put up pictures of their lovely families, exciting trips, or a shiny new and beautiful garment that transformed them into movie-stars. They made it look so easy. There was no sorrow, just joy. No days of nothing, only laughter and good-natured banter. Stella marvelled at the thrilling adventures, the photographs of their flawless faces that always looked far better on the computer screen than in real life.

Stella, of course, never posted anything. First of all, nothing she did was post-worthy, and secondly, she would have been terrified of the response or the lack of it more likely. God forbid, she'd posted a random picture, and no one liked it. It would sit there, in this crazy vortex of social media sites, a forever reminder of her dull existence. She would have to crawl into a hole and die. So, she did not even try. The mere thought of it made her break out in hives.

She was grateful for the little bit of attention she got. She knew, however, that her colleagues quite frequently met up in addition to their Friday night social. Snippets of information filtered through, although her friends tried to be discreet about it. Sometimes they would stop talking mid-sentence when she returned to her workplace, coffee in hand. They would change the subject suddenly, discussing the weather when Stella knew they had no interest in meteorology whatsoever.

She was sure they had pictures of their little meetups too, only she hadn't figured out yet why she did not see them on Facebook.

They felt sorry for her, pitied her, probably crossing their fingers and toes that their children would not turn out like her. A nobody, someone who had nothing to say. Their compassion made her feel even worse as if she was the outcast, the loner in the schoolyard. They thought she would never amount to anything, would never make waves, never have real friends.

In her mind, Stella understood, but her heart still hurt.

She wanted to be different, truly she did. She fantasised about telling a gripping story, a thrilling escapade. . She would have loved to keep them in suspense, drawing out her tale till they begged her to reveal the ending. But existing only in the shadows of others, observing rather than speaking, her dreams remained just that.

So, Stella had to be satisfied with her role on the side-lines, of being part of the gang on Fridays only and gorging herself on her colleagues' vibrant sagas.

But deep within herself, she knew her opportunity to shine would come.

However long it may take. At some point in her life, she would rise above herself; she would reach out and make a difference.

Stella felt it in her bones. She was put on this earth to be seen. This, her current state, was not what she was all about.

She only had to be patient, and her calling would be unveiled.

One day she would rise like a phoenix; she would swoop in, helping someone in need. They would applaud her she would earn gratitude and recognition.

And then she would have true friends, ones that would stick with her no matter what. She would be the fun one, the one everybody looked up to. In fact, she would be so popular she would hardly remember the person she used to be.

Chapter 34

Kelly woke up from a sticky, delicious dream.

Jannick was waiting for her in his khaki green jeep. Hot dust had settled on his forearms, his face shiny from sweat. Kelly walked towards him, and although it was a scorching hot day, she wore an impossibly tight, snake-skin dress in scuba material. Her hips swinging, shaped like trouble; she oozed sex appeal with a hint of danger, stiletto heels sinking into the soft earth, her heart ready and open.

"Hi, baby!" Jannick whispered into her ear, "Let's go to bed." But they did not wait for their bed; instead, they attacked each other in a frenzy, as if they were wild animals in the bush. They tore at their clothes, ripping them to shreds, unable to contain themselves for a minute longer. They made love hungrily, Kelly sitting astride him, Jannick grabbing her boobs, kissing her neck, thrusting deep inside her so that she screamed out with pleasure.

Kelly woke with a groan. For a second, she lay there, suspended in her dream, deeply aroused.

When she opened her eyes, realising she was at home in her bed, she felt like crying. A stabbing pain so severe she thought her heart would shatter into a million pieces. She missed Jannick. Everything about him. His touch, his eyes lingering on her body, his strong muscular chest, and his native land so vast, so empty. She wished for nothing more than being with him, watching the orange sun disappear behind the acacia trees, his arms firmly wrapped around her.

Ben kept his distance, getting to grips with her strange moods. Her kids lived their lives, college and school. They hardly needed her. Soon they would fly the nest anyway. Paige barely spoke to her, so Kelly just let her be and Alexander had his music.

Lucina picked up on the affair in a second flat. That woman had way too much intuition, a six sense when it came to personal matters.

She wanted to talk with Kelly, but Kelly had managed to avoid her aunt. Lucina had invited the cousins for lunch in the city. Kelly had accepted, knowing full well she would not attend.

How could she? She wanted to be left alone. No one would understand how she really felt. That this man she had met wasn't just a passing crush, a holiday fling. Lucina would only remind her about her duties as a wife and mother, she would use Paige as bait to keep her here, claiming that her daughter was troubled and needed her mother by her side.

She was looking forward to facetime with Jannick later on in the day, and she needed to get Ben out of the way. But seeing Jannick's face on her phone was not the same. She longed for him, his large hands caressing her body, every bit of it. She needed to be with him. He was the air she breathed, the water she drank, and the food she ate. He was her everything, the only person on this planet who truly made her happy, who completely fulfilled her. He was the one human being that made her appreciate her own body, who took her to unexpected heights, to places she had not known existed. Never before had she experienced such strong sensations. Not with Ben, not even when her kids were born. Delirious and besotted, her mind floating in the universe, between two worlds, between reality and fantasy.

There was one thing left to do.

She was only waiting for the right moment.

Stella bought the house next to Rosie's five years ago. She would have lived in her rented flat indefinitely had it not been for the financial advisor, courtesy of the firm she worked for. At first, she had ignored the offer to speak with him but changed her mind after overhearing her colleagues praising his good looks.

She wasn't really listening to what he was saying. She admired his soft looking skin and his hazel eyes. She imagined herself on a date with him, the envy of the other women—her own little victory.

They would ask her all sorts of questions, demanding to hear all about the juicy bits.

Her attention only snapped into place when he mentioned that homeowners were regarded as superior, a different league to renters altogether.

She liked the sound of that, and after making a few more inquiries, she decided that it was time to become part of that elite group. Her status would surely rise; she would fit right in with all the other property owners. She would move up in the world and at the same time gain sympathy. She'd kill two bird with one stone. She saw herself huffing and puffing along with the other women, discussing the monthly repayments, she would be part of their group. She mailed her wish list to an estate agent, keeping it modest as she never lived beyond her means. She was surprised by the substantial loan the bank offered her after agreeing to a large cash deposit. The very helpful young bank assistant calculated that her mortgage payments would be less than her rent had been. It was a win-win.

Stella spent the following weekends wandering from one open house to the next.

When she saw the detached single-family home on Darling Road, she instantly knew that this was it, tugging at her heartstrings, the property was made for her.

The neighbourhood was quiet, the house at the end of a tree-lined cul de sac.

The garden, on the smaller side, suited Stella as she was not green-fingered, usually killing every plant in her possession. The previous owners had planted low maintenance witch-hazel near the neighbour's fence and gorse bushes to the back.

The three-bedroom house featured a modern interior, in neutral tones and freshly painted kitchen cabinets. It was all she could ask for, lovely and simple.

She put down a deposit the very same day and moved in four weeks later.

The first time she noticed Rosie was when she was cleaning her windows, after the men of the moving company had carelessly dumped her boxes in the living room, creating a volcano-like eruption of dust.

She stopped what she was doing and watched the woman next door move slowly through her garden. It was a sunny day, the rays glinting off her dull skin, an unflattering bathrobe draped around her wide shoulders, stringy hair sticking to her head , her posture hunched.

She was poking at some bushes, snapping off a thin branch with tiny garden scissors, her lips constantly moving. All a sudden, the woman's head lifted, looking directly at Stella.

Hollow eyes, black empty pools. But there was something else, something far more disturbing.

The look of utter despair.

A few days later, Lucina called in to welcome Stella to the street. She brought a tray of freshly baked apple muffins, the sweet smell drifting through Stella's new home.

Stella made tea, and they sat outside on the patio.

Lucina told Stella about Rosie's condition. She said Rosie had lost a child a long time ago and had never recovered from the shock. The sisters and nieces came in to lend a hand, but, in the end, they were all helpless. Rosie's pain was far too great; there was no turning back. Worst of all, Rosie blamed herself, unable to forgive or to move on; she was trapped in an eternity of dark thoughts and regrets. She was slowly dying. Her life had been destroyed. She would never know what had happened on that fateful day. The uncertainty and her failing as a mother had darkened her soul.

Obviously, the sisters did not blame her, not even in the slightest, but no voice of reason got through to Rosie. In her own mind, she was guilty. Peace would only come when she met Ewan in heaven, when she could ask for forgiveness.

Stella listened, her skin covered in gooseflesh, a shiver slithering down her spine. She felt as if she had known the family all along. She felt connected.

She was unable to take a single bite from the muffin, and when Lucina rose to leave, Stella promised to keep an eye on Rosie.

Sam's revelation was colossal. This could change everything, all the self-destroying hatred, the sadness.

And then it all fell into place. It was a sign, her chance to make things right. Her big move. Stella could finally change someone's life for the better. Not all was lost; her life did have a deeper meaning after all. She had been given the opportunity to rewrite the past. She would be the one who saved them all and therefore she would be put on a pedestal, basking in her glory, becoming part of their family. She would no longer pine after her work colleagues for their snippets of attention; oh no, she would be showered with gratitude and love more than she could ever imagine.

She had to tell Lucina.

She wasted no time digging out Lucina's number, but the landline wasn't answered.

She tried Rachel's next. After reassuring Rachel that all was well with Rosie and that she only needed to speak to Lucina about something trivial, she was told that Lucina was at her house in Italy.

Deflated, Stella put down the receiver but soon another idea formed in her head.

She could not have told Lucina over the phone anyway. A crucial matter as such needed to be addressed in person. She rifled through the drawer again. There it was. In her hand, she held the piece of paper with Lucina's address scribbled on it. Her Irish and her Italian one.

Stella sprang into action with a new-found sense of purpose. Adrenalin shooting through her veins.

She made a list. Get a passport, take time off work, get some new clothes, book a flight.

She decided against calling Lucina in advance. The elderly lady would only worry. She might even have a stroke.

For the first time ever, Stella felt she belonged. She would embark on a journey to deliver life-changing news.

She would be the messenger who would bring relief, entering into their world.

She would play a part in ending the suffering and self-loathing of a demented woman.

She alone would start momentous changes in a family ripped apart by travesty.

The truth would be told, and the healing could begin.

And more importantly, her life would finally start, her fabulous true self unveiled, like a movie star plastered across billboards.

Chapter 35

Lucina is sitting under the shady pergola on the stone patio in front of her house.

Surrounded by her garden, filled with fruit and almond trees , bordering the olive plantation of the neighbouring farm, the ancient trunks of the trees twisted like rope, the olives shimmering black pearls in the sun. She can make out a hare, crouched low on the long, dusty driveway, lined with tall cypress trees, swaying in the gentle breeze.

Flowering bushes in a rainbow of colours and wild capers are growing close to her saltwater swimming pool, and terracotta pots filled with sweet-smelling lavender are dotted around the traditional dwelling with its Trullo.

Swallows circle high above her, their long tails painting curious shapes into the sky.

It is a warm morning; the sun steadily climbing up into the royal blue vastness. And still, Lucina feels a chill in her bones. A merino wool blanket hangs loosely over her knees, cradling a steaming mug of camomile tea in her trembling hands, she sits curled into the large rocking chair. A solid piece made out of birch wood that she had re-painted in a smokie white shade a couple of years ago.

She had spent many happy summers here as a child. Endless days at the beach and lovely pizza dinners that Alfons made from scratch, cooking in the outdoor oven.

After her father's death, she had modernized the building, adding a swimming pool, a glossy, Italian kitchen, contemporary furniture and thick, shag pile rugs in cosy tones.

The house kept its old charms with the original limestone Trullo that served as her bedroom.

Stella had only left yesterday. They had said goodbye at the wrought iron gate when the taxi came to collect her.

Lucina waved after the black cab, disappearing into the distance, sadness engulfing her like a heavy coat.

The minute she saw Stella at her door, unannounced, she knew the news would be dreadful.

Stella had stayed only for two days honouring the purpose of her trip. Delivering the message of truth.

A tale peppered with tragedy.

First Lucina was confused by what she heard, but then all the pieces fit together like a puzzle.

The behaviour of her nieces, their burdens, their oddities, anger and fear.

Her sisters, who had, like herself, accepted the tragedy as an accident, never questioning the circumstances. Had they all turned a blind eye, looking the other way?

And then there was Rosie, who had lived with unimaginable guilt for all these years, destroying her own life, giving up, consumed with regrets. Thinking she had let down her beloved boy, her ray of sunshine, her little gem.

Lucina is grappling with the enormity of it all.

She phones Pietro, and they meet up at the beach, strolling along the edge of the water. Lucina talking, Pietro listening.

They buy gelato and sit down on a low stone wall. For a few moments, they lick the silky soft treats, sweet flavours exploding in their mouths.

When Lucina speaks again, her voice is firm. "I have to tell Rosie," she says, reaching for Pietro's hand.

A shiver runs down her back as the sun is trying to warm her face.

She thinks of Rosie, her sister. She thinks of booking her flight back to Ireland. She thinks of all the things she has to organize to make this trip happen, but she simply cannot move. Her hands feel clammy, her head light. Despite the warmth, she cannot get rid of the coldness that has invaded her body. She is very tired.

Pietro noticing her discomfort insists on bringing her to the doctor. And although Lucina declares vehemently that she is fine, and that the shock was just a bit too much, Pietro gently places her into his car and drives to the clinic.

The doctor checks Lucina over and prescribes some medication. Her condition is treated as flu-like symptoms.

Pietro offers to stay with her in the evening, but Lucina wants to be alone.

She lies in her bed, her mind occupied with Rosie and the rest of her family.

The hours tick away, and sleep does not come. Lucina's body grows weaker, her skin taking on the colour of snow, her chest tightening with pain.

At the stroke of midnight, Lucina knows she will not make this trip. She will never again return to Ireland. She is dying. Her heart defect has caught up with her. There is nothing she can do; it is her time.

She scrambles out of bed, slipping into her plush bathrobe, sitting down at her desk. She switches her laptop on and starts writing.

Chapter 36

I remember a photograph that was taken a long while ago of my sisters and me. We had just come back from an outing. We spent the day at a local vineyard, laughing, indulging in sweet memories of our childhood. The wine was delicious; the sun shone brightly. We were happy, arms wrapped around each other, standing in front of my house, the Trullo rising up into the powder blue sky behind us.

It was the only trip Rosie had joined us on, she must have known, deep inside her that, for her too, this would be the one and only time she'd be able to enjoy a tiny slice of happiness with her dear ones. And although she did not speak much and stayed away from Marie-Anne I understood that she felt content, as much as it was possible for her. As the years went on Rosie deteriorated further, withdrawing completely from life Marie-Anne had been on her best behaviour, not mentioning the past. Rachel had organised it all. There wasn't even an occasion, no birthday or anniversary, just a simple, spur of moment get-together. A quick trip to Italy. These are usually the best moments, the ones that require hardly any planning at all. I can say, without a doubt, it was my favourite day in my entire life. Something so magical, so harmonious, so pure and joyful about us being here, us sisters united. The past was forgotten for just one day.

I had the photograph framed, leaving it on my desk in the bedroom so I could gaze at it always, reminiscing.

I took it into my hand, the night I wrote my goodbye letter, and kissed it.

I wanted to reach out to my sisters, tell them life without them would not have been worth living. I wanted to relive this happy day, feel the peace deep inside me.

I knew I had to speak the truth. I had to say it all. I needed to do this one last thing in my time on earth; I needed to bring them together once more. Only after everything was revealed, they could heal and find one another again. It was not only my duty as the eldest, as the head of the family, it was also my destiny.

I wrote my final letter to my sisters, and I composed another one with detailed instructions about my funeral and the afters, addressed to Pietro and Ilaria, so my lovely friends could fulfil my last wishes.

I knew all would be taken care of beautifully.

It was not an easy task, but one that had to be done.

Tears were sliding down my cheeks as I typed away, reflecting on my life.

My life was an effortless one, no doubt about that. Loving parents, although not together as a unit, they both did everything they could for me. My mum nurtured me, and my dad showed me the world, taught me to enjoy adventures and handle the curveballs life throws at you. His attitude was always forward and positive. His charm and enthusiasm were contagious.

I travelled the world, making great friends along the way. Especially in my later years as I spent more time in my home in Italy. Immersing myself in the culture and language paved my way into the village community, where I connected with the most wonderful, warm people—my dearest friend Ilaria and of course Pietro, my soulmate.

It's funny, I had many relationships during my life, some more meaningful than others, but none of them touched my heart, non except Pietro. And as we met, two people of mature years, our relationship was strong from the beginning. In each other, we found not only a lover but a true friend. We completed one another.

It would be true to say; I was regarded as quite a catch by the opposite sex. Beautiful, like an ice queen when I was young and classy in my later years.

Men wanted to be near me; some wanted to own me, not that I would have ever let them. Every one of my pursuers needed me more than I needed them. They declared love, proposed marriage, promised eternal devotion.

I handled these advances as I did everything else in my life. Straight to the point coated with the most dazzling charm. Men were as bewitched by the golden luminosity of Puglia as they were by my irresistible nature and I certainly cast a spell on them. I say all this without pride or arrogance; it's simply the truth. I won't lie. Their obsession entertained me, and I am guilty of playing with their hearts at times. Games with their minds and souls. I relished peeling back the layers till their vulnerability was laid bare, unmasked, and unprotected. I liked being the one in charge, their princess.

If this makes me a bad person, so be it. I was never afraid of the afterlife, of our Judge, as I know my essence is good. My family always came first, and I would have bent over backwards for my close friends. Steering my sisters and nieces towards the right path became my utmost priority, and I helped wherever I could. But I also had fun, probably hurting some people along the way. Surely I was a little naughty from time to time, but in the end, I always did the right thing. I do not believe that humans can ever be perfect. There is a little meanness in all of us but as long as the good overrides the bad, you are doing fine.

In my case, I did a lot of good; I loved deeply, and I laughed aloud. I spent money freely, and I always gave back.

And my relationship with the Creator was a solid one.

So, when my time came, I was neither sad nor angry, nor had I any regrets. I had done what I wanted to do. I had lived to the fullest. I was looking forward to meeting our Lord, and I knew I would still be present in my loved ones' lives. I would become an angel.

My last task was done: my letters were written.

I will be waiting for my nieces' burdens to lift, for the family to forgive each other and love again. I will be watching.

Chapter 37

The shade was imperial red. Rachel had bought the small bottle of nail varnish in Boots this morning when she dropped off her prescription. She could not shift the persistent cough and had finally seen a doctor. Nothing to worry about, he had said, but just to be on the safe side, he recommended an anti-biotic. Rachel disliked taking medication; she saw what it did to Rosie. It made her lethargic. Rachel preferred to pray her worries and aching away. *For I know the plans I have for you, plans to prosper you and not harm you.*

She held one hand out in front of her and admired the colour. She used to go for ruby and hibiscus shades, but not anymore. These days she was much more of a racer-red lady.

She continued painting the left hand; slow and steady was key. Her nails always looked salon professional.

The doorbell made her jump, and a blob of nail polish landed on her pointer finger, messing up her perfect work . Annoyed, she wiped it off, then went to answer the door.

A registered letter. Quite unusual. Rachel placed the letter on the worktop and finished her nails. One thing at a time.

Only after her nails were shining, the glossy tint dried, and hands moisturised she opened the letter.

"Another trip to Italy?" Ben's frown lines on his forehead deepened even more, his eyebrows shot up, a sign that he was getting very irritated.

"Well, I am not going, screw this!" he spat.

"The letter states that we all have to go." Kelly tried. Her mother had rung her earlier, as she would have every other member of the family.

Lucina's friend had mailed an important letter to Rachel, one that said Lucina's last words would be disclosed. They were all summoned to Italy. One more gathering, a mysterious message. Lucina had always been an enigmatic person.

"It's completely ridiculous!" Ben was fuming. "The funeral was ages ago; why did she not read out her stupid letter then, why now? Make another trip, for what…"

Kelly did not know the answer. Why indeed? Maybe her auntie wanted them to celebrate her life first and have her final words revealed later? Perhaps there was a point to it all, one they would only understand afterwards?

Rachel had made it very clear that all were expected to attend. Possibly not the smaller children, but everyone else for sure.

"It was her wish," Kelly began again, but Ben interrupted.

"She's dead, isn't she? She darn won't know." Nothing was further from Ben's mind than a pointless journey to this hot barren country, his weird children and preoccupied wife in tow. Kelly was so absent-minded lately, even more than she used to be. She clearly lived in la-la land most of the time, not paying any attention to the family around her. He wondered if she was hiding something big. What though? He hadn't a clue.

"Maybe it's the testament," Paige offered. They were all sitting together for dinner, a rare occasion nowadays. "We might inherit everything, imagine that we'll be rich…"

"I doubt that very much," Kelly answered. "If anything, her sisters will benefit, certainly not you."

"What the fuck!" Paige slammed down her fork. "I am not going either."

"We will all go." Kelly's voice was stern, her usual placid, far-away tone forgotten. She had not spoken to them in that way in a long time.

She looked at her family, her face set. "And that is final."

Kelly had successfully ignored Lucina since her return from Africa. She even went as far as hiding in her upstairs bedroom, pretending not to be at home, one day when her aunt had pulled up outside her house unannounced. She had avoided speaking about the elephant in the room at all costs. And then her aunt died, without any warning. Kelly simply had no way of apologising anymore. She had been struggling with feelings of guilt and longing for her lover, all at the same time. She felt drained and exhausted by the rollercoaster of emotions. She had trouble concentrating even on the smallest task. Her mind was distracted and in turmoil. She owed Lucina this trip; she owed it to her to listen to her last letter and bring her husband and kids along as required. Then, she would move on. Her time had come; she only had to set the wheels in motion.

"Do you think auntie Lucina wanted to give all her money to the poor children in Africa?" Noah's eyes looked huge in his narrow face; his small hands were resting on her open suitcase.

Grace had put it on her bed, throwing clothes into it. Not many, as she wasn't planning on staying long. Her hubby and Noah weren't coming; there really was no point in joining her. The testament would be read out, then she'd be done and could go back home again.

Noah hadn't batted an eyelid when she told him she was leaving. He hadn't asked how many days she would be away; he hadn't begged her to stay.

Could it be that he didn't care? She always wanted to be close to her mum when she was a child; only her mother was not available to her.

Noah was so independent, his own little person. Did he not need her? She was his mother; surely, he wanted to be by her side.

"Well?" he was asking now, pushing his fingers into her arm.

"No, honey," she said gently. "I don't think so. Auntie Lucina was not very charitable."

"Was she a bit mean then?" Noah's eyes widened even more. "She was always nice to me."

"No, no! That's not what I meant!" Grace explained. "Auntie Lucina did everything for her family and close friends. She was very generous, with money and everything else. She just did not believe in giving her money to organisations."

"Why? Did she not want to help the starving kids?"

"Yes, she did, but she wasn't sure if the money would really reach those poor children. I suppose she did not trust the people behind the charity."

"So, would she have given money to a child in the street then, if she saw one?"

"Yes, or perhaps some food and a drink, she would have wanted to give the kid something just for him to enjoy." Grace smiled at the thought of Lucina. That is exactly what she would have done. A bit suspicious, a good heart, a fixer, a matriarch. She hugged her son tight, feeling him wriggle in her arms, trying to escape her grip. He was such a thoughtful, sensitive boy, thinking of the less fortunate. His concern for others made her ponder his questions; it made her wonder what she could do to contribute. Maybe there was another purpose to her life other than her son, a vocation, working selflessly for those in need.

It was a two man's job to get Rosie into the taxi. Or, in their case, a two women's.

Rachel had packed Rosie's bag. She had explained to Rosie that Lucina had a letter waiting for them in Italy and that Lucina had specifically asked for Rosie to be there. Rosie had not objected. She had simply nodded her okay. She even let Lora wash her hair. She hadn't said much, only gestured to let them know what she wanted to bring.

Lora had ordered a mini-bus taxi because of Rosie's size. Her aunt was fat, and moving her was like lifting dead weight.

They had finally managed to get Rosie into the cab and the suitcases stored in the boot of the car.

When Lora locked Rosie's gate, she glanced up to the neighbour's house. The curtains twitched, and she saw a pale face disappear. A fleeting moment, seemingly trivial, and still Lora could not shift the feeling that something bad was going to happen.

Chapter 38

The car model Sam had pre-ordered certainly was not the one the rental company was trying to talk her into now.

Sam had been at a conference in Liverpool when her mother rang with the news. She finished up her work and took a flight from the UK, arriving ahead of everyone else.

She did not mind the two full days in Italy before the rest of the family joined her. The UK meetings had been hell, people trying her patience, she needed to recharge her batteries away from the stressful environment. She was looking forward to some quiet time and a good massage.

"This is not the car I booked!" she snapped, stabbing the rental agreement with a long, sage green fingernail. She spoke slowly and pronounced as she knew the agent was not only infirm in English but also a bit daft.

"I ordered the automatic white Audi, two-seater sport." She gave him a stern look, her long, mink lashes quivering dramatically.

Typical Southern Italian incompetence at its best with their la di da attitude towards life. Sam did not have time for this shit. "Where is your supervisor?"

She thought she saw the young man roll his eyes when he turned his back to fetch the other person.

The senior agent explained, slowly and carefully, as he understood that she was a ticking time bomb, one that would write a nasty review, that unfortunately, the car she wanted had not been returned in time. Therefore, they could offer her an alternative and a partial refund.

Still fuming when she crossed the hot tarmac to the car park, she threw her Louis Vuitton bag into the Fiat and zoomed out of the airport area without looking left or right. Deserves them right, she thought, speeding down the national road, if I scratch up that crappy car.

After a while, the GPS told her to make a sharp right onto a narrow street, away from the main one. Sam obliged without taking the foot off the gas, or paying attention to the road, more concerned with changing the radio station from the Italian babbling to some soothing music when she hit a pothole with full force. Sam let out a scream. She managed to grip the steering wheel, straightening the car but soon realised that she had a flat tire; the noise of metal on metal was undeniable.

"Oh, fuck it already!" She got out of the car and even with an untrained eye, she could tell that the damage was extensive.

Scorching hot, and no water at hand, she deeply regretted her choice of the formal outfit restricting her movements, the acrylic material unsuitable for the heat.

She dialled the car company's number and a garage she had found on google maps, but both rang out. This clearly could not get much worse.

And then it did.

Sam saw the beat-up blue Ford appear in the distance; it slowed right down, coming to a halt, Drake cranked up to the maximum, spilling out of the open windows, turning the tranquil countryside into a disco.

To her horror, she watched a burly bearded man climb out of the car that was surely made for much smaller folks. He stood, at least 6ft 4, broad-shouldered with a crooked nose and bushy eyebrows, smiling at her in what she could only describe as unsettling.

Sam started to sweat even more. This was it. The end had come. She would be raped and murdered here in this arid place, her battered body hidden deep within the thorny shrubs. Her family would search, wondering what had happened to her, till one day when a hiker or a dog walker would discover her skeleton. Only bones left behind in the bushes, picked clean by the wild animals that roamed the area. She would be identified by her perfect teeth alone. It would be unbelievably tragic and her family would never get over it, mourning her life, so promising, so talented. Sam shuddered at the thought of maggots invading her body, a lifeless piece of flesh tossed into the wilderness. A tear slid down her cheek, imagining all the tragedy.

She braced herself as the grinning man came closer, the car keys in her fist, ready to stab him in the eye, ready to fight for her life.

"Ciao." His voice was warm and deep. "Problem d'auto?"

"Si," Sam replied, her eyes not leaving his face. "I don't speak Italian."

"Ah Inglese!"

"No, Ireland."

"Irlanda, Bellissimo!" He laughed, and when he did, his whole body shook. Sam did not see the funny side of it. Here she was, trapped in this intense heat with a lunatic who quite possibly was trying to win her trust before pounding her to death with a blunt object.

"I will have a look," he said in a very acceptable English laced with a thick Italian accent.

He walked around the car and bent down to examine the wheel. Sam followed him, checking for hidden weapons but couldn't detect any.

When he looked at her again, he could hardly disguise his amusement. "You must have done well over 100 km to do this sort of damage. The tire is broken, it's unrepairable."

"Yes." Sam had thought as much.

"Are you in a hurry?" the giant asked, a gleeful twinkle in his brown eyes.

"Not really." Sam felt exhausted. "I am here for the reading of my aunt's will. I am meeting my family in a couple of days; I just wanted to get to the hotel and relax…" she trailed off.

"Where are you staying?"

Sam thought his face was kind when she gave him the address. It was probably the wrong move, but she had no energy left. She only hoped it would be fast when he killed her, and that her face wasn't too disfigured, she wanted to remain beautiful, even after death. Everything she had ever seen and read about victims being lured to their deaths came rushing at her, the silly girls who trusted their predators falling into their traps. And now she was one of them.

He looked at her expectantly. "Sorry, what?"

"Will I give you a lift?" he asked again, eyes shining.

Sam nodded; she grabbed her luggage and got into his car. Her defences were down. She never thought that she could feel that helpless.

"I am Leonardo," he said, holding out his hand. Of course, he was. Sam took it, surprised by its smoothness.

"Sam," she said.

"Sam from Ireland," Leonardo repeated with a smirk.

As they drove, Sam became well aware of her sweaty odour, her wrinkled blazer, and her silk blouse clinging to her body, highlighting the undesirable bits around her belly. She pulled out a compact mirror to examine her face. A blotchy, red mess stared back at her. Her mascara had begun to run, leaving black traces under her bloodshot eyes. She looked simply disgusting. And she stank. This was not good. She took out a baby wipe and cleaned her face.

She glanced at the driving Leonardo. He sat, hunched forward in his tiny car, his long legs tucked under the steering wheel. His hands were large, and his nails clean. His beard looked scraggly in a cared-for kind of way, a couple of long hairs poking out of his nostrils and a pus-filled pimple near his ear had ripened in the sun. Unacceptable. Had he not look at himself this morning? Then again, who was she to criticise. Miss puffy face.

Leonardo was not attractive at all. He was not on Sam's level, not up to her high standards, and still, she found it hard to look away. It was as if his messy appearance drew her in, captured her in some bizarre way. She fought back the urge to put her hand on his forearm. What the hell was wrong with her? She must be delusional. Maybe she suffered severe dehydration. She could never date a man who did not take care of himself ; she would not even entertain the idea of sex with such a…

"So, you are only here for a short time?" Leonardo interrupted her thoughts.

"Yes," she said, and continued after a pause, "How come your English is so good?" She hadn't meant to say so good because it wasn't. His English was fine, not great.

"I lived in England for a few years," came the answer. "Didn't like it too much; the weather really got to me. I prefer the sunshine. I teach in the village."

"You might know my aunt then. Lucina."

"Yap," he said. "I knew her, lovely person, a real lady."

She was, Sam thought. Always put together so well, so elegant. Lucina would not have fallen apart because of a minor car incident. She would have stood above it, calm and collected. She would have made arrangements and then cooled off with a delicious cocktail. If only she saw her niece now. Dishevelled, with a perplexing desire to touch a strange man.

Leonardo dropped her off at the hotel and promised to have her car towed and fixed. Sam felt ridiculously grateful as if he had just saved her life.

"Thank you," she managed. All she wanted now was a shower, fresh clothes, and an ice-cold drink.

Later on, she was chilling out on the hotel's veranda when Leonardo joined her table. He sat down without being invited to. The waitress appeared, and he ordered a large beer.

He obviously had no manners, or he thought she owed him now.

"You are staying for a drink then?" Her tone was much more sarcastic than she had intended it to be, and she immediately regretted it. What the heck. Sam hurt people all the time, and she never felt bad about it. Why now, why with him? She was losing her mind. This place was getting to her, the shrill sound of the cicadas, the smell of citrus in the air, the unbearable temperature. There was something so vulnerable about this big, unkempt man. Curiosity made her see past his physical imperfection and disgraceful rudeness. And there was more, a feeling she couldn't quite put her finger on.

Instead of entertaining her smart comment, he let it slide. His eyes lingering on her, unashamedly

"You are very beautiful, Sam," he said. "But you need to come off your high horse."

He winked, got up, lager in hand and went to the bar.

Sam was left speechless. Never in her life had a man insulted her like this. Definitely not a man as unattractive as Leonardo. What high horse? She gawked after him. Was he coming back, or was he just going to let her sit here all by herself? The cheek of him. As far as she was concerned, he could stay at the bar, flirting with the dumb waitress, see if she cared. But she did care; there was nothing she wanted more than him to return to her. She did not understand her feelings, as she had never felt like this before. She had experienced intense lust, hot desire. This, however, felt different and very confusing. It wasn't just passion; it was something far more profound, earthy, a primal urge that erased her list of requirements, tore down her barriers. Looking at him, leaning against the bar's counter, a great tenderness swept over her. She not only wanted to make love to him, she wanted to be with him, wake up next to him, and hold him tight. Why she could not fathom, he was not her type; he did not fit her pattern. Far from it. There was nothing he could offer her, or was there?

Chapter 39

They all met on Thursday in Lucina's house.

Sam spent the previous two days trying to relax by the poolside. She had gone for a massage and had enjoyed, uncustomary to her usual drinking habit, many G&Ts. So much so that the bar staff had a high-ball glass waiting for her when she came down the stairs, just after breakfast in bed.

And still, it was impossible for her mind to wind down. She was waiting for Leonardo; only he did not show up. As promised, he had the car repaired and delivered back to the hotel without showing his face. There was a small, handwritten note left for her which said 'good luck with all'—nothing else.

Sam was furious. How dare he treat her like this. No one had ever made her feel this insecure. She was definitely superior to Leonardo in every way. Normally she would not have glanced twice at someone like him. Why was it then that she could not get him out of her head? Was it because he made himself unavailable to her, to a woman who could have any man under the sun, at the snap of her fingers? Even if it usually only was for sex. Was it that she had seen something unexpected in this man, something she wanted to explore further, something deeper, beyond her usual choices of clean-cut faces and toned bodies? He had bad habits, he wasn't rich or handsome, and still, for the first time ever, she could imagine herself engaging in a proper relationship.

Anyhow, she had blown it. He clearly wasn't interested.

She was in a foul humour when she finally pulled up in front of the Trullo. The hope of Leonardo returning to her, a hope that had not materialised, had drained her, had sucked every bit of energy from her.

She was the last to arrive.

Ilaria had made cannoli and bombolone, the dainty pastries sitting on a sky-blue plate in the middle of the mahogany coffee table. Next to it, a tall carafe of water, cut lemon pieces floating in the liquid, like slices of gold. Ilaria stood near

Pietro, his arms folded, his eyes sad, but he managed to smile as the family trailed in.

Rachel, Paul, Kelly, Ben, Alexander and Paige were seated on the sofa. Marie-Anne, Trevor and Theresa had placed their behinds on kitchen chairs, and Lora, Oscar and Grace were at the far side, next to Rosie, who sat in a wheelchair.

Neither Grace nor Lora had bothered to bring their kids. Sam wasn't surprised one bit that Grace's husband wasn't here either; he never showed up at family gatherings.

"Is everyone here?" Pietro looked at Rachel. His words laden with Italian pronunciation, his bass voice soothing.

"Yes." Rachel nodded; her hands in her lap. "We are all here now."

Sam thought her mother looked aged in her pleated maroon skirt and tan chiffon blouse. Colours which did nothing for her complexion.

Grace was nervously fidgeting with the strap of her purse; she looked like a little woodland creature taking in her surroundings. Theresa sat calmly; the teal green flared dress looked great on her, her long legs stretched out leisurely. Trevor seemed relaxed too. Lora was the only one helping herself to yet another cannoli, a trace of crumbs falling down her mustard boat neck top.

Marie-Anne sat rigid, upright as if she was about to fire a boisterous employee.

She wore a beautifully tailored two-piece wool blend suit, far too warm for an Italian summer's day. She bore no resemblance to her daughter Lora. Marie-Anne had maintained her trim figure, her face narrow with chiseled cheekbones. Rosie looked like a big, brown blob in her chair. There was no other way to describe her aunt, and Sam felt a deep sadness rising up inside her.

Alexander was looking from one relative to the next as if he hadn't seen them in a long time. Maybe he hadn't, and Sam was reminded of how little time she spent with her nephew and niece. Paige wore a ridiculously short leather effect skirt with biker boots and a distressed denim shirt. Her black hair shaved on one side, a big skull earring dangling from her earlobe. Sam made a mental note to bring her shopping. Ben, sweating in his khaki shirt, clearly wanted to be anywhere else but here, the bald patch on his head shining with perspiration, droplets slowly making their way down the side of his puce face. Sam had made sure to stay as far away from him as possible to avoid the pong. How could Kelly sleep with this man? There she was, her sister, as glamorous as can be in a navy Jacky O dress, simple but classic. Her skin radiant, her blond hair cut a little shorter than usual, her eyes bright. *There was no way Leonardo would have rejected her*, Sam thought bitterly. Her goodie-two-shoes sister with her perfect life, her perfect looks. She made Sam sick.

Pietro cleared his throat.

"Thank you all for coming." He began.

"As Lucina was dying, she composed this letter. She felt that it was very important for every member of her family to be here in person. She had asked me to read the letter out to you, so without any further ado, Lucina's last words."

Chapter 40

My Dear Family!

Thank you for gathering here today.

I am grateful to you all.

I know coming to my house in Italy for a second time must have been difficult, but let me assure you, it is of utmost importance that you are here.

My life is coming to an end.

I am dying.

I can feel it in every fibre of my body.

Don't be sad, and don't mourn me. My life was a great one; I enjoyed every minute of it. The good and the bad, thankfully happy times outweighed sad ones by far.

I addressed my last wishes to my dear friends Pietro and Ilaria, who, I am sure, carried out their duties beautifully. Thank you, my sweethearts.

I wanted to give you a couple of months at home, after the funeral, before I summoned you back.

I did not want to rush things as my last letter is far too important. I wanted you to take it all in.

I asked Ilaria to post this letter to Rachel on a specific date, and I asked my dear Pietro to read it out to you.

As I said, I am about to leave this wonderful place. There is no time left to take a trip to Ireland to speak with you all in person.

I feel I will always be with you, my family, my sisters.

My life was good because of you. I love you all dearly. I felt, as the head of the family, an obligation to set things straight, to speak the truth. The message was delivered to me only recently.

I understand there will be anger and turmoil, but please forgive one another and let there be healing too.

My legacy will carry on through you and all that you do.

Our family and our sisterhood were always the most important things in my life. Believe me when I say secrets must be aired in order to move forward in life. My conscience would not be clear, taking what I now know to my grave. My heart is in the right place. I would like nothing better than for you to love one another and yourselves again.

Ilaria, my best friend, I cannot thank you enough for your friendship, our laughs and talks.

I have left you my sapphire necklace; think of me when you wear it.

Pietro, the love of my life, my soulmate.

I met you late in life, and still, you were the only man I ever truly loved.

Thank you for our years together; I cherished every moment.

Please take all my artwork, my books and my Bentley; remember me when you drive into the sunset. I am still with you and I will be waiting for you in paradise. I love you.

Trevor, my darling brother, I am so proud of you and what you stand for.

I am happy you are living a meaningful life; carry on, and always stay true to yourself.

I have listed you and all my sisters as beneficiaries to my accounts.

Marie-Anne, I love you with all my being, but I do hope that you will learn empathy and understanding. People make mistakes; we are allowed mishaps, no one is perfect, not even you. Shielding your eyes from adversity will not solve any problems.

You portray a hard woman, but I know you are soft underneath. Bring compassion to the forefront, and you will shine. Rachel, you are such a good person, always looking out for everyone. And yes, you are next in line to lead this family. Make sure they forgive and find solace.

Help them through troubled times, listen and pray to your God.

I have faith in you, my sister.

Theresa, my darling. I know how much you have suffered through the years; how inferior you feel towards your sisters.

You might be horrified at what I am saying next, but I firmly believe this is the time for your sisters to learn what you have endured.

Our Theresa is not childless by choice, as you all assumed. She tried everything in her power to conceive and become a mother. It was her biggest desire to care for a baby, but it wasn't meant to be.

Theresa felt left out and belittled. She felt like less of a woman than all of you who had no troubles having kids. She was lonely and alienated.

She would have given her right hand to have what you, my sisters, all accomplished so easily. She truly was devastated when her godson was taken from her, and she blamed herself for not spending more time with him.

In the end, she found some consolation in her dog.

Rachel, Marie-Anne and Rosie, I would like you to support Theresa, try to comprehend what she had gone through and the choices she had made. Show tenderness and tolerance, not judgement, and she will open up to you too.

My nieces—Samantha, Kelly, Grace and Lora—I will leave you this house here in Italy.

You may do as you wish, sell it, or use it as a home.

The best time of my life was spent here in these four walls, in this magical place.

But I live on in your memories and will always be associated with my beloved Italy.

Do not fret if you do not feel the same way. My affiliation with this house is not yours, nor can it ever be. Therefore, it does not matter what you will do. The only important thing is that you all agree.

Fill this house with love and laughter or sell it to someone else who will. The choice is yours, my girls.

Samantha, I do love you, but you are a major pain in the neck, if I may be frank. I am not convinced that you will ever be happy and free from your habits if you do not learn to let go. Smile at yourself, you do not have to give 100% every time at everything you do, and that includes yourself. Know that you can slip up and still be desirable. Being that hard on yourself hinders you from building relationships. It also created a wall, one you erected to stop yourself from feeling sadness and regret. Open up and let people in, as I am sure they are trying to. And most of all, stop comparing yourself to your sister. She was the lucky one. Pretty much everything fell into her lap. She is beautiful, but her life is not as perfect as it seems. She is struggling as well. You must understand people will only show you a slice of themselves, a façade, the better side. No one knows what is happening behind closed doors.

You must face the music Sam and then move forward.

Grace, my little pet. I worry about you. You too, must open up and put the past behind you. You must learn to enjoy life and not let anxiety get the better of you.

Every mother loves her child. Every mother wants only the best for him, but you cannot wrap your little boy in cotton wool and hide him from the world. Have faith that he is a good boy, that he will make the right decisions. You raised him well. This is all you can ever do. Now cut these apron strings and start trusting him. There is a whole world out there for you to discover and take part in. Make the most of it, get involved. Give your boy the freedom he deserves, and know I will watch over him.

Lora, my sweetheart. There is so much unresolved anger in you. Your rage grew like cancer, spreading to your family, your lovely kids, your husband and your home. They are good people who have your back.

Let them help you. You are fighting real demons in your head, and there is only one way to make them stop. Fess up, have a clear conscience.. Please believe me when I tell you, it all starts with the truth. Unburden yourself, and you will be able to see the beauty in this world again.

Kelly, my sweet girl. You have been a princess all your life. You never had to work too hard at anything. People always loved you, were drawn to you. You are extraordinarily pretty. I see a lot of myself in you; the way life was easy for us. But you are troubled too. I understand your marriage is not a bed of roses, and I am sure you have tried to make it work. I know Ben can be difficult, intense.

You have created a family; you have a responsibility towards your children. I think you often take a simple way out and close your eyes to many things around you. There are issues in your house you clearly refuse to acknowledge. Look how private your lovely son is. He has suffered at the hands of bullies for a long while. He has kept quiet because he did not want to worry you. He put you on a pedestal. He thinks the world of you, and so he chooses not to bother you with his troubles. He is one of the most sensitive young men I have ever met. Musically gifted. He needs you to step up; he needs your help. His wish is to study at a prestigious music academy.

I am confident Alexander will make his way in this world. He will be a star. Believe in yourself Alexander and stay who you are, my angel. I will leave you my house in Ireland. Do as you see fit, sell it, and use the money to start your career. I wish you only the very best.

As for Paige, a little girl lost. Someone who hurts and damages herself, her mind and her body.

Kelly, you must know that something is going on with your daughter. You must realise that she is not happy. She is crying out for your help, even when she is pushing you away. You took her word when she promised you that she was alright. You did not dig deeper. Paige has not found herself yet. She is a self-doubting young lady who does all the wrong things, hanging out with a bad crowd. She harms herself to ease her pain. Have you ever looked at her arms, Kelly?

I was trying to talk with you about the matter after you got back from your trip. You shut your ears and pushed me away. I tried to meet you and have a chat, but you turned me away, thinking I would give you a lecture about your current state of affairs.

Yes, I can see how falling in love with someone else can happen so easily. Especially if he treats you like a queen, if he promises you the universe. You have not said too much to me about your new beau, but I urge you to think this through. You have an obligation to your children and your husband. Sit together and work it out; go for counselling. Saving your family is worth it, don't just throw it all away. I am not implying that you were the only one who made mistakes; it takes two to tango.

Love can be blind, so be very careful. Be warned not to rush into this new adventure in a faraway place with a man you hardly know.

I am so sorry this had to be said today, in front of everyone, but I saw no other option. I am sure everything else would have been ignored by you. I am hoping you will have the support from your family, your sister, who will now comprehend that you are just a human being after all.

You need to decide, Kelly. If you stay, you will have to work hard. You will have to embrace many changes, but in the end, it will all be worth it.

Understand that I mean well. You will be looking back one day, appreciating what I did.

This leads me to my last but most important piece.

I sincerely hope that you can put yourselves in my shoes.

I believe that the past must be dug up before we can move on.

Revealing the truth will set you free and mend the rift in our family.

As soon as I heard, I wanted to board a plane to Ireland and see Rosie, but my health failed me.

So, I had to write it all down.

Rosie, my lovely sister. You have suffered the most. In this life, you have endured more than anyone ever should have to.

I know you are waiting for one day alone. The day that you will see your beloved son again.

Money and things don't mean much to you, but honesty probably will.

Knowing the truth is the only way to live your remaining days in peace.

You have worn yourself out with grief and guilt. Guilt for not being a better mother. For not being there for Ewan on the day he died. You said the accident could have been avoided if only you had minded him. You felt you neglected your son, the child you were so in love with.

Afterwards, you spent every minute of every day punishing yourself. Giving up, pining to die and join him in heaven and finally ask for forgiveness.

And you will be with him once more, united, mother and son.

But you must know, what happened on that tragic day was not your fault.

Sam, Lora and Grace were out in the woods with Ewan.

He must have been a nuisance to the girls, interrupting their games. I am sure they wanted to play, without him tagging along.

They wanted to teach him a lesson.

They were children themselves. They could not have understood the consequences.

They grabbed him and threw him into the water.

They thought that he would crawl out on the other side, moan a bit perhaps, but leave them to play in peace.

I am sure it never occurred to them that Ewan was in real danger. The current so strong, it simply swept the little boy away, carrying him further down the river. He did not stand a chance, poor little mite.

The girls must have been beside themselves once they realised what had happened, that they could not save him.

And although, I do not know for certain, I strongly suspect that they were terrified. They probably made a pact to never tell the truth.

This terrible secret was like a tumour growing in their hearts. It made them anxious, worried, irrational and full of rage. They lived with their conscience niggling away at them. They developed odd habits and depression. They might even have thought that Ewan was haunting them.

They did something awful and they did not confess. They were afraid. It must have been hell.

Stella, the messenger, came to me in person, filling me in as she had learnt the truth.

My time was limited.

I, too, am afraid of what will happen now, but I had to tell you, there was no other way.

All our secrets, everything we had swept under the rug.

I would not take it back even if I could and I am sure I did the right thing by letting you know.

I pray that you all can come to terms with my divulgence.

I will be with you always, loving you, watching over you.

Yours Lucina.

Deadly silence hung in the room; the air so thick you could have cut it with a knife. No one dared to breathe. Even the birds outside the window had fallen quiet. The letter limp in Pietro's hand, Ilaria was rubbing at her temples as if to soothe an oncoming headache.

Sam glanced at her cousins, who had turned ash grey. A tear slid down Paige's cheek; Ben's face was set in stone. Her sister looked ill, transfixed, her eyes not leaving the floor, hands clasped tightly together, her knuckles turning white.

Sam had no idea what to expect next. Who would speak first? Would she be blamed? Would Lora and Grace ever forgive her? What had she done? She had unleashed the devil. Her head spinning, shocked by the enormity of it all.

They were stuck in a nightmare.

All through the reading of Lucina's last letter, nobody had uttered a single word. Sam could not believe her ears. It was sheer madness. How could her aunt have imagined that this would help in any way? How could there ever be normality again? She mustn't have been thinking straight, death playing tricks on her mind.

All of a sudden, there was a scream, a sound so disturbing you could have sworn it came from deep within a wounded animal. All of Sam's hair stood on end, an ice-cold shiver running down her spine.

The next moment, Rosie leapt out of her wheelchair, as if she was an agile ballerina. She hit the coffee table with full force, still roaring, grabbing hold of the water jug, smashing the carafe against Grace's head. There was an ugly thump. It all happened so fast that no one had time to react.

Grace fell to the ground, blood pouring from her forehead.

And Rosie wailed and wailed.

Chapter 41

It was Ben who knew what to do.

"Call an ambulance!" he shouted at Pietro, who sprang into action. A pillow was produced and gently placed under Grace's head. Rachel cowered next to Rosie, her arms wrapped around her sister, who was rocking back and forth, whimpering.

The paramedics arrived shortly after, loading Grace and Rosie into the van. They made their way to the nearby hospital, where one was treated for head injuries and the other one for shock.

Rachel wanted to ride with Rosie and her niece but was told there wasn't any room for her in the ambulance, so Trevor, Rachel and Marie-Anne followed in a car.

The rest was left behind, stunned.

Nobody said a word. Ilaria began cleaning up the mess, Alexander joining in to help.

Ben's adrenalin rush had passed. The sordid details of Lucina's letter came flooding back to him, his wife's affair, her love for another man. He felt himself grow angry, red spots creeping up his thick neck. He was afraid he would follow suit and throw something at Kelly, so he gathered up his things and left, without so much as a goodbye, engine roaring, gravel flying.

Lora found her tongue again. "We will have to talk later," she said, directing her words towards Sam. "We will give you and the kids a lift to the hotel." She looked at Kelly, who had not moved an inch. "Come on!" Lora pulled her cousin up, thanking the hosts, running for the door.

"I'll bring you back," Paul said to Theresa. "Maybe, we can stop for a coffee and talk if you like."

Paul was a decent man, and Theresa was touched by his offer. She did not want to be alone, shame and humiliation burning in her face. Her vulnerability, her inability to have children laid bare, like dirty laundry airing out in public. Now her entire family could feel sorry for her, poor branded Theresa!

Sam still sat in her spot. The normality of glasses being cleared and tables wiped clean propelled her back to reality. The chaos that was left behind, the questions that, without a doubt, would follow. The aftermath of the mayhem. Lucina's last letter had created havoc, leaving her family in a state of turmoil. Sam grappled to understand it all. Had this really been the only way to mend the family in Lucina's head? And why did she have the urge to fix them anyway, meddle with their lives and make everything worse in the process? What would it achieve? Had dying made Lucina delusional, the chemical balance in her brain destroyed, unhinged her mind? She thought of her sister and her secrets. Her neglected family and how clueless Sam had been. Her own sister! She thought of Ewan and what they had done all these years ago. The truth was, she was not one bit surprised. From the moment she had blabbed to Stella, she knew it was only a matter of time before it came back to bite her. The uncertainty had caused her sleepless nights when during the daytime, she had successfully banished all unpleasant thoughts, pretending her life would go on as usual, the secret safely tucked away. But in her heart, she knew that Stella would talk, she only was astonished that it hadn't happened sooner.

She needed to go. She hugged Pietro and Ilaria.

"Lucina never failed to amaze me," Pietro said, not without pride.

Sam raced back to the hotel, through the crowded streets teeming with unassuming people enjoying the afternoon hours. At the front desk, she asked the girl to locate Leonardo's address, which turned out to be an easy task as everyone knew everyone in this small village. She got back into her Fiat, without looking in the mirror or straightening her hair, arriving at Leonardo's place a few minutes later.

A whitewashed house with terracotta roof tiles. He opened the door on the second knock. Standing in front of her, filling the door frame, in faded jeans and a grubby T-shirt. Sam's senses came roaring back to her, and she threw herself into his arms.

Chapter 42

Ben's suitcase was packed when Kelly arrived at the hotel. He had wasted no time.

"I'm driving to the airport," he spat when she entered the room.

"Our flight isn't till tomorrow," Kelly replied, her hands shaking.

"I don't care," he barked back. "I can't be here with you for a minute longer; you make me sick."

Kelly sat down on the bed. She felt completely drained; it was all too much.

"I know what I did was wrong," she began. "But I wasn't the only one who slipped up in this marriage—"

"You were the only bloody one who had a fucking affair!" Ben bellowed, purple veins bulging. He did not give her a chance to answer, slamming the door in her face.

Kelly stood at the open window breathing in the warm, soft air, the signature aroma of this country, scents of lemons and olives penetrating her nostrils.

This was not how it was supposed to go. Kelly wanted to tell Ben in her own time, whenever that might have been. She hadn't found the right moment, days turning into weeks, but it certainly had not been up to her aunt to disclose her affair.

How dare she? She had made everything much worse.

The whole family would judge her now. And what about the kids? She knew Alexander wasn't fond of school, that there were a few issues. Of course, she did. She had told him many times he could confide in her but he obviously wanted to handle it himself.

Was Paige really cutting herself? How did Lucina know? Admittedly her relationship with her daughter was a difficult one, but surely, she would have seen the signs? There was just no way this happened under her roof without her knowing.

If her aunt had cared that much about her, she would have found another way, a more private one. She could have written her a letter for crying out loud, that way Kelly would have had time to handle things properly. Let Ben down gently, talked to the children.

She was an emotional wreck. But what must be going through her cousins and Sam's mind right now? They had murdered Ewan! They had killed a child and never said a single word about it. They had watched Rosie fall apart and still kept quiet. It was quite extraordinary!

She was related to not one but three murderesses. Her own sister! Unbelievable. Thank goodness she had never let Sam babysit. Sam might have killed one of her kids if they got on her nerves.

Who would have thought? And did anyone have a hunch about this letter?

She dialled Jannick's number. She had to speak to him. His voice alone would calm her down; he would know what to do.

Two days later, Grace was released from the hospital. Rachel had rebooked all their flights; she felt it was important that they stayed together.

Grace's wound had been stitched; her head wrapped in bandages.

But it wasn't the gash the doctors were worried about. As a result of the blow, the optic nerve had been damaged, and her vision impaired. She was fit enough to return home but had to arrange an eye operation as soon as possible. They had bombarded Grace with letters, referrals and aftercare for the time being. Grace had a hard time taking it all in. She was struggling to come to grips with what had happened at Lucina's house. She could not remember all the details and was waiting for someone to fill in the gaps.

Rosie was discharged as well. The police were informed that no charges were pressed.

Rosie was brought up to her room overlooking the courtyard. She watched the birds sit on the edge of the fountain, drinking their fill. She had indicated that she would only tolerate her sisters at her side, no one else. The nieces and her daughter were not welcome.

Marie-Anne booked the trattoria for dinner.

As it was walking distance, they silently strolled along the dusty road, side by side.

Unintentionally, Trevor, Marie-Anne, Rachel and Theresa sat at one side of the mosaic table; Sam, Lora, Grace and Kelly at the other. The jury was in.

Paul and Oscar had taken Alexander and Paige out for pizza, under the motto: "We will leave you to chat."

Sam immediately felt as if she was under interrogation. The jury panel was sitting across from her, watching her, ready to scrutinise. She mentally prepared herself. Her back was straight, and her eyes alert.

Her aunts and mother took their time. Food and wine were ordered, small talk was made.

After a while, Sam could not take it any longer.

"Okay," she said. "Cut to the chase, say what you have to say."

Marie-Anne swallowed her bread. She took a large swig of her Pinot Grigio.

"I think I speak for us all when I say we are still in shock." She looked from one member of the family to the next. Trevor nodded encouragingly.

"Shocked not only by what had happened to Ewan but by all the other secrets and by the way these facts were dumped on us without warning. Good, old Lucina." A quick smile crossed her lips.

"She certainly knows how to make us sit up and listen. I am not saying that I agree with her method, nor do I believe that she could not have found a gentler way of breaking the news. But it is what it is. Lucina was a very special person, and her intentions were good.

She wanted the family to pull together; she wanted us to be more lenient with one another, to help and not crucify each other."

I am not happy about the pandemonium in Lucina's house and I am not sure if Rosie will ever find peace, even knowing the truth.

I think we all have a lot to learn and to sort out in our lives. I do not know about the rest of you, but I give you my word that I will try to make more of an effort with our family.

Lucina was our matriarch, and she is gone now. Even if her practices were a little controversial, all she wanted was for us to be one united group. A real family. The good and the bad.

I know you girls did not mean for this travesty to happen. I know you did not have the knowledge to judge the situation. "Of course, it was an awful thing." Marie Anne trembled, locking eyes on her nieces. "I can see how scared you were and why you did not tell. You held on to your pact for better or for worse. It cost you a great deal of distress, I am sure. You battled your own fiends.

I know in my soul, by not revealing your secret, you have punished yourselves enough."

"Now, hold on a minute!" Theresa's voice was shrill, full of anger.

"I am very happy for you Marie-Anne that you have decided all that for yourself, clearly coming to terms with the situation fabulously."

"There is no need for sarcasm," Trevor intervened, trying to place his hand over Theresa's, but she pulled away quickly.

"I do not know what all of you think and what you have discussed behind my back," she continued, spitting out her words. "But I, for one, am pretty pissed about having my private affairs revealed to the world. And what's more, I also have grieved and tormented myself about Ewan's death. Have you all forgotten what Rosie went through, still is going through? Your girls, they are killers, they murdered…" Her voice broke, and she dissolved into sobs.

"No one forgot Rosie," Trevor tried again. "And, yes, what the girls did was terrible, but we are here to mend this family, not to break it apart."

"Easy for you to say," Theresa managed in-between crying. "She had nothing bad to say about you…"

"Your daughters should be punished…"

"Don't you think they have been punished enough?" Marie-Anne's voice was climbing up an octave. She had lost her cool, she had started out calmly, but Theresa really had aggravated her by simply refusing to see the bigger picture.

"Punished my arse!" Theresa jumped up, sending the chair flying, storming out of the restaurant.

"We are a family!" was the last she heard. She would refuse to speak to them; they had managed to avoid addressing the elephant in the room till Grace had come out of the hospital; they might as well ignore it forever. Not speaking of what their wretched daughters had done, making excuses for them, protecting them, when these girls were pure evil. Surely, they had talked amongst themselves all agreeing to brush Ewan's untimely death and the devastation that had followed under the carpet. She harboured no desire to forgive or spend time with any of them again.

"Thanks, Mum" was all Lora could say, and for the first time in years, she yearned for her children. Grace was silently weeping, Trevor's arm draped around her shoulders.

"It won't be easy," he whispered in a soft voice. "But we will get there."

Kelly looked at Sam and thought she noticed a triumphant flicker in her sister's eyes. Had Sam no heart at all, no remorse? What was going through that girl's head? Kelly could not wait to get out of here; the possibility to turn her back on her dysfunctional family seemed within easy reach, the dream of living another life only too enticing.

"Say something!" Marie-Anne nudged Rachel, but Rachel was frozen in time. She felt like her organs would fail, one by one. Lucina was gone; she had left them, although meaning well, in an awful state of affairs. Rachel was the eldest now, she needed to step up and bring the family together. But the truth was, she had no idea how and she could not say if unity could ever be achieved again.

Part Three

Chapter 43

My life on earth is done. My family is falling apart; there were too many secrets, too much hurt.

I had no idea if my letter would make a difference. If calling them to my house in Italy, revealing the truth would help matters. But I was hopeful, and I tried. I thought it was the only way to make things right.

I had no time left to fix our troubles in person, and although I agree, I could have done things differently while I was still alive, I did not. My answer to the dilemma was the letter. A last attempt to bring peace and understanding where there only was speculation before. I was certain there would be an outburst, and I was right.

It is funny, when I think back, what I perceived the afterlife to be. I imagined floating around in space, in a good place, still able to see my loved ones. I was not wrong. It is all that and more. I can get a glimpse of life on earth. I have ways of guiding my dearest, but not in a conventional way. I can be with them, make them aware, I can throw out lifelines and hope that they will take them.

Now, I have to contain myself by sitting back and waiting. Waiting for them to come around, to comprehend. Good things can't be rushed, and I have all eternity.

They will accept responsibility; they will learn solicitude, which will alleviate the horrors of the past.

And one day, we will all meet again, my family, my pride and joy in this celestial place.

Chapter 44

Waiting never was her strength, and she had waited for a long time now. Her eyes skimmed over polished surfaces, a spotless coffee table, freshly arranged flowers and sparkling windows.

Everything was done and had been for a couple of months. Work, her house, the garden, there simply wasn't another thing she could think of to occupy her mind. Except waiting, waiting for the day when they'd finally knock on her door.

The message had been delivered so long ago, and Stella had expected an immediate reaction, an outburst of gratitude and praise, words saturated with love.

But none of that happened. Oh no, Lucina had to die. As far as she understood, straight after she left the old lady. Stella briefly contemplated if she had killed the woman bringing her the disturbing news, but she quickly dismissed these thoughts again. It purely was a coincidence; surely, it had just been Lucina's time.

Not what Stella had anticipated at all. In her mind events had unfolded quite differently.

She did not know how to respond to Lucina's death when Rachel told her over the garden fence.

Had Lucina confided in anyone? Would the travesty be revealed? Or had her efforts been in vain? It was all Stella could think about. Thoughts were spinning in her head, going round and round like a carousel.

She decided to let them deal with the funeral first. To let sleeping dogs lie and weigh up her options later.

The day of the burial came and no one said another word to her. Life resumed.

It had been an excruciating wait, thoughts of the unknown tormenting Stella day in and day out. She felt like a caged animal, and she knew she had to make her move before she would go insane. The uncertainty was killing her, the not knowing driving her mad. Hundred different scenarios of what could have happened or what was said were playing out in her mind.

One hot and sticky Saturday, she had enough; it was time to confront them.

She decided on the following Monday to set her plan in motion ; she would get to the bottom of it. After all, she deserved it. She would be the star of this story, no matter what.

But Stella's prayers were answered before that day.

Sunday evening, just as twilight gave away to darkness, there was a sharp knock on her door.

She opened her nightly Lambrusco in hand.

It was Rachel. She asked if she could come in for a minute and then explained that an important letter had been delivered. Lucina's last words. They were all summoned back to Puglia once more.

Stella was speechless. This was it; it simply had to be. She eagerly agreed to keep an eye on Rosie's house. Rosie, Rachel informed her, had to make the trip as well; Lucina had asked for her specifically.

That last bit of news confirmed it for Stella. The big revelation. She only had to wait a tad longer, sit tight till they all came crawling to her, thanking her that she had mended the family.

Yes, she could see it very clearly. Lucina's words, the truth, Rosie would finally understand that none of this had been her fault. The girls' devastation, begging for forgiveness. Rosie and the others finally making sense of it all, the burden that would lift from their shoulders, the discussions that would follow, all leading to the grand finale. The reconciliation. The family unit restored in all its glory. Rosie's immense relief that she was not to blame. She would still mourn her child, no doubt, but she would now know that she had been the best mother to her child. Stella hoped that the girls would pay their deed, but that there would also be forgiveness.

A beautiful picture formed in Stella's imagination. She felt relaxed and excited at the same time.

Soon she would receive her well-deserved bouquet of laurels. The ultimate prize. She would take a bow, smiling, assuring them that she was only glad to be of help. They would embrace her with open arms, and she would become part of them.

Another couple of weeks passed. Rosie had been returned to her home. It was hard to judge by Rosie's slow movements through her garden if her spirit had been lifted. But Stella—who watched her from the upstairs window, thought she detected a lighter spring to Rosie's step.

But nobody came to her door.. Not Rachel, as she had expected, not the other sisters, and the nieces were nowhere to be seen.

Doubt creeping back into Stella's mind. Apprehension spreading out like molasses, conspiracy theories confusing her brain, niggling away at her.

She had to grab the bull by the horn. Her time to shine had come, and nothing was going to stop her now.

She would go and see Rachel.

Chapter 45

After hanging up on Paul, Rachel had no idea what her husband had said to her. Something about dinner, chicken perhaps? She hadn't heard a thing. Her head was still buzzing. She felt faint, bewildered, and very disturbed.

First, when she opened the door to Stella, she thought something terrible had happened to Rosie. Why else would the neighbour stand in front of her house? As soon as the woman explained that she wasn't here because Rosie had fallen ill, Rachel was overcome by a dreadful feeling. Surely, the neighbour could have rung her on the phone. What made her come all the way over to her in person? Rachel had the distinct impression that the other woman was after something in particular; the situation seemed threatening, and Rachel's first reaction was to refuse her entry.

But Stella had none of it and pushed past Rachel into the hallway.

"Goodness gracious!" Rachel exclaimed her hands fluttering to her neck.

"We have to talk!" That was all the neighbour said, and she did not sound friendly one bit.

Rachel bought herself some time by making tea and arranging digestive biscuits on a porcelain plate.

When she sat down next to Stella, smoothing down her house frock, she had composed herself a little. She had prayed silently that she would stay strong, so help her God.

Stella's eyes rested coolly on Rachel's face; her voice sounded strained as if she was trying to suppress here anger.

Rachel felt very worried, the palms of her hands beginning to sweat, a faint ringing sound in her ears. She knew, after all, that Stella was responsible for telling Lucina the truth about Ewan.

To be honest, they had not paid much attention to the messenger after the pandemonium in Lucina's house and certainly not after the horrible fight in the restaurant that divided her family even further.

They had not spoken to one another much after returning from Italy; everyone was still trying to make sense of the fiasco. Everybody had their own views, and nobody had the strength to take the first step. None of them had given Stella another thought.

But it was crystal clear now that Stella had an agenda. Her being here was not a random act; it was calculated. She wanted something from them, and whatever it was, it wasn't good.

When Stella's car finally disappeared around the corner, Rachel sank down onto the sofa and cried. She simply did not know what else to do.

Stella's request was delivered in an indisputable manner.

The neighbouring woman had explained how Sam had exposed the secret and how she had made the trip to Lucina to set the record straight. Her aim was to bring clarity and healing. She was sure that once they learnt the truth the family's burden would be lifted, that they could come together again. She alone was responsible for mending the rift. It had cost her precious time and effort, not to mention the money she had shelled out. A selfless act.

When Rachel interrupted that the disclosure had brought more turmoil and devastation upon the family, that Rosie was raging and Theresa was furious, and that none of them were speaking, Stella turned violent.

She slammed her cup down with such force that the delicate china split in half, tea seeping into the tablecloth.

But Stella did not even bat an eyelid; she yelled right into Rachel's face that she did not care. She did not want to hear about their troubles; the bottom line was that she had stepped up to help. It wasn't her fault that the family could not get it together. She had made it her business to tell the truth, to bring harmony. And so far, she had not heard a single word of appreciation, not one bit of recognition; God damn it!

They should be thankful that someone cared that much about their stupid family; she was infuriated by the lack of gratitude.

Rachel sat frozen next to the incensed lunatic of a woman, unable to utter a single word, too afraid the ticking time bomb would explode, there was no telling if Stella would grab her by the neck or slap her across the face.

The threats came fast and hard. Stella would inform the police; she would make them pay. Or even better, she would bring the story to the newspaper's, surely, they would have a keen interest in the matter. Their family name would be ruined, their reputation dragged through the dirt. People would turn away from them in disgust; they would never live it down. Branded forever.

"Call me." Stella had hissed through her teeth before she left. "And don't take too long."

Rachel's whole body was shaking, and she felt sick to her stomach, fighting the urge to vomit. She managed to light a candle and prayed.

Lord give me strength to carry on, to lead my family, please bring us peace.

She had to get in touch with the others.

Chapter 46

With trembling fingers, Rachel texted her sisters and nieces. She mentioned a time and place for them to meet, without asking if it suited them. She only stated that it was urgent; they had to talk. She did not include Rosie as there was no point. Rosie would refuse to sit in the same room as her nieces and Grace. That ship had unfortunately sailed.

When Paul returned home, he found his wife collapsed on the couch, shivering and visibly upset.

Paul, a man of a view words, wrapped a soft blanket around Rachel, made a fresh cuppa, and sat with her stroking her back, waiting for her to calm down enough to speak. It took a long while, but Paul was a patient man. If life had taught him one thing , it was that some things simply could not be rushed.

Finally, Rachel sat up, hugging him, sobbing into his neck.

"There, there!" was all he said, ignoring his rumbling stomach, knowing that tonight's dinner would consist of a ham and cheese sandwich and some crisps instead of the roast chicken. Rachel managed a sip of the herbal tea, then she began to talk, slowly and miserably.

Paul had to suppress his flaring anger towards the woman who had caused so much grief. A woman who did not think of anyone else , and was only interested in applause.

But feelings of rage would not improve the situation, so much was clear.

What he wanted to do to Rosie's neighbour was one thing; what he was going to do was another thing entirely.

After he ran Rachel a nice bath, adding soothing lavender drops to the bubbles, he fixed them something to eat, turned on the gas fireplace and lit a few candles, transforming the living room into a tranquil sanctuary. Only then, when Rachel seemed relaxed, huddled in a thick bathrobe, nestled in the large wing chair, he urged her to pick up the phone and find out what Stella really wanted.

The day was dull, as were their moods, slate grey skies and plummeting temperatures in the middle of the summer.

No surprise here, thought Sam, wrapping her mulberry pashmina tightly around herself. She adjusted the unnecessary sunglasses on her head as she walked from the car park to the cosy restaurant her mother had requested they should meet in. Her mind drifted to Puglia, not to the chaos Lucina's letter had created and not to the meeting that was about to take place but to the red earth, the ancient olive groves, the language that sounded like music, like poetry in her ears.

She would have never thought that she would fall in love with a place so unsophisticated, so raw, so different from everything she normally liked. But she had. It had hit her hard, the Italian charm worming itself deep into her bones. And it wasn't only the location either. A man had captured every bit of her being, and she could not even say why. There was not a single shred of evidence to support her feelings, the crazy, out of control pounding of her heart every time she looked at him.

Something had changed within her, her emotions, perspectives, her core. It happened in the blink of an eye when Sam had least expected it. She wasn't sure what had triggered the change; she only knew she no longer was who she used to be.

She was curious about this meeting. Her mother had been very brief on the phone, when Sam had rung her back after receiving the curious text message, and she had not allowed any questions.

The small private function room to the left of the restaurant was dimly lit, a round of drinks had been ordered, and to Sam's astonishment, everyone was already here.

Rachel sat at the edge of the long table, smoothing out the sherbet orange tablecloth in a slow-motion, an untouched cup of tea in front of her.

She did not know what to feel anymore. She was confused and scared; she felt helpless and, most of all, numb. It was as if someone had taken away all her senses. She was lost. Her head ordered her to take action, to lead the family , to speak, but her body shut down. She could not address them, words stuck in her throat, she had been frozen in place since Stella's visit.

Everyone she had asked to come was here, all except Kelly. Her daughter had simply told her that she would not participate. She was quite happy to let them sort out their own mess, and she did not want to be involved with the people who had murdered a child and had kept quiet for so long. She wanted no part of a family who chose to ignore an act as vile as this. Her extended family was no longer a concern of hers. Rachel had been shocked to learn of her daughter's infidelity, and she was even more puzzled by Kelly's hard and selfish reaction. Kelly was prepared to leave them all, her own flesh and blood, and embrace an, in Rachel's opinion, uncertain and very risky future.

Rachel had always thought Kelly was the softer one of her daughters, the one with the good heart. But what did Rachel really know? Not much as it had turned out. Disappointment and shame mixed with feelings of complete loss, sadness and defeat.

Paul greeted the family, thanking them for coming together. He did not explain why Rachel wasn't talking, as it was clear that she no longer could speak.

He briefly mentioned that he was saddened by the family's dispute, that he understood their shock over Lucina's revelation but had hoped that they could talk it out and find forgiveness for one another. Unfortunately, his hopes had not materialised, which brought him to why they were here.

He breezed through Stella's visit, describing the unstable, greedy woman who had threatened the family and given them an ultimatum.

Stella was prepared to drag their good name through the muck, exposing what the nieces had done, informing the newspaper and, therefore, the world. The story would surely cause a shit storm, reporters quizzing every aspect of their private lives, their kids would be affected, their jobs, their daily routines. People would whisper, pointing fingers, making a wide berth around them. Friendships would be lost, neighbours avoiding them, and worst of all, the stigma would stick, like sap on a tree, the ever-present shadow. Not only the nieces would suffer, but the entire clan would be dragged down.

Paul painted such a horrific picture of how it all would unfold that Marie-Anne became hysterical and Grace started to sob.

Sam watched Trevor's efforts to calm Marie-Anne, holding a glass of water to her lips, rubbing the small of her back. Grace was beside herself, crying uncontrollably into an already soaked tissue. Sam had expected nothing else from her cousin. Ever since the truth had been told, Grace dissolved into tears at the drop of a hat. Her head wound had healed up, but her eye was permanently damaged, never to regain full vision. Lora had pulled the platter of finger food over to her side and was methodically demolishing every morsel.

Rachel sat stock still with a faraway look on her face as if she wasn't part of this crazy scene. Theresa's eyes bored into Sam's, ice-cold, arms folded. She appeared unmoved by the outcry, giving nothing away.

It was Paul who spoke again, this time in an effort to salvage the mess, to instil calm and order. "Please," he said. "Let us talk about this like adults."

But there was no adult-like talking as everyone started to voice their opinion at the same time. Marie-Anne addressed Theresa in a frantic manner, begging her to reconsider. Lora put her two cents worth in, between bites of sausage rolls and smoked salmon canapés. Grace wept, and Sam shouted for everyone to simmer down.

The waiter, who stuck his head around the corner to ask if more drinks were needed, disappeared quickly again, hoping that the rowdy crowd would not start throwing things.

Paul, a normally composed man, finally lost the plot.

"Would you all just shut the fuck up!" he yelled suddenly, making everybody jump. They held their breath, too afraid to speak another word. No one had ever seen Paul that upset. His daughters had sailed through childhood, without him ever raising his voice at them and his own wife thought that he was incapable of feeling anger, she had only known him to be kind and understanding.

This was very bad and they understood they had to zip it and behave.

But most of all, they had to listen to what the man had to say.

And what he said was not exactly flattering.

He told them to start acting like grown-ups, to consider their mistakes, and to stay calm and collected. He said that it was time for this family feud to come to an end. It was time to make amends. All of them. It was time to act like a family again and fulfil Lucina's wish. He reminded them that life is precious and short.

Then he disclosed what Stella wanted in return for her silence, in return for keeping their secret and letting them move on.

When everyone was leaving, Paul took Theresa aside, urging her to think about her family and their future. He asked her to consider Stella's request, as it was the perfect punishment.

Then he gave her the name and number of an acquaintance of his, a man who worked for a newspaper and could share his experience with her.

"Call him!" were Paul's last words to Theresa.

Chapter 47

Jack Hennessy wore an Oxford-button down, flannel shirt and jeans.

He was most comfortable pottering around in his garden and tending to his pet fox Ruby. He took the vixen in when he found her injured at the side of the road, and since she was only a pup, she responded well to the care, healing quickly and adopting Jack as her father.

Jack's friends call him the silver fox behind his back, not only because of his unusual pet but because of his grey sideburns and salt-and-pepper hair.

His relaxed manners made him likeable; his courteous ways were popular with the ladies, but Jack wasn't interested in seeking out a lady-friend. His wife had died a few years back, and he had been quite content by himself, working at the newspapers, meeting up with his friends, and caring for Ruby.

There really hadn't been a need, much less a want, to start a new relationship.

That is till Theresa walked through the door.

He had agreed to do a favour for an old friend. He was asked to tell this woman how a tragic family story, thrust out into the open for the world to absorb, could cause devastation. And he knows he had seen it many times. Lives turned upside down, never to be the same again.

But when Theresa approached, shaking his hand, all words vanished, and he could not speak. He managed to squeeze her hand in what he considered to be a manly grip and signalled the waitress.

Theresa ordered, and Jack took a big gulp from his beer.

Finally, he found his tongue again.

Without a proper introduction, he started to chatter about families that had been disgraced in the public eye, rambling on, words spilling from his mouth that did not make sense, not even to him. He did not know what was happening to him, first the loss of words, now the diarrhoea of the mouth. He thought his mind was failing him; he was starting to sweat perspiration forming on his upper lip. Perhaps he was suffering a stroke?

Theresa could not decide if Jack's eyes were hazel or green. It was an in-between, a brownish colour flecked with shamrock green.

She felt his discomfort; his random prattle amusing her.

She had thought about the family's dilemma all night. Her sisters, the nieces. Ewan and Rosie. What was the right thing to do? What had Lucina hoped to achieve in blurting everything out without a filter, without thinking of the consequences, their feelings? And still Theresa knew for certain that Lucina's heart had been in the right place, even if her mind hadn't been. Did the truth set them free? Maybe. Had the nieces suffered enough? Would they pay their debts? Most likely. And still, Rosie would never recover, and Ewan wasn't coming back.

They had all hurt; they had lied, and tortured themselves.

It was time for all this to stop. To start the healing, Lucina had so wanted to happen for her family. Could Theresa begin the process?

She glanced at the man who was sent here to make her see. To make her understand how all could spiral downwards even further. She paid attention to his voice, watched his eyebrows slope together when he spoke, saw his pain.

Tenderness overwhelming her, a feeling of joy spreading through her body.

She had no choice but to look forward.

She reached across the table and took Jack's hand. He did not have to go on convincing her. She was ready to make a change; she was ready to give her family a chance.

She would, however, let Jack believe that it was his influence that had turned her around. She would let him bask in his glory for a little while anyway.

At this moment in time Theresa only knew one thing, she would try, small baby-steps and she would do it with Jack by her side.

This time they met at Theresa's. Her aunt had sent them all a message on what's app. Sam was slightly surprised by how quickly Theresa had contacted them , and again she had no idea what to expect. The meeting could have gone either way, but it went smoothly, and it was brief. Theresa filled them in on her chat with Jack, the newspaper guy, and what he had told her. Sam thought she saw a glimmer in her aunt's eyes when she spoke of Jack.

"Ah, love!" Mused Sam, love could change anything.

Theresa was prepared to leave the whole episode behind her, to start afresh. Be a family unit again; have sisters once more.

She wanted them all to do their bit, learn from the past but move forward. They needed each other.

They all agreed that Rosie was a lost cause, even if it pained them greatly to acknowledge it. They knew Rosie only lived to die, to see her son again. The sisters would continue their duties, helping out in Rosie's house, making her life as comfortable as possible.

The nieces would fulfil Stella's request, their punishment.

They would take tiny steps, but they would take them together.

It was a hazy afternoon, the sun sinking into the horizon, leaving golden streaks across the sky.

The family stood around the cherry tree they had just planted.

Everybody had come, except for Rosie and Kelly.

Marie-Anne had said a few words and Rachel a prayer.

Grace had insisted on the wreath. 'Our little angel' was printed in blue letters on the ribbon.

Sam had to admit, the arrangement of purple irises, white zinnias, and pale asters was beautiful.

Noah had placed a scruffy looking teddy bear under the tree, and even Paige managed to look sorrowful in a grey kaftan peppered with gothic looking daggers.

All eyes were on Sam. She had informed them that she would like to make a speech. It was one of these new, strange things that happened to her lately, when out of nowhere her brain came up with these maddening sweet gestures. When sugar-coated words fell from her lips, dishing out compliments before she could stop herself. It was the new Sam, and she did not know if she liked her yet.

Anyhow, it was too late now; she had to deliver.

"Dear family!" she began, a lump rising in her throat. What the hell was wrong with her? Where had the strong Sam disappeared to? Who was this weak and fragile person?

"I am so glad we came here today, not to sort out another disagreement as thankfully we have put that chapter behind us now, but. to remember and celebrate Ewan. He died far too young because we wanted to teach him a lesson. I think I speak for us all, —Lora, Grace and myself—when I say we have regretted our doing ever since that day. We have punished ourselves by living with secrets and guilt. This, of course, does not take away from our terrible, careless act. Ewan was part of our family, son, nephew, cousin, and brother. I can only say how sorry I am. May he rest in peace till his mother comes to find him."

And then, to Sam's horror, she started to cry.

Leisurely stretched out in the yellow sun lounger, arms high above her head, face warmed by the midday rays, Stella purred. Life was good.

Scrolling through her Facebook news feed, she no longer felt obliged to like every post. No, not at all. In fact, she had her own photos on the site now, showing off her new friends, happily posing for the camera with Grace, Sam and Lora by her side. Smiling into the world, letting everyone know that she had arrived. What's more, all her colleagues liked her posts now, commenting on them, jealous probably, the silly cows.

She felt like a cat high on catnip. Every day was an adventure. She only had to pick up the phone and call one of the girls. They were there at her beck and call. Friendship in return for silence. A mighty good deal. It was all Stella ever wanted. She was part of a gang, accepted, valued.

Sure, the women hadn't exactly wanted the friendship, some may say it was forced upon them, but Stella saw it in a different light. The girls would come around, that she was sure of. They would start to really cherish her, appreciating their time together. Stella had needed a start, a way in, and she had gotten one.

These three women were now her social circle; they completed her.

If Stella would have ever allowed herself to dig deeper, to examine why these women hung out with her, she would have had to admit that it was a facade. Friendships built on water, a mere obligation.

But Stella never did think about it. She simply refused to. In her brain, everything was packed away in boxes, labelled and, if needs be, forgotten.

In her mind, all was good. She had asked the girls to be friends in return for keeping her mouth shut. They had willingly accepted. They were starting to get to know and like her. With time, the ultimatum would slip away, and only their strong bond would remain.

Stella had won. She had compartmentalised all her actions and happily lived into the day without any worries. Her new life. Any further thinking wasn't necessary; she was delighted with her own truth.

Chapter 48

It wasn't Rachel, as Theresa would have thought, who provided the most support for her. Since Lucina had made Theresa's feelings of insecurity and inferiority towards her sisters clear in her letter and had thankfully not elaborated on her many sexual liaisons, Theresa had to face the facts. She had to take a hard look at herself, but she also found that exposing the truth eased her stress and that her sisters were far less judgemental than she had originally thought.

But out of all of them it was Marie-Anne she could really lean on. Her sister had somehow softened to the world. Marie-Anne was there to talk about everything that was going on in Theresa's head. She did not judge Theresa or push her to understand or commend what the girls had done. Marie-Anne just let her know that it was okay to take her time, that they all were wrestling with the enormity of the crime committed, the secrets and pain and that the transition from turmoil to a more normal life would be a hard one. One that would take time. She even got herself a dog, a little Westie, so that they could take their four-legged friends for walks. Theresa suspected that her sister only bought the animal because of her, although Marie-Anne denied the allegations, claiming that she had always adored dogs, and that it was about time she went out and got some exercise. Obviously a complete lie, as Marie-Anne was as skinny as a pole.

Either way, the sisters enjoyed their strolls and their chats, their pets happily running ahead, sniffing at all the curious smells.

They talked about Lucina and her way of mending the family. They discussed the girls and Ewan, the incident that had changed and shaped their lives.

They both were in agreement to look ahead, to take events as learning curves, and make the best of every situation.

Theresa started to slowly come to terms with Lucina's last words. The exposure of her infertility had made her recoil in disgust. The mortification had been immense. The ignominy had felt like a prison. One only she could break out of. She started to own her inability rather than hide it. There were millions of women out there who could not have children. She was not alone.

And although she was way too advanced in age and kids no longer were a possibility, she joined a self-help group of infertile women. They were younger than her, by a long shot, but welcomed Theresa, nevertheless. She was finally given the chance to openly talk about her grief. And what's more, she felt she was heard. Taking part in this group outweighed the benefits of therapy by far. Her counsellor had been helpful, but she had never walked in Theresa's shoes.

Through sharing her story, she was forced to take a long, hard look at herself. Her wish for becoming a mother had taken over her life, had made her blind, had driven her to be ruthless and selfish. She had only cared about her agenda and not the people around her, not the men she had used for her purpose. She hadn't looked inward, had blamed everybody else but herself. She had been so absorbed in her pursuit that she never entertained the thought that the inability to conceive lay with her. Not until it was medically confirmed in New York.

Her support group helped her work through the pain. She was on a journey to recovery, admitting to her past mistakes but with a positive outlook for the future.

She approached her family in the same way. They were taking small steps, each one of them.— A chat over coffee, a long walk, a lunch. Trust had to be rebuilt, and it would take some time.

The biggest joy in her life was Jack. He hadn't suggested the women's group but welcomed her decision. He listened when she needed to talk, only giving advice when asked for it and never with judgement.

Theresa loved his company, but they both had agreed to keep their own places and not move in together. Maybe one day they would; for now, they were happy with their arrangement.

Bruno Mars and Ruby had not exactly seen eye to eye on their first playdate, with Ruby snarling and Bruno cowering in a corner. But Theresa and Jack were not concerned. "Give it time!" they said to each other and kissed under a velvet sky full of stars.

Trevor had taken his part of the inheritance and gone on a once in a lifetime trip to Las Vegas.

He booked Gary and himself into the Bellagio's penthouse suite, right on the Strip, with its own wet bar in the spacious living room. Complete with an emperor size bed in the master suite, where they spent many happy hours.

They ate and drank like Roman kings, indulged in shopping sprees, and blew the rest of the money in the casinos. Ten days of glitz and glamour, of burning through cash and throwing caution to the wind.

They toasted to each other in their first-class seats on the way home, their champagne glasses clinking together. They had shared so much laughter, their memories were priceless and theirs to keep forever.

Trevor briefly pondered if Lucina had intended for him to spent his money wisely, to invest perhaps or save it for a rainy day. But as soon as the notion entered his head, he dismissed it again. His older sister knew that he would behave outrageously, go on a vacation extravaganza or buy a Porsche.

As Trevor leant back, sipping his bubbly, he smiled, thinking fondly of Lucina and her crazy way of trying to bring the family together. Thankfully, it had all worked out in the end. They were all stronger now. "To Lucina!" he said. "You truly knew how to have fun."

It was none of Rachel's business what everybody did with their share of Lucina's money.

Although she rebuked Trevor for his wasteful nature.

Her money was in the bank, where it belonged, a nest egg for her daughters as she did not need very much. Of course, she had given the church a healthy donation; after all, the church community was always there when she needed them.

Sam was doing ok, but maybe she could treat her elder daughter to something special. Sam had surprised her; she had not only stepped up, but she had also shown her true colours. Compassion, regret, and she had taken responsibility. Her harsh exterior had melted, giving way to a much more lovable Sam. Rachel had always known that her daughter had a soft centre , even when everyone else had labelled her as uncompromising and resolute. A mother knows best, after all.

Kelly, however, had greatly disappointed her. She had probably been too lenient with her younger daughter, letting her get away with far too much. Rachel felt helpless thinking of all the mistakes her daughter was about to make. Kelly was literally running into the lion's den. But what could Rachel do? She could only be there for her whenever Kelly's dreams would fall flat. And still it pained her so to see this side of Kelly, the selfish side, the way she only saw what she wanted to see, disregarding her family's problems, her marriage and most of all her kids. How could she just abandon Paige? The girl clearly wasn't right. But there was no talking to her daughter as she brushed off every bit of advice. Paul was of no help to Rachel either. He firmly believed that Kelly had to make her own errors, even if it was blatantly obvious to everyone that she was about to make the mistake of a lifetime. She is an adult. He kept reminding Rachel. Well, her daughter certainly did not behave like one. She acted like a love-struck teenager without a care in the world. There was a family to consider, children who needed her mother. But all Rachel's conversations with Kelly fell on deaf ears and Rachel was forced to watch the sinking ship. The only thing left for her to do was turn to God.

Rachel went to see the father and asked him to pray with her. She asked for protection for both of her girls and for wisdom for Kelly. She had been so completely horrified by what her daughters had done. One a murderess, and the other an adulterer. She had blamed herself for not raising better Christians. But the father put her worries at rest. He reminded her that God had given free will to His sheep and that He moved in mysterious ways, Rachel needed to hold on to her faith and pray.

Besides her daughters, Rachel also needed guidance as Lucina's words, naming her the head of the family, were still ringing in her ears.

She had not managed to lead them yet. She had stood back and watched. The thought of taking the reins terrified her.

Together, they asked the Lord to grant absolution.

She realised there were two crucial tasks ahead of her, to secure a promising future for the family and guarantee her entrance to heaven. One, she would gather the family together as often as possible, to rekindle their connection and keep an eye on her granddaughter.

Two, she would pray much harder.

She had often thought about the truth coming out, especially when Grace had urged her to spill the beans. Lora had refused point-blank. She had always fobbed her cousin off, intimidating Grace by threatening her with prison and the loss of her son.

She had however envisioned the secret being disclosed. She had imagined being furious, completely out of control. She'd be enraged, flying into a frenzy, tearing someone apart. Most probably the talebearer.

But Lucina was dead, so she could not shred her to pieces. The strange thing was though, she had no desire to rip anyone apart. She was not mad; neither did she feel any resentment towards her aunt or Sam. What she felt was relief. An unexpected calm sensation had washed over her. She had found repose. When the weight shifted from her shoulders, the tension and anger she had held so close, faded away too.

It was an astonishing development. One she had not anticipated one bit.

When the family dispute was settled to some extent , she put her new self to good use. Her kids had suffered, exposed to her violent temper tantrums. She needed to show them that they could trust her again. Lora started by encouraging them to sign up for some after school activities and promised she would be there to collect them and to watch a few of their games. She booked a weekend away with Oscar and even opened up to him about her food related problems. He was surprisingly understanding, coming up with some good suggestions.

And then there was the neighbour, the very demanding neighbour. They needed to keep the woman sweet. She didn't like spending time with Stella, never being able to say no to any of her requests, being under Stella's thumb. But Lora had resigned to the fact that this was her duty now. She just had to get over herself Grin and bear it.

She had hated the last few months, the funeral, the revelation, the crazy that followed, her family torn in all directions. It was hard and frustrating. But they had all promised to make it work , to get to know each other again. She felt bad for how she had acted around her family and the grief she had caused. She had shot their beloved dog. Only she had known that it was Ewan, an evil form of Ewan obviously. To the kids, it had just been a pet. She wasn't sure if she regretted it or not; after all, she had to save herself. And she did not allow another animal. It was far too soon to make such a big decision.

And then, one sunny morning, she did something she had not done in over 35 years. Without overthinking it, she drove to the Waterford cemetery and before she knew it, she found herself at Ewan's grave. She would have sworn that she could not remember the location of his grave, but her legs had walked her straight to it. She lit the candle she had brought and placed it on the ground.

"You will always be my sunshine," read the inscription on the headstone.

Tears welled up in Lora's eyes. Ewan was exactly that to his mother. Sunshine. She felt a deep pain within her. They had caused this. For his life to end so prematurely. She could never go back, never make it undone. She could only try to be a better person.

For the first time she asked her cousin for forgiveness. She had lived with her burden, rage and obsession rearing its ugly head.

"I am sorry, Ewan," she said aloud to the boy who would stay a child forever. "I am so sorry for what I have done; please find it in your heart to forgive me."

At this very moment, a bird fluttered from a nearby elm, startling her. But as she watched the small creature soar up into the sky, circling high above, she understood that this was her sign.

Through a flood of fresh tears, she thanked her cousin, kissed the grave and left.

The feeling of relief stayed with her, and even when a storm was brewing in her belly, and an outburst apparent, she managed to keep herself in check. She would think of Ewan and the load he had lifted.

She felt happy now, as she was wandering through the supermarket, selecting items for their dinner. She rolled a honeydew melon in her hands; she tossed some fresh spinach into her trolley.

She thought of skipping dessert altogether but came to a halt when she passed the cake aisle.

There were cream buns, eclairs, and sugar doughnuts staring right at her, beckoning her to grab them.

Oscar had vowed to support her in her diet.

He said he would slim down with her. But then again, they could always start tomorrow.

"There you are!" The face of the nurse was uncomfortably close to Grace's.

She was in recovery after her second eye operation. "Now, will I bring you a cup of tea?"

Grace could just make out the nurse's lady-moustache and the large pores on her nose. She shook her head slightly. "No, thank you," she mumbled. She wanted to be left alone.

She had endured numerous tests after her return from Italy. In the end, the doctors decided to operate in hope of fixing her sight. They could not promise a positive outcome, they had made that very clear.

It was far too early to tell whether the operation was a success, as her eye was bandaged up and she needed to rest.

Her surgeon had given his all, but if she was left blind in one eye, she would have to cope. Grace had not condemned her mum, not even for a split second. If anything, she thought she deserved it. She was surprised by her aunts, except Theresa of course , who forgave them understanding that it had been a terrible accident, a situation they could not have judged as kids. They did question them why they had not fessed up sooner, as in their opinion, staying silent had made everything much worse. But they had been terrified. Terrified of being shunned by their family, as the heinous crime was unforgivable. Grace's guilt however had nearly killed her, but she had been unable to stand up to Lora, too weak to go against them both and the pact they had made. She had watched her mother deteriorate before her eyes unable to help. And since Rosie did not know of her part in Ewan's death, Grace harboured some hope that her mum would love her instead, even a little bit. But the love never came, and Grace was cast aside together with everything else. The only consolation was that her mother did not know the truth about her. That she did not know how vile her daughter really was. When their secret was unveiled Grace was glad it was finally over and at the same time, she understood that her relationship with her mother was finished. . Her mother had broken off all contact with her and the cousins. She never wanted to see any of them again.

This too, Grace understood. But it hurt. She had never been the favourite child and had vanished from her mother's radar after Ewan's death. Grace should have known. She knew Rosie well, and forgiveness was not in her books.

She would never be able to reconcile with her; she could never again speak another word to her mother or ask for leniency.

St. Peter surely would not call her name.

This was her fate. She had to make peace with it and live with her punishment till her death day. Stella's request, on the other hand, was only a minor inconvenience to Grace. She certainly could not call it her penance. She humoured Stella, taking part in outings and visiting her in her home. It really wasn't all that bad, and Grace had developed a strange fondness for the peculiar lady.

Her own future was uncertain, but she was determined to move heaven and earth to make it a good one. Her family had finally reconciled, and Grace swore, she would do her best for them and her child and beyond that, for the suffering children in this world.

Whether her eyesight was restored was irrelevant. She now knew what to do with her life.

She would start with volunteering in her local area. Later on, when Noah was older, she would go abroad working for a charity in a third world country. She would teach Noah all there was to know: how to stand on his own two feet, to make good decisions, and be a kind human being at the same time. This was her mission.

She could not make amends with Rosie, but she could still be useful.

And she would do it alone. She had decided that her husband no longer needed to be part of her future. They had grown apart a long time ago. She was better off without him as he would only hold her back.

Grace would plough on. She would become strong for herself and her boy.

Chapter 49

Marinated in her own sweat, not only because of the impossible heat that streamed through the open window, but because of the intense sex, Sam lay tangled in her sheets, outright ecstatic. Her arm flung across Leonardo's soft belly; her fingers tracing through moist, curly chest hair. A slow grin appeared on her face; she could not remember a moment in time when she had been that content. Employing her critical eye Leonardo was a five out of ten when it came to looks, no more. He was a ten in everything else though. His personality had captivated her; his laugh was contagious, and his smile wicked. Sam would have never thought it possible, but she was besotted with this man. The sex was beyond words. He did not need to be handsome as he was sure of himself and all that he stood for. This quality alone drew Sam to him like a magnet. She had never met anyone as confident as him, someone who had rejected her initially even though he must have found her beautiful.

The last few weeks had been nuts.

After Lucina's letter was read, chaos broke out. The altercation in the restaurant, a war of words, personal views clashing. Then they flew home and tried to make sense of it all till the second bombshell was dropped. Stella's warning, her demands.

Rosie did not want to see her or Grace and Lora anymore. There was no calling round to her house any longer. Her mother had forgiven them, even related. It was quite bizarre. Maybe her God had advised her to? True Christians must forgive the sins of others. Sam was sure her mother lived by that principle. Rachel would pray away their wrongdoing, would ask for redemption. Her mum had accepted the truth and her eyes had been opened to see Kelly's true colours. See that her younger daughter was not without flaws, that she was an egotistical, thoughtless little bitch.

Sam's prediction had come true. It was nearly a given after her slip up with Rosie's neighbour. She did not blame the woman for it, but she hated her for tormenting her aunts, cousins and herself. Of course Sam obeyed Stella's request, spending time with this deranged creature, smiling for yet another selfie. What choice did she really have? She only hoped Stella knew that none of it was real. A bought friendship. Stella had uprooted their past, their secret. But the truth was Sam, unlike her cousins, had never been afraid of breaking the promise to keep the events of that tragic day to themselves. She did not pursue it, but she also did not worry about it. When it did happen, she was initially horrified, she had let the cat out of the bag. She was concerned what Lora and Grace would say, more Lora perhaps as she was short-tempered. Grace was probably glad. Sam had always thought that Grace struggled with the secret. At first neither one of them addressed her. Much later, Lora confided in Sam in private. Lora told her that she felt free inside, rather than angry, that calmness had taken over. Sam had never toyed with the idea of telling, it just happened. She had quite successfully banished the whole episode from her mind and she believed that Ewan would rather pity than ill wish them.

She realised what they had done to Ewan was horrific indeed, but part of her had wanted to punish him so badly for being such a brat. She wanted to put the fear of God in the little bugger. Did she want him to die in the process? No, although she really had loathed that child. During the last months, the arguments in her family, Stella's bullying, and most of all, falling in love with Leonardo, had encouraged her to go back there—back to her childhood and her role in the calamity. And although she had shoved the images away, her guilty conscience had manifested itself in her anxiety. She certainly had never wanted to cause that much hurt, the domino effect of their action that plunged the family into turmoil. She had to accept her past; she also had to be there for her family. It became apparent that they looked to her for direction, for help, as her mother wasn't quite capable. She needed to be the glue that fused the family together again. Her tough shell had ebbed away, the flood gates had opened, and so she gave herself permission to cry in Leonardo's arms, tears of sadness and regret.

She had discussed Lucina's property with Grace, Kelly and Lora. As none of them were interested in keeping the house, she had offered to buy them out and had already spoken to a lawyer.

Kelly had mentioned something about giving her share to Paige, as her daughter had not benefited at all. Sam had no idea what was going on in Kelly's head. Her sister had turned 180 degrees and Sam decided to stay out of it but, at the same time, be there for her kids when they needed her. In Sam's opinion her sister had burnt all her bridges and Sam could not help but feel a sense of schadenfreude. Kelly who had the world at her feet had really blown it, had disappointed and hurt people around her. They had finally seen through her, recognised her for what she was. Self-centered. Neither she nor her life had been perfect. Kelly had fooled them all.

The connection Sam felt to Lucina's house was strong, but it hadn't been an immediate reaction. She had barely glanced at the place during the funeral, but the site cast a spell on her when she returned for the reading of the letter. The beautiful surroundings of old olive and lemon trees, the smell in the air, the small and charming village nearby, the way of laid-back Italian life, the slowness of it all. For someone like Sam, an on the go, high powered person, it was a stark contrast to her normal pace and maybe the one thing she really needed in her life right now.

She still worked as hard as ever at her job, but she made sure that she took time off too. Her holidays were now exclusively spent here in Italy, with Leonardo. Their relationship was only at an early stage, blossoming but neither one of them wanted to make any promises for the future. They simply took it one day at a time. Since Sam felt so comfortable with Leonardo, she allowed herself to open up to him and rethink the goals she had set for herself. She had lived with her tunnel vision for so long. The ivory tower she used to reside in had collapsed. She had cancelled her appointment with Dr Leg in Paris, and although she continued to dress with style, she no longer obsessed about her appearance. She accepted that she smelled unpleasantly in the fierce heat of the south, she handled her red cheeks with grace, and she kept calm when Leonardo gazed at her bald eyes and bare face adoringly, first thing in the morning.

What's more, she confided in him about her OCD behaviour. She had never gone there with another human being but with Leonardo she dared.

He listened without judging and without advice. He simply accepted her.

Later on, he asked Sam how she would feel about giving up her little wooden block, her safety line. Sam mulled it over for a while before deciding that it was time. Together they tossed it over Lucina's laurel hedge. Admittingly, Sam experienced a strange sensation, but she vowed to stick to her guns. It was not an easy task, one she had to deal with every single day. Her new safety net was Leonardo, on standby whenever she needed him. In person or a phone call away.

Sam had never been one to believe in destiny, in things happening for a reason. She had always worked hard for what she had. But the more time she spent in Italy, her body becoming accustomed to the tranquil setting; the more she grew receptive to these ethereal notions.

She was at peace, finally embracing who she was.

Chapter 50

The seat next to Kelly stayed empty. She would not have to engage in chit-chat, and she could spread out. It was a long flight from London to Johannesburg, where she had to switch planes for Windhoek. Jannick would be waiting for her in the arrival's hall, looking great in his khaki shorts and tee. Her insides lurched in anticipation.

It had been far too long. She longed to take refuge in his muscular arms, feeling his strong biceps against her body. She could not wait to rub her face against his stubbles, to trace his sunburned neck with her fingers. She had been doing nothing else but dreaming of him.

After the shocking revelation in Lucina's letter, there had been no going back for her. It was a done deal, and as far as Ben was concerned, their marriage was well and truly over.

Her daughter was as furious as Ben. Not only because of her mother's affair but because of being excluded from the will. Lucina had literally forgotten about Paige. Except, of course, declaring to the world that the girl mutilated herself.

Kelly had been and still was disgusted with her late aunt.

Firstly, she had publicly shamed them. She had laid her affair bare when it was none of her business. She had then proceeded to tattle on Paige, claiming that she self-harmed.

Ben had cursed Lucina and her gossip, and he refused to speak with Kelly, he did not want to listen to her. There was no reasoning with her husband anymore. He was quick to hire lawyers and start divorce proceedings. Alexander seemed lost and hurt. Of course, she had tried to speak with her kids. Alexander said that he understood, that he wanted her to be happy. At least someone did. The rest was not so easily swayed. Paige took her father's side, one hundred percent. Her own mother was appalled. Rachel went to church every day of the week to pray for Kelly, to hold the father's hands and beg for absolution. Rachel would pour her heart out, begging the priest to shed some light on her daughter's ghastly actions, blaming her own parenting no doubt. Always the martyr. But there was no blame to dole out, it wasn't her parent's fault or anyone else's. Kelly had fallen in love, why was this so hard to understand? And Ben wasn't exactly an innocent party either. How come no one pointed the finger at him? Years of neglecting Kelly, pestering her with his ridiculous demands for perfection. Nobody understood her. Her aunts did not comment much, but she could feel their disapproving looks upon her. Lora only wished her well, not seeming to care and Grace was on a journey of her own, ditching her husband, immersing herself in a new cause. Giving her time to the disadvantaged people of society. Of course, everyone thought that Grace was great. Recovering from an injury, coming to terms with Rosie's rejection, making the world a better place. Yes, Grace got everyone's sympathy and the fact that she was separating from her husband was not even mentioned. Grace could do no wrong, and Kelly was the evil one, the disappointment who, willy-nilly, cast aside her family. They could all go to hell. And Sam? Who knew what Sam made of Kelly's turbulent life. As usual, her sister shielded herself, taking the easy way out. She said she'd be there for Kelly, but Kelly knew this was just an empty promise. Sam was too self-involved to care.

All her sister wanted was her new Italian lover. "Just give it a few months." Kelly mused and Sam would get bored and dump him like she had everyone else before.

Her sister did not give a shit, not really. Just take a look at her childhood; she had murdered their cousin in cold blood. Of course, most of the family had been oh so forgiving, so bloody understanding—all except Rosie, who never would, not in a million years.

It wasn't right. On one side, there were her violent cousins and sister; on the other side, there was Kelly, someone who had tried to make her marriage work. Someone who was lonely and uncared for, someone who had found the love of her life. Why would she not be with him? Why did she not deserve to be happy? Ben and she had been over, long before the affair had started.

Kelly had done everything possible for her kids. She had not only provided for them, but she had been a damn good mother too. She was not the neglectful person her aunt made her out to be. She had bent over backwards for these kids.

Lucina had been an attention seeker. She had made up a story about Paige to get back at Kelly. Kelly had questioned Paige about it, and Paige vowed that she had not harmed herself in any way. Kelly and Paige had never been close, but surely, her daughter would have told her if there was a serious problem. Kelly did not force the poor girl to show her the arms, as she chose to believe her.

Anyhow, when Sam offered to buy her out of that stupid house in Italy, Kelly had arranged that the money would go to Paige.

Again, she had done the right thing. Did she get any credit for it? No!

The entire family was against her. Well, fuck them all; Kelly did not need them anymore.

Her kids were practically grownups; Ben would make his way in life without his pretty, little wife. Their finances would be sorted.

She was on the way to Africa. A new chapter.

Jannick had said that they would have to get married for her to stay in Namibia. It hadn't been a proposal as such, more a statement out of necessity. In her mind, Jannick would have asked for her hand in marriage anyway. If it had to happen sooner rather than later, so be it.

Her life would be one most people could only dream of. Every morning she would wake up to the African sun, next to the man she adored—a man who would protect and cherish her till the end of time. Every single day would be an adventure, out in the bush. She would relish every moment. Her life was only beginning.

Lucina had not wanted to help Kelly at all. All she wanted was to spread vicious rumours, blacken her reputation as a mother and wife. Lucina had wanted to destroy, not bring together.

Even if her aunt would have had the chance to speak to Kelly before, she would have still written this rotten letter under the pretence of helping. Kelly seemed to be the only one who saw through Lucina, the one who understood her true intentions.. The jealous bitch! Kelly was kicking herself that she had not copped on sooner to her aunt's malicious schemes.

Now Lucina was the hero of the family who spoke the truth and saved them all. She was glorified as their saviour. What a joke!

Every one of them had been blindsided by Lucina's words, her declaration.

But Kelly would not dwell on it. Her family already was a distant memory. Alexander could come and visit whenever he wanted.

Kelly was entitled to happiness. She did not need Lucina's blessings.

She would get busy living.

Kelly had made a conscious choice, one she felt was the absolute right one.

Chapter 51

It was coming up to her mother's first anniversary of leaving the country. Leaving them.

Alexander was doing okay, he did not let the bullies get to him during his last year of school. He loved how Lucina had called him strong and smart. He had told her that Lucina gave him strength. Good for him. The house in Dublin was rented out for the moment, bringing in extra cash. Alexander would sell it soon. He got an acceptance letter from the school he so wanted to attend. Paige had forgotten the name of the place. Alexander was happy, his schooldays were over. Her dad did pretty well too. He was divorced from mum and had moved on. He was out on a date with the lady who owned the barbershop down the road. "First date only," he had said with a wink, but Paige had watched him get ready. Nice shirt, expensive cologne. He never talked about Kelly. It was like he had erased this episode from his life. Paige got along much better with him now. Her dad had calmed down, he rarely shouted, and he spent actual quality time with them. He went to all of Alexander's piano performances and no longer mentioned his lack of enthusiasm for sport.

He encouraged Paige to finish her course, and he even bought her a motorbike. She didn't cringe at his caution to take it handy. Paige had confided in him a fair bit. She told him about the cutting and had started, after her father's urging, counselling sessions. They went surprisingly well, even though the therapist was an old bag.

Paige had finally broken up with Reuben. She had decided to stay single for a while. Plenty of fish in the sea and all that. In hindsight, she understood where her friend Emma was coming from. Reuben's controlling behaviour, and so on. In fact, Emma turned out to be a pretty decent best friend.

Her mother had become a total stranger. She never called to check in with them; she clearly assumed that they were fine, flying at it. It obviously did not occur to her that there had been plenty of tears along the way. A bad taste was left in their mouths, and they had to deal with the bittersweet memories of a woman who had once lived here.

Once in a blue moon, they received a letter with a strange African stamp. She wrote a lot of blah, always ending the note saying they could visit any time.

Paige knew that this should make them feel better. Her mother wanted to give the impression that she cared for them, that she missed them. Paige, however, appreciated what the sentence really stood for. Her mother only wanted to make herself feel better; she wanted to feel okay about abandoning her family. Deep down, even a selfish person like her mum must know what she had done was wrong. As far as Paige was concerned, her mother could rot in hell.

Paige did not reply to the letters. She gave them to Alexander.

To Paige, her mum was dead; she no longer wanted to include her in her life. She was better off without her.

Lucina's letter had set a lot in motion. Most of it was good.

Was the family coming together? Paige was not sure. Some of them tried anyway. Rosie was as bad as ever. Was Paige better? Ya, she was on the right track now. Would she have gotten there without Lucina's letter? Probably. Things happened, and you had to deal with them. Life was not all sunshine and lollipops.

When she needed to clear her head, she'd take her motorcycle for a spin, riding along the country roads, feeling the wind brushing against her body. It was the only time she truly felt at ease; her thoughts unwinding like thread from a spool. Brodie still held a special place in her heart and probably always would. Her mother was a cloud drifting away, and Paige's life a series of unpredictable events.

Only one thing was certain: Lucina had been the biggest shit-stirrer!

Chapter 52

Rosie felt more tired than she had the previous days. Rachel had been in, changing her bed, arranging fresh flowers on her kitchen table. Rosie did not care for flowers in her house. The odour annoyed her. She appreciated her plants outside in the garden, where they belonged.

It had been a long time since their trip to Italy. The last time she had set foot outside her house. She refused to go anywhere now, not even to the doctor's office. What for? Her sisters came and went, occupying themselves with chores they considered to be important. Cooking meals she did not eat. Washing clothes she did not wear. Badgering her to take a bath when she did not give a toss.

Her teeth were as rotten as her skin and hair. She knew she stank, and her house was in disarray, but she had no energy left to pay attention. She was waiting for one thing only.

She hated the fuss her sisters made, and she had forbidden her nieces to ever enter her home again.

The letter had been a great surprise to Rosie. She had not known what to expect from the trip to Italy, but she understood that she had to be there.

She learnt Lucina wanted to hop on a plane to tell her in person, but it wasn't meant to be.

Poor Lucina. She had tried so hard to make this family work, even from beyond the grave.

All of Lucina's intentions were good. She had always felt that it was her duty to fix everything, but some things could not be mended. Rosie missed her sister, dearly. Lucina had been the one who used to sit with her, in silent agreement. A lovely soul through and through. But what good did it all do, the revelation? Rosie had found no peace even after hearing the truth about her horrid daughter and nieces. The monsters. How could they kill her small boy? All he had wanted was to play with them. They had excluded him; no wonder he had acted the maggot. They must have known that he would not stand a chance in that river, the current so strong, pulling him to his death. Yes, they had known full well. They had just wanted to get rid of him. Calling him a nuisance and all. They had also known that they'd be in all sorts of trouble afterwards, so they had kept their little mouths firmly shut. Letting her believe that it was an accident, a disaster she could have prevented. Sure, she had been busy at that time in her life, the endless task of making cakes, demands of her husband, God bless him, the struggles of daily life. She did what she could, and she knew that she had loved Ewan with all her being. He had been her sunshine, her favourite person in the whole wide world.

They took all that away from her, and they did not even care. They didn't bat an eyelid. Fighting their own demons? Oh, please, they could not begin to imagine what real grief was. They had never experienced true hardship. Never had to receive such awful news, feel the terror burning in the pit of their stomachs. They did not have to bury their child, their flesh and blood. So young, deprived of all that was meant to be. A future, laughter, friends, and his own family. No, they had no idea. How could she turn a blind eye, how could she ever forgive them? She was not that good of a Christian. Sam, Lora and Grace would roast in the eternal hellfire. God would have no mercy on them.

Lucina had wanted Rosie to know the facts, what really had happened that tragic day.

Rosie went from tormenting guilt to white-hot rage. Neither was good. Neither brought closure. Nothing brought back her son. She died the moment he did; her life was over; it was as simple as that.

The rest of the family could go on with their days as they pleased, finding themselves, bettering themselves.

Rosie loved Lucina for her kind heart, for the effort she had made. Rosie longed for the day when she could see Ewan again.

She fell asleep one night, her body calm and relaxed, her house tranquil.

She drifted off into another world, the one she had been dreaming of, experiencing a lightness she had not known before, marvellous light engulfing her, propelling her into eternity. She felt tremendous, hopeful and blessed.

And there he stood, in his divine brilliance.

Her boy, arms open wide, ready to embrace her.

The End